alter
ego

alter ego

helen heckety

RENEGADE BOOKS

First published in Great Britain in 2024 by Renegade Books

10 9 8 7 6 5 4 3 2 1

A CIP catalogue record for this book is available from the British Library.

ISBN 978-0-349-13062-0

Typeset in Berling by M Rules
Printed and bound in Great Britain by Clays Ltd, Elcograf S.p.A.

Papers used by Renegade Books are from well-managed forests and other responsible sources.

Renegade Books
An imprint of
Dialogue
Carmelite House
50 Victoria Embankment
London EC4Y 0DZ

www.dialoguebooks.co.uk

Dialogue, part of Little, Brown, Book Group Limited
an Hachette UK company.

PROLOGUE

It's quite odd to see a fox carrying a pair of scissors in its mouth. Sharp teeth poking through the hand holes, the silver bolt between the blades glinting in the last of the sun as the fox turns toward the woods. That's how I imagine it, anyway. I can't know, because no one was around that evening. I had been there, in that field, but by the time the fox arrived, I was long gone. Possibly still in the back of the ambulance, but more likely in the hospital, stuck on the ward, trying to get a grip on what had happened, wishing I wasn't so far away from the vastness of the hills and the sheltered woodland, from the orange sky and the cool breeze of dusk.

But since I was far away from it all, I can only imagine it. How the fox's nose would have been close to the grass, picking up the scent. How it would have pawed at the strange object with its claws at first to try and work it out, because it wasn't like anything it had seen before. And then deciding to carry it home, jogging along, as foxes do. Past the wild daisies, through the springy moss and onto the dirt of the woodland.

I imagine a rabbit heard the vibrations of the four legs and darted down into its warren before the fox could catch it. Not that the fox would have been interested, then. It already had its prize, and although it was like no animal it had ever seen before, it was clearly a bodily thing. Dead, but bodily: the silver parts were heavily stained with the unmistakable, beckoning smell of blood.

Into the den under the tree, stepping over the roots before ducking its head, the family wouldn't take long to start gnawing at the handles, trying to break it apart, before relenting, and fighting over who would be first to lick the blades.

1

#OUT

Offering a dehumidifier to a homeless person wasn't cool. There's no excuse. If there is a heaven, I can imagine her at the gates with God, explaining how she could never catch a break; that too many people treated her with too little care and too much aggression. But there was one thing that *really* got her, that fundamentally made her realise that the world is a dud and totally unsaveable. It was when a skinny white girl with her hair in a messy bun, struggling to fit a dehumidifier in her already crammed Ford Fiesta, took a step back to consider her options, looked around the car park for an answer and apparently found it in a homeless woman, twenty feet away and picking the cheese from a discarded Burger King wrapper. The girl genuinely decided it was worth asking – while holding the power cord and gesturing toward the half-metre high, white, wheeled appliance – 'this any good to you, mate?'

It goes without saying that I regret the whole incident, and if I could take it back (the event – not the dehumidifier), then I would. It was an impulse that came from desperation. I felt, as I tried to wedge it in-between the clothes dryer, the torn vacuum-packed bag and the storage box of cards, photographs, cough sweets, travel kettle, swimming costume, goggles and inflatable lilo, that I was running out of options, fast. Options and energy. While it was helpful of Ella to carry all my packed belongings down the two flights of stairs, she felt it was more than fair enough that I then carry them to my car. But having to heave them along the pavement, over the road and into the nearby car park was chaos for my body. On each trip, I could feel my fingers slowly collapsing as they tried to hold the weight of the box, slipping in the sweat of my fingerprints, my wrists buckling, my arms falling into a slight tremor. The reality of my body made me feel a little sick. A little bit worried about what I was planning to do.

As I stood breathless by the car, I thought of the time a therapist asked me to write a letter to the non-disabled version of myself. I remember my initial reaction: 'why are you interested in someone who doesn't exist? It's me here, you know, sitting in front of you. The disabled one.' Not that I said that, of course. I seem to remember I just swallowed. And then of course, I did it. I wrote the letter to that version of myself, and in doing so, made her real. Or as real as she was ever going to get . . .

By the time I grabbed that dehumidifier, the very last item of my life in London, the corners of my vision were edging out. I tried to shove everything into the passenger seat footwell and strap it in like a robot child that showed its love for me by drinking the water in my bedroom walls, but the seatbelt failed to hold it in securely. I had visions of having to suddenly brake for a stray sheep and the thing smashing through the windscreen, sprawling itself all over the road. There was no option but to leave it behind.

Yes. I know, I agree with you: nice attempt trying to justify this irrational thinking, but it's no excuse. I will be reincarnated as a naked mole rat for what I asked that homeless woman, a naked mole rat living in overly damp conditions.

'And he's not got any social media?'

'Nope.'

'And you're sure about this?'

'Yes, Ella. Yes I am.'

'Because you know I've already agreed with Poll—'

'The room is hers. Stop worrying.'

Ignoring me, she went on, 'But you're not *living-with-him* living with him, right?'

I took my best friend's hands and moved them up and down with the syllables of the words, speaking extra slowly, 'On-ly. Un-til. I Get A Job. And. A Flat. Of My. Own.'

She laughed and I let go.

'I need to be getting off.'

'I know, I just don't want you to go.' She gave me another hug, as her eyes filled with tears, and I tried to ignore the tightness in my chest.

Taking in the front room for the last time, I imagined the furniture looking back at me: my bedraggled brown hair that was now half in and half out of the bun, smudged mascara, my small frame in the same navy-blue hoody I always wore – no bra, slight shadow of a nipple in the right light – and my denim jeans, complete with a butter stain from that morning's hurried bagel. Here I was, in front of all that furniture: just another person who used it and left, never to be seen again. The television would be pleased that it would finally get a different face to look at; it gave us all those channels and it only got three in return: Ella, Me, Me and Ella. I imagined the wooden kitchen table wouldn't miss my sweaty palms, but perhaps would fondly remember the time I fell asleep underneath it: a bad mixture of too much vodka and a thunderstorm had me convinced the building was under threat, much to the confusion of the boy I'd brought home (he left as soon as I crawled under the table whispering, I unfortunately recall, 'Blitz! The Blitz!').

The sofa was probably used to the comings and goings more than anything else. Four people squeezed onto it, one on the arm and a few sitting crossed legged at its feet. This was the usual set-up, whether it be Ella and our work friends from the salon, Ella's gang from basketball, or the mates I made from Eco Society at Uni (we talked a lot about how to save the planet, but the only action we ever took was the slightly misguided adoption of a penguin from London Zoo). It was a lively house, always busy in the evenings and far too quiet in the mornings as Ella and I inevitably overslept for work.

The last thing I looked at was the corkboard of photos, all ready for Ella's birthday party (she had, classically, started prepping very early). Right in the middle was the two of us at college in our costumes for World Book Day, both characters from Jacqueline Wilson books. There she was: seventeen-year-old me looking at her future twenty-nine-year-old self, who was only half smiling.

Ella gave me one final hug and asked me to message the minute I arrived at Oliver's house. And that was it; I turned around and walked out, stopping the door from closing just in time to say, 'Oh, and try not to walk in on Polly wanking like you did with me.'

'HATTIE!'

'Twice. It was twice. That's one and a half times too many.'

Her laughter was cut abruptly short as the door slammed shut, louder than I'd ever noticed before.

Outside, I abandoned the dehumidifier in the corner of the car park, got in the car, checked my phone and scrolled through the forty-seven messages on the group chat: Our Son Mr Jonathan. There were seven of us in total, mostly my friends from Eco Society (our icon was the adopted penguin, Mr Jonathan), Sam, Bea, Georgia, Pete, Pearl and Ella too – an honorary member since she never attended Eco Society, but often came on nights out with us.

After a triumphant story from Sam about successfully getting a date with a guy he met on a speed awareness course, a couple of '*Hattie – today's the day?!*' and '*Gah I'm going to miss you sooo much*' and '*But Wales is so far! Whhyyy??*' appeared. I heart reacted to them and replied:

Yep, that's me! Off to follow my heart and this whirlwind (but very nice and good and lovely) romance. Just like Sam. Speedy.

GEORGIA: And you're sure he's not a murderer?!

PETE: Who? Sam?

GEORGIA: I mean he was famously going 34 in a 30 . . .

BEA: Murderer awareness course

SAM: She meant Oliver but thanks guys, thanks a lot

BEA: Guess there's only one way to find out . . .

GEORGIA: I'm going to keep asking until you tell us . . . what's his address?? What if you disappear?? I want to look like a nice helpful friend on the news

Ha! Sorry – it's:

I wrote his full address and pressed send.

Then I typed a totally different one in the Sat-Nav. Anxiety bubbled in my throat. But I knew I was doing the right thing, and it would, of course, be ridiculous to put in Oliver's postcode, because Oliver didn't exist. I had completely made him up.

2

#BETWEEN

As I headed onto the motorway, one of the shoeboxes I'd chucked into the back got dislodged and sent my printer careering toward me, wedging itself between the front seats, above the handbrake. I couldn't shove it back while I was driving; black ink had started to slowly seep out of its mouth.

I pulled over at the services and tried to sort it, stuffing in tissues to soak up the leak. As I moved it into the back again, the scanner lid lifted to reveal the folded sheet I'd hidden in there. If you need to hide something, hide it in a scanner. No one ever looks there.

I could see the words I'd written at the top of the page through the other side of paper: The Plan. I reached out for it, but before I touched it, I realised I had black ink all over my hands, so I grabbed my keys and made my way into the loos. As I turned on the taps I thought of The Plan, so precious to me that I didn't want to muddy it with black smudges. It had to be perfect. It had to stay intact. I pumped the soap dispenser and went over it in my head.

LEAVE OLD LIFE
WITHOUT
ANYONE KNOWING THE REAL REASON
AND THEN
FROM THE DAY YOU ARRIVE IN WALES ...
YOU ARE NOT DISABLED
WELCOME TO YOUR NEW LIFE!

Not quite in Wales yet, but having left London, I was in some sort of grey zone. A purgatory: my old life was over but my new life hadn't yet begun. The liminal space of that service station bathroom. I stared in the mirror and I realised I'd got ink on my lip.

I wouldn't say that my disability is invisible, but it's not immediately obvious. This means I can 'pass' as an able-bodied person, which was of course integral to The Plan to live as an able-bodied person in a New Life away from London and everyone who lived there.

The New Life part of The Plan only worked because of people's ignorance. Part of the reason I can 'pass' is because a lot of people assume that all disabled people are in wheelchairs, and since I'm not in a wheelchair, they don't immediately see me as having a disability. They just assume I'm very thin and don't eat enough, rather than having muscle-wasting limbs. It also depends on what I'm wearing – if I wear my long black boots, a long-sleeved dress and a chunky cardigan, you can't see it so much. While packing for my New Life, anything that showed off my body too much went in the bag for the charity shop.

As I pulled at the paper towels and they refused to budge, I tried to ignore the look from the woman waiting behind me.

The ink on my hands had only faded to grey, and my skin was red from all the scrubbing. I yanked at the towels again but something was stuck. The woman behind me took a small step forward and asked if I needed some help.

I wasn't in Wales yet. This was the in-between. This would be the last time.

'Thanks – yeah – I have a disability that affects my hands, so—'

My throat burned as I spoke and I felt in my pocket for a cough sweet. She gave a small, confused 'Oh?' and looked at me the way people always look at me once they find out, reframing me according to what they consider 'disabled'. It's never a good thing; the word is drenched with negativity. Trying to make it fit, she looked at my hands to see if she could figure out exactly what it was that was 'wrong' with them. She took in the ink as if it was part of it; a mark on me, like a curse.

She pulled the handtowels with ease and gave me one quickly, avoiding my eyes, as my cheeks grew red and I turned back to the sinks again.

Like I said: The Last Time. This was what I was leaving. I could have cried at the relief of it. However, I still had a lot of work to do. If this situation was going to happen in my new life – the situation of me not being strong enough or fast enough – I would need to have an excuse ready.

For example, it's difficult for me to sit on the ground and get up again; if I do find myself on the ground, I have to crawl towards something, like a table, and use it to push against so I can get up. I just don't have the strength or the balance to get up otherwise. I also wouldn't be able to run, or lift anything heavy, or balance, or climb. I hadn't figured out all the solutions to these problems yet, but I thought I could probably get quite far with simply avoiding these things, and perhaps saying something quirky like, 'Oh, I won't sit on the ground in case I traumatise an ant.' Quirky was fine, disabled was not.

As I wet the towels and tried to scrub harder, I saw the woman's reflection as she adjusted her hair before leaving. The contrast of our two bodies in the mirror distracted me so much I scalded my hand under the hot tap. As the paper towel disintegrated in the water, I repeated 'The Last Time' over and over. I told myself that I could do this, because I had always done this: a part of me thinks I've forever been trying to hide my disability, even before the age of two, when I was diagnosed.

I've always pictured a tiny embryonic version of myself sitting with a box of chromosomes: coloured beads you had to string together correctly. Maybe that tiny embryonic version of me got distracted by a new finger, or the sniff of a heart, ready to beat. So I put one of the beads on wrong, and only realised when I'd already added more to the string, and it was too late to change it. I imagine I thought I could keep my mistake on the down-low. I probably felt a pang of guilt when my parents were told the diagnosis. I do wonder whether a part of me wanted to own up and say, 'Sorry lads, that's on me.'

Had I had the words, that is. But even when I learnt to speak, finding the words for this stuff was difficult. In school, on days when we got a supply teacher, the other staff would often forget to tell them. Once, I was asked why I wasn't getting changed for P.E. My reply would physically hurt as the words scratched themselves out, as though going over the same old wound, in preparation for the awkward response, the confusion, the stares. Even at the age of twenty nine, I feel like I'm back in that classroom, the teacher looking at me, wondering why I'm not doing the same thing as everybody else.

Hands dried and out the door, I was leaving the grey zone. No more explaining to do, and no more sore throats every time I tried. I would be free from using cough sweets to soothe the pain. All I had to do was keep to the story and make sure my friends in London never found out what was really happening. I couldn't go there, couldn't explain it all. Especially not to Ella. Not now, not ever. And I certainly couldn't ever, ever go back.

3

#HUT

Our Son Mr Jonathan

PEARL: Argh sorry I've been AWOL Hattie, Lena's had chicken pox

Ah shit Pearl that sucks!! No worry at all

SAM: Hattie are you in Wales yet??

GEORGIA: What's Oliver's house like?

Ella

[Missed Voice Call from Ella]

Sorry all good, just catching up with Oliver ;-)

Yessss girl

GIF of woman hula hooping in hot pants

House so empty without you!

Awww no – let's catch up soon,
just watching a film xx

It had started to rain heavily, water distorting the letters on my phone screen. I wiped it with my sleeve and put it in the pocket of my coat.

'The Shepherd's Hut' was situated on the edge of rolling hills and woodland, a full hour away from the fake address I'd given to everybody on WhatsApp. I knew I needed the fake address to be real, just in case anyone looked it up on Google Street View. It needed to look like a convincing place that Oliver would live, not too out of the ordinary or sensational, ideally on a busy residential street where you couldn't quite make out the house numbers so you weren't entirely sure which one it was. I also wanted it to be far, far away from where I *actually* was, which is something I would later come to regret. But at the time, I was led by my gut instinct to be away and removed and out of reach. It's why I chose Wales in the first place – it feels a long way from London, and no one really seemed to know much about it, according to the undercover research I conducted when I was coming up with the plan. Scotland, for example, was ruled out quickly, after Bea revealed she had family there, and then Georgia pitched in that the only porn film she had saved on her laptop was by a Scottish feminist filmmaker in which a woman undoes the fastening of a kilt using nothing but her tongue. Wales, however, seemed to bring little up in the way of conversation, or kilts.

It was dark by the time I got to my actual new address, and I had to use the torch on my phone to walk from the edge of the field where I'd parked to the hut in the centre. Despite the bad weather, the air in the country felt richer than anything I'd been breathing back in London, even on the days I went to a park and told myself I was 'getting back to nature'. It was almost like an entire new chamber in my lungs had opened up, unlocked by the quality of the dark, earthy air. I shone the torch at the hut and smiled, before realising I had a small challenge to complete first: there were three wooden steps up the small, decked area by the door. I climbed them slowly, one step at a time, pausing in between, due to the lack of a handrail.

I had of course started the beginning part of The Plan months ago, when I realised, without question, that I needed to leave and start my New Non-Disabled Life. But I had to leave with subtlety. I had to do it without explaining, particularly to Ella, why I needed to start again without delay. While I was busy making her think I was seeing this guy Oliver, I was secretly applying for jobs and searching for Airbnbs that I could stay in long enough to get a job, so I could get a flat and lock myself into a lease far, far away.

The day I found out I'd been offered an interview was the day I booked the little hut in the middle of nowhere and immediately went running into Ella's room to say Oliver had asked me to move in with him. Make her think I'm moving for love, and she'd find it difficult to question me. It had worked, thank God.

The owners of the hut had texted me the code for the lock-box, and I'd managed to get the key out, but when I put it in the door, I struggled to twist it. The metal held firm against my fingers. I gave it another go. And another. By the sixth attempt I was giving it everything I had, but I couldn't turn the key far enough to unlock the door. I let go, key still in the lock, and took a deep breath. I pulled my cardigan sleeve over my hand: a skill I'd learnt in childhood to stop the pain of the metal digging in and to enhance my grip.

The sleeve seemed to do the trick and the key started to turn, but not enough. I checked there wasn't another keyhole I'd missed, I tried my other hand, I tried two hands, I tried taking a deep breath, then taking the key out and putting it in again, but no luck. Using the torch on my phone, I noticed I'd missed another call from Ella and felt a sudden rush of tears; panic was setting in as I was so far away from a room I felt safe in and a place I knew well. I was so far away from how I thought this new life would be.

WELCOME TO YOUR NEW LIFE!
YOU CAN'T EVEN OPEN THE FRONT DOOR

With my phone back in my pocket, I took another deep breath – whatever that 'extra chamber' in my lungs was, it seemed to be closing up. As a last resort, I gripped the key with my teeth. My face was wedged in the 'shabby chic' doorframe – grimacing, biting down hard, tilting my head, trying to make the damn thing turn, with saliva dripping and my tongue wincing at the taste of metal. For a second, I thought I'd done it. But when it still wouldn't turn, I hit at the door with the palm of my hand.

WELCOME TO YOUR NEW LIFE!
YOU ARE ALONE IN THE DARK

The unmistakable feeling of wanting my mum seeped into every part of me. I stared at her name on my phone, wishing I could just video call her, and her strong hand could reach out of the screen, dry my tears and turn the key for me. But there was no calling Mum and Martin, I had told them the same lie I had told everyone else. They wouldn't understand my reasons for leaving even if I explained it.

I kicked at the door frame again, hard.

WELCOME TO YOUR NEW LIFE!
YOU NEED TO FIX THIS

The only thing left to do was to call the owners. The thought of it made me want to throw up, and the sound of the phone ringing could have honestly killed me there and then. Cause of Death: Had to ring stranger after 9 p.m. and ask for help.

When Nancy picked up, I gushed an introduction.

'Oh, hi, Hattie, everything okay?'

'I'm just having some trouble getting in the door.' I closed my eyes at this point, knowing that she would start talking about the code, the importance of pressing the hash – which is exactly what she did.

'No, it's the – the key, actually, I can't seem to turn it in the lock. It will only go so far and then, I can't . . . get it to open.'

She was baffled.

'Yep, yeah, I'm turning it the right way, it just won't go, I didn't know . . .' Normally this would be the time I'd say I was disabled. But not anymore. 'Is it a tricky door or something?'

Nancy started talking to her husband Christian, 'I dunno, she says it won't turn in the lock? – Sorry, Hattie – yeah, I mean it can be quite stiff but we've never had anyone—'

'I mean, it's just not—'

'Lord, okay, Christian says he'll drive down to you now, but it's going to be about fifty minutes.'

'Ah, okay thanks, yeah, God, so sorry.' I hung up, carefully made it down the steps and headed back to my car. Sitting in the driver's seat, I switched on my 4G and put on an episode of *24 Hours in A&E*, playing The Game. It started as something that used to calm me down as a child when I was panicking at hospital appointments. The Game was looking at people in the waiting room to try and guess why they were there. Then I started playing it when the TV show came along, because I found it calming. The good thing about the TV version was that I found out the answers; I would often sit with a notebook to keep a record of my guesses:

> The Game: Notes
>
> Woman clutching her jaw – she's tried to pull her own tooth out?
>
> Toddler appears fine. Parents very worried. Had a seizure-like episode?
>
> Man looks very pale and sweaty. Reminds me of picture of Dad?

My dad died when I was three, so I don't really remember him, but I do remember, and often think about, what happened. As I got older, my insistence on Mum telling me the story of how he died took its toll on her.

'Darling, you know that bit. Did you want to hear other stories? Look through the pictures again?'

But I would always end up flicking to the photograph tucked

in the back of the album, the one of him in the hospital bed, smiling but looking pale.

Mum let out a heavy sigh. 'Darling, you have it, okay? You have that one. I don't know why ... I don't like to see that one so much.'

After a major operation on his abdomen, Dad woke up complaining of intense, unrelenting pain. The doctors upped his morphine, and after a few days, sent him home with a couple of boxes of Oxycontin and instructions to take it easy. Long story short, the pain got worse, and after passing out in the supermarket, he got blue-lighted to A&E, where they discovered a surgical sponge had been left in his body and was going septic. They did their best to save him, but it was too late. He spent the next few weeks in and out of consciousness, complaining of green giraffes trying to 'lick his life away'. Until, apparently, one day, Mum put me down beside him, only just three and not understanding what was happening.

As I snuggled into his neck, he said, 'Ah, Hattie ... here you are sweet girl ... here you are but I think I'm going.'

I wish I could remember it, but I don't. I just remember being told Daddy was in the sky now. Because of the sponge, I thought. Because of the sponge that was hiding.

Mum's friends flew in from all corners, and I had special sleepovers with the neighbours when 'mummy needed quiet time'. I grew up around the grief like it was a stuffed toy I clung on to, barely noticing it was there until I needed to use both of my hands.

Mum met Martin when I was ten, and he was nice enough. The introduction was gentle and without any pressure. He didn't move in for a few years, and I always called him Martin rather than Dad. He was, and is, a kind man, who is supportive, and completely understanding that I will always go to Mum first. I liked that Mum seemed happy and I liked the sound of his radio on Sunday mornings. I could have done without his legal lectures; as an employment lawyer, he was a little too fond of the idea that one day we would sue some big organisation. I made the mistake of letting him read the contract for the job I got with Ella at the salon – and I will never, ever do that again. The phone calls. The ludicrous edit suggestions. The desire to read everything four times over and explain every legal term.

Sometimes we'd all go on holiday; sometimes they would go on holiday just the two of them, and I would stay with Ella. When Mum got back, she would go through the photos with me. I would always make her beaming smile fade when I got out the same old album again – 'since we're looking at pictures . . .'

She would sigh. 'Darling, you know the story.'

But I just couldn't stop thinking about the sponge, how it got sewn up inside my father and no one had even noticed it was missing.

I don't really tell people that Martin isn't my dad, I just let them assume until they start asking questions. Like how I have the money for XYZ. Being an only child, Dad's death brought a financial safety net. By the time I was in my late twenties, I still had enough to be able to stay in a hut in the middle of nowhere for two months because I needed to get away and start again.

4

#KEY

I stretched out in the car seat and hoped it wouldn't be too long before Christian arrived. Another episode of *24 Hours in A&E* was just starting when Ella messaged again, and I swiped it away with more force than necessary, at which point another message came in, and I hit my phone screen – hard – to read it.

Ella

Good film? X

Horror to cuddle up or romance to get sexy?

UMMM actually something to do with outfits for dogs

Was boring. So banged again, obvs

Bloody hell

A film about dogs and you bang

You going atttt it

Yeaaaaaah baby

Jealous

I will admit that these texts made me completely, utterly, fundamentally regret naming my made-up boyfriend Oliver because it was my dad's middle name. I had not really thought it through. It was just as I was looking through my things and working out if I was truly going to put this plan into action, when I found the photo of him in the hospital bed. I was staring at it, like I always do, as if one day I will notice something new, as if one day I will see the sponge in him . . . Anyway, his first name seemed too obvious. But his middle name – well, at the time, it felt right. And now here I was talking about my imaginary sex life with my imaginary boyfriend named after my very real dead dad.

Our Son Mr Jonathan

Pearl, how's Lena doing?

PEARL: Not too bad. The spots are scabbing over

ELLA: Gross lol

GEORGIA: Yeah ok Pearl was eating dinner but fine

I dropped my phone next to the handbrake and let the screen turn off by itself. I gazed into the blank, moonless sky, waiting for the glow of headlights.

*

The hut wouldn't have been my first choice, but it was the only reasonable place that let me book a two-month stay. That said, two months was the limit. I needed a job before then so I could afford somewhere to rent, otherwise I'd be living in my car, which was very much not part of The Plan. I was on edge as it was, sitting there for about an hour, waiting in the darkness for Christian.

When I saw his headlights, I opened the car door but waited until I felt confident it was him before jumping out into the dark. Christian was over six-foot with very neat grey hair. He made little eye contact and spoke curtly, calling, 'Hattie – yeah?' as the light inside my car illuminated my cautious expression, hand still on the door in case I needed to slam it shut.

'Yeah, hi, hiya Christian, sorry.'

I handed him the key and tried to keep up with him as he walked toward the hut.

'Just couldn't ...' I called, as he made it to the door before me.

He opened the door, first time, with ease. 'What was the problem?'

The rain was only spitting now but I shielded my face and squinted at him as though it was still pouring.

'Like I say, it just couldn't – wouldn't – turn, Nancy said it could be a bit stiff?'

He hardly let me finish my sentence.

'Well, you're in now.' His eyes darted in the direction of his car. 'Okay?'

'Yep, thank you.'

He jogged down the steps and looked at me quizzically,

wondering why I wasn't going in, but I was reluctant to slowly try and climb the steps again with him watching. He'd turned the light on so our faces were gently lit by the warm glow of the hut.

'God! Really coming down, thanks again!'

The rain was still very lightly spitting but for some reason I decided that since it was dark, I could keep pretending it was pouring so Christian would leave faster. Trying to convince someone light rain was an onslaught was a concerning tactic, possibly verging on a messiah complex.

Christian gave me another confused look and turned back to his car. I stood by the steps, looking into the small building I was set to call home for the next eight weeks.

I took another slow, wobbly walk up the three steps into the hut. At the far end was the bed: a single, with a bedside table up against the mattress. The duvet and pillows were bright white, crisp and freshly laundered, a chunky knit grey throw on the end of the bed. A table jutted out of the wall at the other end, built-in benches with grey cushions on either side, although the table only really had space for one. A wood burner sat beside it, and there was a proper sink with running water and a wooden cover, so you could use it as a worktop. I could see a cooker, a little fridge, no freezer, no washing machine. In the kitchen along the back wall, there was the slightly weird addition of a pink helium balloon with a note at the bottom, weighted with a stone. I lifted it off and the balloon bobbed against the roof.

WELCOME HATTIE!

Odd move from them, I thought. A balloon? Who pumped it up? Did they get it done in a shop? And then carry it all the way across the field in the wind? Do they do that every time they have a guest? Or do they have their own helium cannister? And if so, is it here, in the hut? I looked around but the hut was clearly too small for such an item. The logistical implications made me bite the inside of my cheek. If only they'd spent their energy making sure the door was easy to open.

I went for a wee in the bathroom tucked in the corner and decided that this would do very nicely. I put the kettle on, knelt down and opened the door of the wood burner, then whacked a log in from the little basket by its side. I had no idea what I was doing, but I assumed it couldn't be that difficult. I scrunched up some kitchen paper and put that in, then reached for the box of matches. They were only short ones, and my fingers found it difficult to grip them properly. After a few failed attempts, one finally lit, but the shock of the flame made me drop it on the mat. A tiny scorch mark was left as the match sat extinguished. I decided I'd just go to bed rather than continue this mission. Imagine if I accidentally set the place on fire thirty minutes after needing help getting in the door? 'Hiya, Nancy, bit of an update . . .'

I pulled the extra blanket over the duvet and tucked myself in. Before I turned out the light, I looked at the balloon, still sitting against the curved ceiling, with the note dangling from its string. Something inside me was desperate to see if I could reach it from the bed and play with it, pulling it down and letting go of the string. I shut off the light and promised myself I'd pop it first thing in the morning.

5

#BALLOON

When I was four, I broke my leg trying to catch a pink balloon. I still remember the carpeted classroom, the way the light shone through the floating sphere as I jumped up to catch it, and the way I crumpled down, the hot pain of the broken bone and the teacher who thought I was crying over nothing and made me get up and walk on it. I didn't tell her that I couldn't; I just tried to do what she said and I was back on the floor again in half a second, howling.

It had been a special afternoon; we were holding our very own pretend wedding in the classroom, which looking back seems a bit wrong, but back then, my main issue was that I wasn't the bride. Claire got to be the bride; Claire with the beautiful, black curly hair who never invited me to her house after I'd invited her to mine. Rumour has it she had a quad bike, which, again, looking back, makes four-year-old Claire seem like a bit of wanker, but at the time, it gave her an ethereal aura of freedom: maturity and the open road.

Mum was called; she wrapped me in a blanket, lay me down in the back of the car and drove to A&E. I still remember every jolt. A doctor had a look at both legs and asked me if I could lift, bend and straighten them. I wanted him to give me a sticker but instead he sent me to X-Ray in a wheelchair and Mum wasn't allowed in with me. The lady in X-Ray asked me if I could get out of the chair and get on the X-Ray table, and I didn't say anything because I didn't know what the right answer was. Mum would know what the right answer was but she was outside. Eventually I got lifted onto the table and had to lie still, which was a bit difficult because I was crying. I distinctly remember thinking that I wouldn't be in this situation if I had been the bride.

I went back into the doctor's room and it was too full of people and too hot and I was too tired and too sick of the pain and the antiseptic. I remember a lot of words I didn't understand. What I did understand was that things were a lot more complicated because I already had a disability.

They told me I had to stay in the hospital for a little while, and then one of the people in the room dropped all their money on the floor and I remember looking at the shiny fifty pences and hoping that she would give me some, because that seemed fair after such a bad day, but she didn't, and next thing I knew, Mum was leaving and I was on a ward with a boy groaning into the dark because all his ribs were broken after a car crash. I never saw anyone come to visit him, which could make me seem empathetic, but actually I just kept hoping someone would come to get him so he would go away.

Nurses would often ask me if I was in any pain, and even though I was, and the cast they'd put on my leg was itchy and heavy, I said I wasn't because I wanted to go home sooner. At first, I was honest about the pain, but it only meant more strange faces would gather around my bed, ask more questions, try and test my movement again, talk of sending me back to X-Ray, talk of just 'a few more days'.

When I was eventually allowed to go home, Mum had moved my bed downstairs and I had to stay off school for a whole term. One day my class came to visit and I lay there as they ran around the living room acting out their favourite bits of *The Jungle Book* that Mum had put on in the hopes of calming everyone down. As the room filled with the leaps and screams of wild animals, I looked down at my body and saw how broken it was compared to the others. I thought about how, even when my leg was healed, I still wouldn't be 'better', not really. Not like the children in my class. None of them were breaking their legs now, in my lounge, as they jumped about, and danced, and did handstands with their legs kicking in the air. I thought about being on the ward and the nurse who asked me how I ended up with a broken leg. When I told her, she said I had to try and keep my feet on the ground from now on.

THE NIGHT THAT CHANGED EVERYTHING

23:32

The waiting room is extra busy. Time of year probably. Receptionist has her head down and doesn't seem to be making eye contact with anyone. Medical staff are only seen in small flashes, as they move from treatment rooms to the main ward and back again, calling names that barely register, because it's never my name, and that's what I need. I need my name to be called. I need to know that someone is calling out for me and hoping I respond.

6

#PLAN

Our Son Mr Jonathan

PEARL Ha Sorry

ELLA It's okay Pearl I have recovered

GEORGIA Less scabs more Oliver's house!

PETE Yeah what's it like?

Give me a sec guys I'm knackered

The drive was so tiring

GEORGIA Yeah but picturessss

I clicked off the chat.

Ella

Morning lovely!

Urgh it's so quiet here without you

Polly's coming later THANK GOD

There's no one to talk to

[Missed Voice Call from Ella]

Sorry I missed you!

Actually quite jealous of the peace

Just had brunch with Oliver's family

CHATTY BUNCH

OMG you've met his family already??

Need updates!

Don't worry, full story coming

Need a nap but we're all on a dog walk atm – his mum has a husky!

I was still in bed and hadn't even opened the blinds. All that packing and driving had worn me out, and I couldn't face talking to Ella. I don't really know why I added in the husky, but she didn't try and call again. I looked over to the large piece of A2 paper propped up by the kitchen table. There in bold, black sharpie was the heading: The Plan.

I had managed to leave my old life: tick. My friends did not know the real reason, but I couldn't tick that off yet: there was another element to that part. When you start a new life, it means the old one has to end. I had, in a sense, died, but Ella didn't know that yet. Ella thought she was still chatting to me, but I was just a ghost. I was planning to exist only through flashes of sound and sight – messages here and there, a phone or video call once in a while. I would find a job and get set up in Wales with a flat and then go quiet when Oliver and I eventually 'broke up', saying I needed space to get over him. And then there would be mentions of new boys, new friends and being busy, slowly but surely drifting apart until we weren't really friends anymore. This way, I didn't have to explain anything to Ella; I didn't have to go through the grisly post-mortem as she poked and prodded and asked, 'Why?'

I couldn't explain what had happened. About how there was a moment I knew, for sure, that I had to leave. That would have killed me. Even thinking of it here, all those miles away, in the hut, made me feel sick. Keeping Ella from knowing The Real Reason was an ongoing challenge.

I had arrived in Wales: tick. And so far, as far as anyone else knew, I wasn't disabled. The incident with the door had rattled me, but Christian didn't know. I didn't tell him, I didn't explain, the words didn't have to drag themselves up my throat and hang in the air while he took me in as a whole different person.

I picked up the sharpie on the table and added a line underneath.

WELCOME TO YOUR NEW LIFE!
WELCOME TO FREEDOM

Then I underlined one of the bullet points I had made a few weeks ago.

Interview for reception job at Hospital!!
  Get Job = Paycheque
  Get rental = Yearlong lease = SECURITY

The interview was tomorrow and was also, concerningly, the only one I'd been offered. I was still applying for other things when they came up; there was a teaching assistant job, a librarian, a police admin assistant, but it was slim pickings in terms of jobs where I could get away with hiding my disability. But the reception job would be great. I just needed to absolutely nail it.

I had, naturally, lied on my application. My previous experience working as a receptionist in the beauty salon with Ella became a *Private Healthcare Clinic*. I was fairly confident that when they rang my old boss, Gareth, he would go along with it: he was obsessed with marketing us like we existed in the medical world.

'Hey, here's a thought,' he'd start, as I was checking our bookings for the day, 'I'd like a poster about our eyebrow treatments. But tie it into mental health, if you can?'

When I went to him an hour later to say I was struggling, he started rubbing a spot behind his ear.

'Self-care equals feeling better equals less depression, yeah? It's not about the eyebrows; it's about how they've healed your PTSD, you know?'

Once I'd gone over my application, I needed to find the perfect outfit. As I was rummaging around one of the three suitcases I'd dragged from the car (and very sketchily up the steps), I started thinking about what it would be like working in A&E every day, and the 'live' rounds of The Game I'd be able to play, noticing the symptoms, trying to work it all out: pale skin, washed-out eyes, an arm gripped tightly, close to the body. A burn or a break?

I came across another wash bag and, once again, the sponge was back in my head. Sitting in my dad's body all that time. Silently. I put the bag to the side and reached for a black dress.

It was tight, shift-style in thick matte fabric, with a zip at the back that I could only do halfway up. I wondered if I could get away with throwing on a large cardigan but the fabric gaped too much around my boobs without the zip done up properly. This was not a dress for someone currently living alone. As I looked through the other options, I was disappointed to see it wasn't the only one with a fastening at the back. The pale pink blouse that I was considering had a high neck with three clasp buttons at the back; something I'd usually ask Ella to help me with. Never mind, new beginnings would mean a new wardrobe, just as soon as I got a job. I discarded them and tried on the only option left: a cotton, stretchy swing dress in burgundy. It didn't look bad, and if I got any blood on me while in the hospital, at least it wouldn't show.

I balanced my phone on the bed, hit record, and managed to just about squeeze in a full body shot from the other end of the hut. I walked towards myself then watched the video back.

I put on a pair of black tights and my knee-high boots, hiding my lower legs. Even though most people don't think I'm disabled, I couldn't risk anything. The way interviewers look at you is different from the way most people look at you.

They're really, *properly* looking. I couldn't risk my legs, or my walk, giving the game away. My legs that, as a doctor once described, were like 'upside down champagne bottles' – and I said, 'Woah, sounds like my legs are calling for a party?' They didn't get the joke.

As a kid, I was often told to walk up and down one of the many hospitals. Once they even painted my feet and asked me to walk along a strip of paper whilst they studied the marks I'd made and made notes. They never shared those notes with me.

I chucked my phone down on the bed and opened the doors to the hut, breathing in the cold air. Crows flew from the trees in the woods nearby, as if shot from a party popper, out into the sky. I could feel that extra chamber in my lungs opening out again. The patches of dewy moss looked so comforting compared to the chewing gum stuck on the pavement in London. I could hear birdsong rather than angry motorists beeping at someone for taking a second too long to move at a green light. I'd always think, 'Give them a chance, we don't all move at the same pace, you know.' Here, surrounded by rolling hills, with the woods to the side leading down to a small, quiet village, I felt the space and the air that I had been yearning for. That's what I needed – to surround myself in the very present, mindful world of nature.

As I went to grab the keys, my heart dropped. I took a deep breath and in an act of denial tried to twist the key in the lock again, this time with the door open. Maybe it was just because it was dark and I was tired the first time? But no, I still wasn't strong enough.

Back inside, I opened my laptop to try and research some sort of disability aid that might help me open the door, but soon found myself on YouTube watching more clips of injured people in waiting rooms.

'Susan has come in with an—'

I paused it. Her left leg was stretched out in front of her. Swollen ankle? Foot? No, it's probably her ankle.

'—infected toenail.'

Damn it.

I punched the pause button and scrolled to find another video until I found a patient I could guess correctly. I got out my notebook and played The Game until I convinced myself I could work anything out. Whatever the problem. Even not being able to get into my own front door.

After about ten minutes, I was clear headed enough to be comparing two 'key turners' that I could pick up at a local hardware store on the way to my interview the next day. A key turner was a device that, once you had fixed the key to it, basically gave it a long handle that made it much easier to turn.

I scrawled an extra bullet point on The Plan:

> FIND WAY TO HIDE DISABILITY AIDS, NEED EXCUSE READY IN CASE THEY ARE FOUND

One more A&E video, and then it was time to work out the rest of my appearance. My hair was in need of a brush and littered with split ends that splayed out just below my shoulders. I put it up in a bun and threw on some large hoop earrings. I studied my hands, wanting them to look natural. Bit intense to wear gloves in an interview so, as long as the interviewers didn't see me grip or twist anything, I thought I'd get away with it.

I set up my phone again and practised walking a few more

times. I practised sitting down and standing up, trying to reduce the chances of me wobbling. I practised opening the door to leave. I practised smiling. I filmed my eyes close up and watched the video back, staring into my pupils to make sure they didn't give anything away, my irises tight around the black abyss, dotted with flecks of dark and light brown, like the colours of a snail's shell.

7

#DEN

I was carefully inspecting a snail when I first met Ella. It was mini-beasts week and all the Year Five classes had come together to, as Mr Margrove kept repeating, 'Explore, Find and Record'. I was very excited about finding a snail, in part because it meant I could finish the worksheet and get to eat my snack, which today was a fruit winder that I'd promised to share with Nina. I remember this because Nina was taking ages with her mini-beasts so I scoffed the whole lot and when she found out, she cried, and told Mr Margrove who told me to apologise, which I did, but I got a detention seconds after the sentence, 'Sorry Nina, I've been a bit of a twat,' came out of my mouth, because I made the mistake of thinking that 'twat' was another way of saying 'twit'. The next day, Ella presented me with a 'With Sympathy' card she had made herself, apparently deciding that an unfair detention was akin to a death in the family. I loved it so much our friendship was cemented then and there.

But our conversation over the snail was the thing that sparked our friendship into light.

'Oh my gosh, you found a really good one!' she said, a look of wonder on her face.

We sat on the grass, noting the features of its little stalk eyes and spirals, with Ella lending me her silver gel pen so I could make the picture of its body all sparkly.

When we hit Year Six, the school bought a new field, creating a larger outdoor area for breaks and lunchtime. The edge of the field was lined with trees, and you could explore them for a few metres before hitting the blue-stringed boundary.

Here began the creation of dens, to the point that the field looked virtually empty at lunch, while everyone gathered on the edges. Ella and I took the creation of our den very seriously. The day after we got to check out the new playing field, she arrived armed with secateurs and a full-on grim reaper scythe. The scythe was confiscated the minute a teacher saw her walking through the locker room with it, and Ella had to have three meetings in the headmaster's office to make sure she hadn't been radicalised – by a gardening club or otherwise.

Our parents discussed it at length one evening when Ella came round for tea.

'I mean, come on,' they said, leaning on the kitchen counter as we tucked into turkey dinosaurs, 'the girls haven't got a violent bone in their body.'

'Exactly,' agreed my mum, 'I mean they're not even angry. We don't do anger here, do we love?'

She smiled at me and I nodded back. This was a common phrase in our house. The way my mum dealt with me getting in a strop was to simply deny it was happening.

'We don't do anger here,' she'd said, when I was getting

particularly riled up about having to be the umpire every sports lesson rather than being allowed to do art inside.

'But it isn't fair,' I muttered, 'and it does make me angry.'

I was in Year Six, and tiny, but the feelings inside were too large and too heavy to stay submerged forever.

THE NIGHT THAT CHANGED EVERYTHING

23:54

We're not going to do the countdown, are we? People in A&E don't do the countdown, even on New Year, right? I feel like I've slipped into a parallel universe. This is where the broken people are. The ones who didn't make it to see the fireworks, who don't get to look into the night sky. We sit together in limbo, but I don't feel much togetherness. Everyone else seems to be here with someone. Someone who will pull them out of the brokenness, back into the morning of New Year. But I'm here on my own. I've got no one to hold on to.

8

#BOLT

Unfortunately, your application for 'Teaching Assistant: Wales' has been rejected. Please log in to your account for more details.

Ella

[Missed Voice Call from Ella]

Mum

Hey love how's it all going? X

Hey muma pyjama xx Yeah it's all going well, lovely to be actually spending proper time with Oliver!

Will call you at weekend

Might have job news by then!

Oh that's great

So glad to hear it

Only when you have time, no pressure x

Ella

Sorry I missed you, on way to interview!

How's Polly settling in?

Oooh what job??

Let me know how it goes

Yeah Polly great

still weird without you

Someone in Oliver's family knows someone who needs a dog walker

Having another brunch to discuss

You're literally just having sex and brunches

Hey what else is new

I didn't tell Ella where I was actually having an interview in case I got the job, and then she could just walk in one day as a 'surprise'. As I waited to be called into the interview, I had to admit it was nice having someone to talk to. I really hoped I'd get the job, so I could start making new friends as the new me. I just had to absolutely smash the next half an hour.

LIT

You have a new match!

I swiped the dating app notification away out of habit. I was completely bored of the apps, but not quite bored enough to delete them entirely. I thought I'd probably start again when I got properly settled in Wales but was in no hurry. I was more than capable of wanking my way out of the desire to message back a boy who was over 6ft but 'apolitical' and 'not sure' of what he was looking for. Now was not the time for dating. It was the time for a job.

Has your heart ever thudded in your chest so hard you're convinced other people can hear it? Edgar Allan Poe wrote a story about a guy who murdered someone and hid the heart under the floorboards. When the police came round, he was convinced they could hear it beating.

The minute I got in that interview room, it felt like my whole body was a floorboard, and the heart thudding underneath it was going so fast that it felt alien to me. I was told that one of the interviewers, Jackie, would be my line manager if I got the job. I mused about commenting on how much I liked her blouse, but then thought better of it: it was a peculiar beige, one that's difficult to describe. You've heard of Elephant Grey; this was Starving Camel. The other interviewer was a man called Warren who kept holding onto his pen even when he wasn't writing. Warren's shirt was a genuinely nice pale pink but he had the look about him of someone who would take a compliment from a woman as a confession of undying love, so I steered clear.

At one point they gave me a hypothetical scenario: 'Working in an A&E department, obviously you'll come into contact with patients who are in very heightened states of emotion. What would you do if a patient started to get frustrated with how long they'd been waiting, and came up to you at the desk demanding to be seen by the medical team?'

I wanted to say: 'The way I keep myself calm is to watch videos of people in A&E and work out what's wrong with them, so this job will be like meditating for me.'

But I knew that wouldn't float. Instead I went with: 'Aggressive behaviour would not be tolerated as I have a duty to keep the other patients and staff safe.'

I sat in silence, absolutely thrilled with my answer. Confident. Assured. This girl takes no shit.

'Okay, yep, I see your line of thought. How would you communicate that with the patient?' asked Warren.

'I'd tell them I'm calling security.' Bad. Ass.

'Well they're just raising their voice a little, let's say. Do you think perhaps a warning might be appropriate in that situation?'

Bugger. Clearly they wanted me to show that I do, in fact, take some shit.

'Oh! If it was just a case of a raised voice, then that's something I can deal with. No problem. I am used to having to raise my—' I stuttered. 'I am used to difficult customers.'

'And what if they asked to be bumped up the list?'

'I would tell them that unless they are experiencing new symptoms or a worsening of their condition, they need to wait their turn.'

'And what if they say, "Well yes, actually, I'm feeling really faint"?'

'I'd advise they sit down with their head between their legs.'

Warren gripped his pen a little tighter. I glanced down at my bag on the floor and wondered how much longer the interview was going to take. They moved on to asking me about my availability, and wanted to confirm that I would be okay to work night shifts.

'Ab—' I cleared my throat 'Absolutely,' I nodded.

'You have a good stamina?' they asked, and I nodded again. My throat was starting to get scratchy. The memory of driving into the hospital car park and realising I couldn't use my blue badge flashed in my brain. It was now hidden in the glove box.

When they asked me why I wanted the job, I couldn't help but let out a cough. A part of me just wanted to say: 'Look, I won't go into the details but something happened back in London and I knew I needed to start my life again and I do have some savings stored from when Dad died, but that's going to run out soon and I can't stay in Airbnbs forever, so I need a job so I can pay the rent.'

But I couldn't say that, obviously.

Instead, I said, 'There's nothing more important than being part of a team that looks after people on the worst day of their lives. And it's that team I'm really looking forward to getting to know, socially, too, as I've just moved down here.'

I was genuinely hopeful for the social side of things – with the other staff, not the patients, because I assumed no one would really want to chat with a smashed-up eye socket.

When it was over, I walked quickly into the toilets. My mascara had smudged a little, and my hair had started to come out of the bun I'd put it in, strands flying in all directions. But on all accounts, it hadn't gone too badly.

Instead of going back home straight away, I decided to take a trip around the hospital, because the lure of seeing how it felt to wander around without an appointment looming over me was overwhelming. It certainly had a sense of nostalgia, but it was a different feeling. This is how it is, I thought, to be non-disabled. To be here as a person with a job, not a person with a body that was of medical interest.

I reckon you could spend every day of your life going into a hospital, and wandering around the corridors, occasionally sitting in a busy waiting room, killing time in the café, and no one would ever notice you. The cliché is that the woods are the place where people get lost, but that's not realistic. Hospitals: they're the place you can really get lost in.

I looked at one of the maps, studying the coloured squares and the key in detail, imagining myself in the A&E department, all the patients coming in at the door and ending up going deeper and deeper into the hospital. Do you know they never put the morgue on a hospital map? I always assume it to be in the basement, just in case one day the floor collapses. Imagine all that careering down into cardiac care. Hell of a test for the pacemakers.

I went round the corner and found a bench. Sitting down, I took out the key turner I'd bought from a mobility shop on the way to the interview. I needed to put it together before I got home, in case it was faulty or something. When I got to my actual flat, I'd make sure that I could get through the door with ease, and then I could dispose of this long-handled cat-out-the-bag. No one would ever need know.

I was just unscrewing the little bolt that you use to fix the key to the handle when it flicked out of my grasp and went rolling away in the direction I'd come from, spinning at the corner and disappearing from sight. I clutched the key turner and gently put it in my bag before I lost any other part of it and attempted to very smoothly walk in the direction the bolt had rolled, trying not to draw too much attention to myself.

I turned the corner and that is when I saw, to my horror, a porter picking up the bolt and looking worriedly at the wheelchair and its patient he had parked by the hospital map. He didn't see me looking, instead crouching down by one of the wheels and checking to make sure the bolt hadn't come from there.

And then he put the bolt in his pocket.

HIS POCKET.

The only way I was getting back into the hut was IN A STRANGER'S POCKET.

I studied him as he turned to look at the hospital map. He was fit, about my age, although maybe a little older, just over thirty or so. He had a closely shaved head, brown skin and very sexy forearms with tattoos of flowers and thorns and rain clouds.

I needed to get that bolt back.

'Excuse me,' I started, and he turned round. God. He was phenomenally hot. 'I think you have my bolt.'

I tried to style out the sentence as though it was a very normal thing to say. He looked confused.

'My bolt,' I repeated. 'You just put it in your pocket.'

He clicked onto what I was talking about with an 'OH – right – this –' He held it toward me, 'this is yours?'

'Yes. That's my bolt,' I said, taking it from him. 'Thanks.'

There was a pause. I didn't mind looking into his beautiful green eyes.

'Where's it from?' he asked.

I had not thought this far ahead.

'It is from.' I stopped as though it was a complete sentence. 'My . . . skateboard.'

His brow furrowed for a second before melting into a gorgeous smile, one that made his eyes seem even more radiant than before.

'Oh, nice. You skate?'

'Yes. I am a skateboarder.'

'Cool. Where is it?'

Yes Hattie, where exactly was this skateboard? Why not give him a demo, do a cheeky little flip?

I stood there silently, my face growing red.

'Can we get a move on?' The voice of my saviour, my guardian angel, sitting in the wheelchair and patiently waiting.

'Sorry,' I said. 'You should get going.'

I turned on my heel and went round the corner, praying to every God going they weren't about to come the same way. After a few minutes, I cautiously poked my head back around to see that they had disappeared. I scurried back, gripped the plastic of the key turner in my mouth so I had two hands free to screw the key in tightly, and worked as quickly as I could in this quiet moment with no one watching me. Thankfully, I managed to put the thing together okay, and found my way out of the hospital. I did, very subtly, go on to the dating app to see if I happened to stumble across the porter after a few swipes. But no, and I got off my phone when I saw my new match was from London, anyway.

It'd been raining while I was inside, and the gentle swish of tyres going through puddles bounced around the car park, a backdrop to the beeps of machines and shutting of doors. As I walked towards my car, a lady in a grey jumper pushed a buggy in the direction of the hospital, her daughter kicking her legs and singing, before hurling her bright orange soft toy onto the wet ground. I bent down to pick it up, her mum smiling a thank you, as I looked at it properly. A jolly, smiley, big-eyed llama.

'Lam-Lam,' the toddler called, her arms stretching out toward me.

I held the toy for a second too long, and the call became a shriek.

'Sorry!' I said, handing it back to her. 'It's just a very cool llama.'

9

#LLAMA

I got very angry whacking the piñata at Ella's eleventh birthday party. With the 'we don't do anger here' line still holding firm at home, getting angry was something I tried to do away from Mum and Martin, but this did mean that it inevitably came out at the wrong moments.

Ella's parents had booked people to run the party: both of whom were called Katy and kept asking us if we were 'ready' for the various activities they had planned, including manicures, dancing and a cupcake decorating contest. Fair play to the three boys that turned up and fully engaged with everything, especially when they figured out that you trip out if you take a massive sniff of the nail polish remover.

It was a classic pre-teens birthday party as we all arrived trying to look as cool as possible: myself in a lilac floaty number from BHS, a lilac hairband with small diamanté detail, and very gritty lip gloss that I'd got free in a magazine. This desire to be cool was precariously balanced with still being kids, and being very swayed by the promise of stickers, prizes and sweets. Nothing demonstrates this better than a llama piñata.

There it hung in the garden in all its pink and orange glory, tiny strips of paper starting to curl up toward the sky, its eyes two perfect black circles, its ears far too upright, as though it sensed its fate: the predators were coming. We all encircled the poor paper beast as Ella went first, blindfold on, stick in her hands. Her parents stood a little way away, taking photographs, while one of the Katys spun her around as music blared out from the other Katy's phone. Two misses and three direct hits maimed, but did not break, the llama, much to the pleasure of the girl waiting to go next. We counted out the number of goes as she flailed the stick in the air, the sun blinking out as it disappeared behind a cloud and came back out again.

'Five!' we all shouted as she made her last hit, a poor show if I'm honest, and the llama held firm. As I twigged that the llama was going to take some beating, I counted the number of kids in the circle before it was my turn, and slyly moved further away, next to a boy called Omar, during a moment of cheering for a particularly good hit.

As the minutes went on, the impatience of the kids started to show as the circle moved closer to the target, and the number of swipes became less clear, merging together in a kind of battering when the stickholder had figured out where to aim.

When Peter Banbury's blindfold slipped and there was no intervention from anyone, I had a moment of relief when I thought I would get away without having a turn, but the llama, although clearly emotionally, physically and spiritually broken, was still refusing to haemorrhage. It was now lopsided, literally hanging by a thread, and one of its eyes had fallen off, staring back up at its tortured body from the ground. I reluctantly moved toward one of the Katys and, just before she put my blindfold on, I remember looking to see if the llama had been given a mouth, but I saw no line or obvious break in the tissue paper squares below its nose.

My voice shook as I tried to ask her quietly not to spin me round. The words were so worn, so heavy, and once again they scratched my throat.

'But that's the game!' she said. 'Got ourselves a sly one here.' She laughed and spun me quickly.

Ella's mum started calling, 'Oh! Careful, careful!' as I struggled to keep my balance. Then Katy stopped spinning me and handed me the stick, with a jokey, awkward, 'sorry!'

There was a heavy silence in the air as if I had personally inhaled the party atmosphere and everyone was waiting on me to breathe it back out.

As I was given the stick, I heard groans around me, and that was when I started to feel really irritated. I was wobbly on my feet, and disorientated. I'd asked her not to spin me around. Why did she still do it?

I took a swipe and it felt good, but it only hit the air, and no one seemed to be counting my hits. That made it worse, and I gripped the stick tighter, swung harder. I started to shout a little when I swung. No hit.

A 'three!' was called, their silence broken as I brushed the llama, and the feeling of hitting something was liberating. I gave another swipe, hard, and screamed as they yelled 'Four!', excited at the prospect of what might happen next.

'Five!'

The last one was a full-on whack with a guttural 'RAAAAAA' that I didn't even realise I was screaming until it was almost over. As the llama dropped, the crowd shrieked.

I kept hold of the stick and pulled the blindfold down, but seconds after my eyes had adjusted to the light, I felt a weight hit my lower legs and I was on the ground, staring at the hands grabbing the sweets between the blades of grass. A girl jumped over me and as I felt the echoes of her feet around my head, I let go of the stick. I tried to roll myself over and away from the wrestling bodies, but I was too dead-centre to have space, as everyone crowded around me. I started to feel as though I couldn't breathe, and made an attempt to call out, but no sound came. My eyes strained for Ella, or her mum, or anyone who knew I'd need help to get up, that this wasn't rough and tumble and none of this felt like a game. For far too long, the only eye I could meet, in the small space between bodies and blades of grass, was the one that remained on the llama. After what felt like forever, I heard Ella's voice and her arm was reaching out for me, telling everyone to stop.

'You're hurting her!' she yelled, trying her best to get me off the ground.

Next thing I knew, Ella's mum called for everyone to stop as she pulled me up. I felt my face go red as everyone stared at me, and the tears came soon after. I was escorted back inside where the other kids fiddled with their sweet wrappers.

'You really went for it there, Hattie,' her mum said, looking concerned. 'Overdid it a bit, eh?'

I didn't say a thing. I had hit that thing hard, with anger running through me, but at the end of the day, that was the game. I only did the same as everybody else.

Ella sat down next to me in the hall, her mum hovering nearby.

'Thank goodness for our Ella, eh,' said her mum.

'I got these for you,' Ella held out her hand and offered me two clammy Chewits and some sort of unbranded boiled strawberry delight, saved especially for me from her hoard.

I took them gladly and thanked her for helping me up. I went back outside, deciding just to watch this time, as they played a game of tug of war with a 'special' pashmina a Katy had provided. Ella sat with me too, insisting she'd rather be with me than play a silly game.

'I could have not had this party at all and just sat here and chatted to you, and it would have been the best,' she said, licking a lollipop. 'Are you sure you're not hurt?'

'I'm fine, really.'

'Does it hurt more when you fall over? Because of what makes you poorly?'

She asked the question with genuine, kind curiosity, but I didn't like the way she said poorly.

'Well, I'm not poorly, really, am I? It's a condition with my nerves. And I think so. I think I'm not as strong and I wobble.' I felt the same burning in my throat that I'd felt when I spoke to one of the Katys, the pain of the words coming out as they went past the place that was already sore: the place where I'd had to drag out a plea not to spin me around, to have to try and explain why I was different.

'Oh yeah, your nerves. God I'm really so sorry, Hattie. I'm just bad at biology.' We both laughed. 'Hey, apparently we get to learn about sex next term.'

I was pleased at the change of subject. 'I'm still confused about how long it takes to have sex, you know?' I started unwrapping one of the sweets.

'I think it's like three hours? It must be quite a long time.'

'Yeah, that sounds about right. That's why people do it at night.'

Ella nodded in agreement.

We went back to watching the game of tug of war and as both teams held on tightly, I sucked the strawberry sweet and felt the liquid pool in my mouth, finding, as I swallowed, that it soothed my aching throat.

I wonder if I would have believed it if someone had told me, right then, that nearly twenty years later, I'd be constructing a plan to covertly end our friendship completely – slowly pulling on the rope that connected us, getting further and further away until eventually, it snapped.

THE NIGHT THAT CHANGED EVERYTHING

00:12

No, we didn't do the countdown. Just a few mutters between people, tired smiles. A small 'woo!' from two girls. I expect it's too early for rowdy drunks with nosebleeds and bruised fists. I keep checking my phone, but nothing. How can this be happening? I send another text. I've sent so many now. No response. I try calling. Nothing.

I hold onto my ribs as the pain seems to double with every heavy intake of breath, tears making my eyeliner run into my eyes, leaving them red and stinging.

10

#BRITNEY

> Unfortunately, your application for 'Police 999 call operator: Wales' has been rejected. Please log into your account for more details.

Mum

Just booked a last minute few days walking holiday with Martin

Be good to chat before we leave?

Absolutely!

Ella

How'd it go??

??

Okay I think!

[Missed Voice Call from Ella]

I gave my phone another heavy hit to swipe Ella's name from the screen.

The evening after the interview, while I was waiting for some pasta to boil, I scrolled through the messages I'd missed on the group chat. Sam was getting ready for his date, posting pictures of the same shirt but with a different number of buttons fastened in each one, ranging from top collar to none at all. It was important I still kept in some kind of contact with my London friends so they didn't get too suspicious, and I had thought the group chat would be relatively easy.

Our Son Mr Jonathan

No buttons, tie the ends #Britney

PETE: She lives!

SAM: Knew she'd appear when it really mattered

GEORGIA: How is it?

SAM: Have you been murdered yet?

Yes! Murdered yesterday, now ghost.
But back to the buttons.

GEORGIA: Pictures please

Of what? My murder? Bit grim

SAM: Hahaaa

BEA: Oliver's house! Is he rich?

UM seriously Sam's a priority atm

SAM: THANK YOU

My pasta boiled over so I went about sorting it, trying to make sure it didn't leave a mark on the hob. By the time I looked again at the chat, Sam had left for his date and conversation had, unfortunately, turned to me.

ELLA: Photos of Oliver's house pls Hattie

BEA: Do you think he got you to move in with him
cos of your blue badge?

They were all fairly obsessed with my blue badge and it was a bit of a running joke. But in all honesty, who wouldn't be?

Hahahaaa

ELLA: House!! House!!

GEORGIA: CAN I JUST say

I still don't actually know what he looks like

BEA: Yeah me neither

GEORGIA: Him IN his house pls

He's out just now

PEARL: OMG guys just watch homes under the hammer if you wanna see a house!

Obviously, Oliver *in* his house was never going to happen, and while I appreciated that last message from Pearl, they weren't letting this one go. Pearl had once told me she found the group chat a bit intense, and I hadn't really understood what she meant.

'It's a lot of requests for gossip and pictures and . . .' She'd trailed off at the time, seeing my blank face.

Yeah, I'd thought, *that's why it's fun*.

But now I started to see her point. Wondering if it was believable enough, I took a few pictures of my surroundings and studied them, before deciding that no, I fundamentally couldn't. It very much looked like a hut.

I looked on Airbnb for some believable photos of living rooms that weren't too artistic but crucially did look really nice. I sort of needed everyone to think I was in a kind of paradise, so it would seem obvious that I wasn't coming back. Rightmove did not deliver the goods of paradise – there was either no furniture, or weird furniture, or mould, or occasionally an awkward shot of the estate agent in the bedroom mirror. Eventually I found a lovely living room, and then after some more scrolling, a fancy-looking bathroom, and screenshotted them both.

If you insist...

The images sent, and I held my breath.

GEORGIA: Fanncccyyy

SAM: Oh v niccee

The screen flipped to an incoming call from Ella, and since it was obvious I was online, I couldn't ignore it.

'You're very lucky you've caught me in the gap between brunch and sex,' I said, answering.

'I mean CLEARLY. You are absolutely on track for a UTI.'

'Omg I know though. The banging, the apple juice, it's not looking good.'

I tried to keep details brief about the interview for the dog-walking job, simply saying it had gone well but I didn't know yet, and then I tried to move the conversation on to Ella.

We talked about the salon, about Gareth, she complained about the tube, told me she was going out for drinks with Polly tonight, and that she wished I still lived with her.

Considering that I was telling her such a big lie, I still found it tricky telling little ones over the phone. Ones like, 'I know, I know, I really miss living with you too'. The guilt started to make me feel anxious, and I opened the doors to the hut and looked over at the woods. The natural shelter they formed looked so inviting. I bluffed about Oliver when she asked, saying he'd 'just got back' and I'd have to talk to her properly when he wasn't around, because I was still trying to play it cool.

'But,' I whispered, 'I really, really like him.'

'Like really, really?'

'Yeah, mate. Exactly like that.'

When we hung up the call, key turner – that worked a treat – in hand, I headed down towards the trees, and all I could think was how much space I had compared to London. There was no one rushing me down the slope, I wasn't trying to keep my balance while also making sure I got to a platform on time. The woods were open to me at all times, ready when I was ready, no hurry, no rush.

The air smelt earthy, full of green, rather than grey smoke and sweat. I was alone and yet, in that moment, as I dipped under the canopy that left rays of dappled sunlight falling softly on my face, the least lonely I'd felt in a long time. The birds, the beetles, the buds on the trees: they moved as they moved, and so did I. Somewhere, up above, a chick could have been pecking at a shell, ready to breathe in the air of this new world we both were hatching into.

'You're heading towards something so much better,' I told myself, looking up at the speckled sunlight. 'Away from cough sweets, from London, from Ella, from having to explain everything. Away from it all.'

And that day in the bliss of the woods, I really, truly believed it.

How could I be so wrong?

11

#THROAT

I was referred to a specialist about my sore throats when I was twelve.

'Can I watch it?' I asked. 'Can I see what you see?'

The ENT doctor was getting a little tired of my questions, but since I was only a kid, and my mum was sitting right by me, she managed to remain friendly.

'Alas it won't be possible, I'm afraid, and I can't promise the tape will be released on DVD, either. Now I just need to spray this numbing spray into your throat . . .'

Before I opened wide, I asked for a detailed commentary of what they were looking at. She told me she'd do her best and gave my mum a look.

'Less of the questions now, love,' Mum said.

After they stuck the camera down my throat, they told me there was nothing 'of note' to see. I wondered if that meant they had found something but had decided it wasn't worth telling me about it.

I quizzed my mum on the way home in the car.

'What do you mean you tried not to look? I want to know what I look like on the inside!'

She laughed and apologised for being too squeamish to study the screen.

'The main thing is there's nothing wrong. So you need to stop with the cough sweets, don't you? As Dr Frond said, they'll be making it worse at this point.'

Ever since that strawberry sweet at Ella's party, I thought I'd found a miracle solution to the burning sensation in my throat. The one that came when I was inevitably asked why I couldn't run by some new kid, or had to explain to a teacher that I wouldn't be in school because of a hospital appointment, then tell friends what would happen at the hospital appointment, and then what did happen at the hospital appointment and what was it, again, that was actually wrong with me. That syrupy liquid seemed to soothe things just enough that I didn't find my hand constantly rubbing at my neck, my teeth on edge in response to the pain.

Mum and Martin didn't really notice at first, it was a pretty normal thing for a twelve-year-old to take a packet of sweets into school every now and again. It's probably not that normal for a twelve-year-old to keep them in her school bag at all times, and to start using them as a sort of medication.

'What are you sucking on?' Ella would ask at break time while we were working out furniture arrangements for the den one day.

'Just a sweet,' I replied.

But as the months went on, I found that the boiled sweets were losing their power. I asked Mum to buy me some cough sweets in the weekly shop because I'd been getting sore throats. She quizzed me a little but agreed. When I asked her again the following week, she'd said I'd have to see the doctor if it was still going on. I bought them myself with my pocket money after that, pretending it was 'on the mend actually' when she asked a few days later.

The cough sweets seemed to work much better, but the taste was disgusting. I'd have to get used to it, like I'd heard Mum talk about with olives. I started having one every day, lying in bed before school, promising myself I wouldn't spit it out. When Mum found the wrappers hidden between my bedside table and my bed, the appointment for the doctor was made.

'You should have told me, darling. If it's that painful we need to get it sorted.' I was rarely in trouble and most things were dealt with by a conversation. She did at least stick to her side of the 'we don't do anger here' deal.

I managed to stop taking the cough sweets for a few months after seeing the ENT specialist, pretending the pain had stopped altogether. In reality I was just learning to live with it. Well, until we went on a family holiday and I met a boy called Eliot. After that, I found myself in the same old corner shop, staring at the same old packet, and promising myself that this time, I'd do a better job of keeping them hidden.

THE NIGHT THAT CHANGED EVERYTHING

00:30

A nurse stops and asks me me if I'd been given any pain relief.

'I can get you some paracetamol?' she says.

All I can do is shake my head and say, 'That's not why I'm crying.'

12

#FIRST

Mum

Lovely to chat darling

Here we are after today's walk/hike!

Aw yay! Great pic

Ella

[Missed Voice Call from Ella]

Sorry mate – bit hectic – got the dog walking job!!

Three days after the interview, I got the call to say the A&E job was mine. I danced around that tiny hut like a worm on MDMA. The turnaround was tight, though, and my first day was after the weekend, a week after arriving in Wales. Apparently, someone had left 'unexpectedly' and they were badly in need of staff, so I was warned my first shift would be a long one and I may be 'thrown in at the deep end'. No trouble, I had told them, I am an excellent swimmer, pushing away the images of me grappling onto the side of the pool in my pyjamas, while someone demanded I dived for a plastic brick. I had no use for the brick, I thought. If you need a brick, get it yourself.

And so, on my first day as an A&E receptionist, after a forty-minute journey that felt more like an hour, I was back in the hospital, pumped and ready to play my first real life version of The Game. It was particularly good because I was just shadowing a lady called Daphne, so I had a lot of time to concentrate on the waiting room. Daphne was white, middle-aged, had been working the job for sixteen years and had a strong Welsh accent. She had a receding hairline and wore a thick black velvet hairband to disguise it. She nudged it back as often as she said the word 'babe'. I spent a lot of time standing behind her, trying to guess what was wrong with patients before they spoke.

I was meant to be paying attention to how she sent notes over to the triage team and worked with whoever was 'out back' – a room behind the desk where we did extra admin and monitored the number of available beds in the various wards. However, I had changed my outfit six times that morning, convinced everything showed too much of my body, and by the time I got into the hospital I really needed The Game to distract my racing thoughts about how obvious it must be that I'm disabled. I was also beginning to regret triumphantly throwing away the cough sweets I'd found in a trouser pocket, as the anxiety was making my throat feel itchy.

The Game was extra fun to play in a live setting, and I started coming up with a points system:

> Woman-mid-forties-blonde-hair-clutching-arm-with-frozen-peas. Burn? Kettle?
>
> 'Hi I think I need to see someone quite urgently, I burnt my arm—'
>
> Yes! Get in. '—with quite a lot of bleach . . .'
>
> Shit. Fucking bleach. Chemical burn. Why do I never think of a chemical burn? Five points for burn, zero for the cause.

And then, even though I wasn't meant to look at patient notes in this way, I could find out if my guess was right too:

> Discharged tonight with burn cream and dressings, no follow up needed with plastics. Five more points.

An hour in and it felt like I'd landed the best job in the world.

Daphne seemed to know every single member of staff in the hospital, always stopping for a chat as they walked past and trying her best to loop me into the conversation, which I enjoyed. Her speed of typing was a worry though, as was the fact that when I did finally get to sit down, I wasn't strong enough to adjust the office chair that was far too low: how long would it be before people started to notice? Would they say something? The question was buried by a woman running in with a sick bag.

I recognised him the minute I came back to the desk after lunch. Of course, there he is, the very fit man who thinks I am a skateboarder. Phenomenal.

He was resting his chin on his hands, his flower and thunder tattoos on radiant display. I naturally wanted to get to know him better, but was still a little wary in case he asked me to do a kickback flip or something. If he found out I did not skateboard, he might ask, 'So why were you running around the hospital looking for your bolt?' What would I say then? That I was secretly a robot?

I tried to move quietly into the spare seat next to Daphne, but the chair was far lower than I had anticipated, and I lost balance trying to sit down. The chair juddered back as the wheels went spinning, and they both looked over at me as I clamped my feet to the ground. I made a horrendous 'woo!' noise in recognition and tried to gracefully wheel myself closer to the desk.

'Easy does it, babe! Aiden, love, this is Hattie. First day here in the chaos!'

I nodded a hello and tried to look busy on the computer that I didn't have a password for yet.

'Hey Hattie. Think I met you before – was that you, the other day – you were looking for your—'

I interrupted before he could get any further. 'No.'

Daphne blinked at me and looked back at Aiden.

'Oh – I thought—'

'Daphne, can you help me get set up with my login?' I asked.

There was an uncomfortable pause and I kept my eyes on the computer screen.

'I'll leave you to it then,' said Aiden, tapping the desk as he walked away.

Daphne wheeled her chair a little closer to me.

'Babe, don't worry about chatting when there's no patients waiting, like. Good to get to know everyone. Porters can do you a solid when you're in a bind and all.'

The minute he had gone I tried to make up for my sudden rudeness. Daphne had been nothing but kind to me all day.

'Oh, okay, he seems lovely. Sorry, just first day nerves and all!'

'You'll be okay, love,' she said. 'How about we go for a drink over the road when we finish? Just a quick one mind, but sure some of the other girls will be up for it, and you can get to know everyone, and settle a bit.'

Oh, absolutely, get in. Less than a day on the job and I was already well on my way to making some new friends in my new non-disabled life. The relief of a first day in a new job and not having to even mention my medical record. WELCOME TO FREEDOM. My throat had never felt better, and I was glad I'd thrown those sweets away. I was smashing it.

Quite a few people had been up for drinks, and as we left the hospital, I was trying to work out who everybody was. There was Daphne, of course, and then Melissa who I had briefly met as part of the reception team too, Anne who apparently did work on A&E but wasn't working that day and was meeting us there, three porters: Bhavin, Neil and Will, and then Zoe who worked on cleaning. I was sad to hear Aiden wasn't coming and had actually already left for the day.

While Daphne and Anne were middle-aged, Melissa was in her thirties, and I thought would make a good mate. The porters were similar and Zoe was early twenties. They seemed a good bunch, and I wondered how often the 'drink after work' thing happened. Would I be invited every time? To fully start this new life, with new friends, I needed to make sure I was.

The one problem was that the pub turned out not to be 'over the road' but a good ten-minute walk away, and I found it impossible to keep up with the group. They all set off at speed and my legs just couldn't keep the pace, so I faked a phone call and said I'd catch up with them.

'Here she is!' Daphne yelled when I made it a good ten minutes later than everyone else. 'Took your bloody time.'

'Sorry, I know, it was . . .' I stuttered. 'The ex. Whole reason I moved over here and he's still calling me.'

'Oh, can't be having that, love,' Daphne said. 'But since you're the last here I'm afraid it's on you to get the round in.'

I had no choice but to agree, so I made my way to the bar, which was quite a way from the table. I had eight drinks to get. I asked the barman for a tray, but wasn't sure if I'd be able to carry them all on that, so awkwardly took four of the drinks off, said I'd be back for the rest, and he gave me a wearied look.

The beers immediately sloshed over the sides as I walked, and it was all I could do to stop the wine from toppling over all together. A tremor started in my hands, needing to keep steady, but only having limited time before my arms gave out altogether.

When I finally made it to the table, Melissa piped up, with a smile, 'God, you do take your time, don't you?' I tried to swallow the shame that squirmed in my stomach and reared its head into my throat.

'And you're a few drinks short!' joined in Neil.

I put the tray down on the table with a clunk and more beer sloshed over the sides. Swallowing again, I could feel my cheeks getting hot. I looked back to the bar area; it was a lot more crowded than it was a minute ago.

'Well, for that, you can go and get the rest of them,' I said, motioning toward the bar with the dripping tray. I hid my shaking hands under the table.

'That's my girl!' said Daphne.

'Guy at the bar was taking ages. I told him I'd give him a minute. Probably his first day. Not sure bartending is for him,' I said.

'I'll let you off because you're new but next time I'm not having it,' said Neil.

The table laughed and I started being introduced to everyone.

'And you've met Neil, of course,' Daphne said, while he was still at the bar. 'Currently single I might add, if you need to get over that ex.'

I pretended to look slightly horrified, which got another chuckle from the table and inside I was delighted. The plan was working, because new people never usually talked to me about dating if they knew I was disabled.

'What about you, Bhavin?' asked Daphne. 'What's the news with that girl?'

'I'm getting there, I'm getting there,' he said, nodding with a smirk. 'Paul, bless him, was trying to give me dating advice earlier.'

The table laughed again, and Neil came back with the drinks.

'First day? That was Ian at the bar, he's worked here all his life.'

The table went quiet as everyone looked at me for an answer.

'Bloody hell – I . . .' Words started to disappear on me. 'I don't know, if that's – if that's fast service in Wales then I miss London!' Then I giggled far too loudly, to only small titters from everyone else.

My heart started beating faster as I tried to change the subject.

'Why is Paul bad at dating advice?'

I got out my phone to try and calm myself down and temporarily remove myself from the conversation.

'Urgh, he's nineteen and thinks he knows it all,' sighed Bhavin.

'Not as bad as Aiden though,' piped in Melissa.

The table cackled again, and I looked up from scrolling.

'He's a weird one, isn't he?' said Neil.

'Lovely though,' said Bhavin. 'But yeah, bit odd.'

I wondered why they thought he was odd, but at the same time felt a little bit relieved that they didn't necessarily take him that seriously, in case he started talking to me loudly about skateboarding or something. He knew I was Bolt Girl, but maybe I could just pretend I had no idea what he was talking about?

I put my phone away and seeing the key turner sitting in my bag, closed it quickly. I needed to relax. Taking a sip of my wine, I settled, and started chatting to Melissa about our shared love of dogs. She had a whippet and said I could walk it with her sometime. She was also arty, like me, taking a pottery class on her day off. What a win. I had my whole new life ahead of me, full of opportunity. The world was my oyster, bobbing along at the bottom of the sea.

13

#DANGER

My first-ever romance was with a boy who wouldn't go in the ocean because he was frightened of mermaids. I was twelve, and me, Mum and Martin were on holiday with Martin's best friend Keith and his family. Keith had two older teenage sons, one of whom, George, I fancied like crazy. I would fantasise about him passing me a note at the end of the holiday saying, 'I'll wait for you', such was my deranged understanding of relationships at that age. But the logic was there: the chemistry we had playing Uno? There was nothing like it. Wild card? You said it, mate. Pick up four? Yeah I'm reading this right. Him shouting 'Uno' while looking directly at me? That's right, baby, I am the one.

By the time I got to fourteen, and we all went on holiday again, he'd dyed his hair green and had a girlfriend who he spent the whole time talking to on MSN, and I had developed an understanding of how far apart fourteen and seventeen was – AKA he refused to join in a single game of Uno, which I found to be an incomprehensible decision.

But back to the holiday where I met Eliot. Eliot was twelve and staying at the same resort as us in Portugal. We would see

Eliot's family most mornings at breakfast, and – looking back, probably in an attempt to get me away from George – Mum had pointed him out and said she bet he'd be up for hanging out on the beach, and why didn't I invite him along. He seemed to be an only child, like me, so I thought it might be worth a try.

He agreed to my invite, and we made plans to meet on the beach in an hour. George asked me if Eliot was my holiday romance (oh, George. Jealous much?). I just shrugged and said I'd see how it went, but I wore my favourite lilac dress and silver sandals in case it was a date.

When I arrived on the beach, Eliot was wearing a shirt and shorts. And I mean, a short-sleeved dinner shirt. It dawned on me that this was indeed a date, and I may have been fast approaching my first kiss, which I was absolutely buzzing about. Just wait until I got home and told Ella.

We walked a little way along the shore and found a good spot to build a sandcastle. Our parents could still see where we were, but in my mind, I had basically left home in my first car and was at a club drinking cocktails with my fiancé.

It was then that Eliot started talking very seriously about mermaids.

'Mermaids are in the water and they sing a song and you think it's really beautiful and lovely and the mermaids have really nice hair and everything so you go closer, to listen to the song, but then it's all a trick and you drown.'

'Oh,' I said. An open-mouthed, panting dog weaved in and out of us. 'But I think that's just a story?'

'I think that you have to be very careful of beautiful things, very careful, because what you think is good might not be good.'

'Are you saying you don't want to go swimming, then?'

'Yes, and also I'm trying to teach you about the mermaids.' He looked sternly out on to the horizon as though he was sending the message he wasn't going to be fooled. 'We should build a trap!' he said, getting on his knees and piling up a mound of sand. 'Come on!'

It was decided we would decorate the big mound of sand with the most beautiful shells, to play them at their own game and lure them on to the beach.

'And then they will die because they'll be out of the water!' shouted Eliot.

He definitely had a look in his eye that told me he genuinely thought he was about to bring down an entire epoch of the mermaid population.

When the last shell on our structure had been placed, we sat back to look at our hours and hours of work, and he put his arm around me. My heart leapt.

'Hattie,' he said, 'I know we've only known each other for a day but I really like you.'

'I really like you too,' I said.

'And I'm not frightened.'

I paused for a second, trying to work out what he meant.

'What do you mean?'

'Your mum told my mum about how you have something wrong with you, like with your legs she said? And that it's going to get worse as you get older. And I'm just saying, I want you to know, that's good for me because I won't have to worry about you being beautiful, which would make you dangerous.'

I didn't know what to say. He went on.

'When we were looking for shells, I found this one, and I wanted to save it for you.'

And then he kissed me, quickly on the lips, as I sat there, completely still.

'Oh Hattie, don't cry. I know it's sad,' he said, getting up from the sand and waving to his parents.

I wiped my eyes and got up too. We walked back to the sun-loungers and I held on to Mum tightly, the tears flowing.

'Oh sweetheart. Aw, I think she's really going to miss you, Eliot.'

Later that night, I turned the shell over in my hands as I lay awake in bed. The words 'something wrong with you' rang in my ears and only faded when the tiredness took over and I slipped into sleep.

The next morning, I put on my silver sandals and placed the shell on the floor when Mum wasn't looking. The sound of the crunch was addictive, and I stamped on it again and again until she looked over, horrified, and told me what a terrible thing I'd done to break something so pretty.

THE NIGHT THAT CHANGED EVERYTHING

00:34

The nurse didn't have anything to say to that. She didn't say, 'Oh love, then why are you crying?' She just left me sobbing, and now I'm worried the other people in the waiting room are getting annoyed about the noise I'm making. I'm trying to breathe through it, trying to stop, trying to hold myself together in the quietest, smallest way I can.

14

#LIFT

Mum

Great you've found a job!

Martin says dog walking sounds quite casual and have you got a contract?

Thanks!

Tell him not to worry xx

Ella

WELL DONE ON THE JOB

What stuff do you have to do??

At the moment it's a lot of brunch

Hate you

Potentially might walk a dog later

Is that the husky??

What husky lol

The one you were with the other day

'Shit,' I muttered, as I put my phone under my arm and pressed the button on my car keys.

Oh hahaha yeah no not that one sadly

When you arrive for your second day on the job and your line manager immediately calls you into her office, you know the day isn't going to be a good one.

'Slight change of plan for today,' Jackie began before I'd even sat down on the blue plastic chair. 'I need you to shadow the porters.'

My eyes widened. 'Oh, okay, they didn't mention – in the job description – just reception, I thought?'

'You're still on reception but there's a new strategy for emergencies – if a coach trip careers off a cliff, I need to know I can switch out someone on reception and get you pushing beds and carrying oxygen tanks. Like I say, emergency protocol. We need to maximise the time you're officially on training. It's just for today.'

I nodded slowly.

'Okay? So you're shadowing Bhavin – he should be up on the floor any minute,' she gestured to the door.

'Great, thanks Jackie.' I smiled and left the room, hoping that Bhavin would somehow be inexplicably delayed by eight hours. But as I turned the corner, there he was, waiting by the desk.

'Hear you're with me today.' He smiled. Bhavin was a little older than me, perhaps mid-thirties, was clean-shaven and clearly hit the gym most evenings.

I nodded again and tried to keep up with his pace as he walked down the corridor. As he turned to take the stairs, my heart dropped.

'Do we take the lift?' I tried to sound casual. 'You know, I just thought, when we're transporting—'

He did a part laugh, part scoff as he went up the stairs, taking two at a time. 'Lifts take forever, stairs quicker – but yeah, if we were moving a bed – obviously.'

He was already at the top before I was on the landing between flights.

'Obviously!' I shouted, hand gripping the banister and trying to move my legs as quickly as I could, ignoring the feeling of my balance blinkering out like a radio signal, my muscles pulling heavily against the extra strain. I tried to go over yesterday's rounds of The Game in my head: 'Detached retina, haemorrhage, potential TIA: Come on, Hattie, you can do this, you can work this out, you work everything out,' but somewhere deep in my gut came the reply, 'You couldn't even open your front door.' I bit into my lip to stop the surge of tears that threatened to tip from the brink.

He waited at the top for me, and I had to concentrate extra hard to keep my balance.

'We're gonna have to start calling you the snail,' he said, laughing.

It caught me hard and I didn't respond quickly enough. I didn't laugh along, but just averted my eyes.

'What?' he asked.

'It's just . . .'

Hospitals are meant to be busy places, but in that moment, it was just me and Bhavin, standing at the top of the stairs, as The Plan lay in a corridor, its heart rate crashing out.

'I'm really hungover.'

This was only half a lie. I had only had one glass of wine but one glass can have quite the effect on me: my balance is like a tipsy person when I'm stone cold sober. Normally I wouldn't drink at all if I was driving, but I didn't want to raise suspicions. When I said goodbye to everyone yesterday, I walked back to my car parked at the hospital, and realised I was absolutely not safe to drive. This meant I had to google the buses, walk to the stop, get the one that took me vaguely in the direction of the hut, and then call a taxi to take me the last few miles. I was exhausted by the time I got back and had to get up extra early to do the same thing in reverse.

'Really? I thought you only had, like, one? Lightweight.'

'I went somewhere else after with this guy I met at the bar.' I started to breathe at the fact he seemed to believe me.

'Ah, you kept that very quiet,' he said, ahead of me again in the corridor.

'Yeah, well. I'm regretting it now.'

He was holding the door open and shaking his head at my speed again.

'We've all been there,' he said with a smile.

Hattie: congratulations. You did it. The Plan hangs on.

'So what's first?' I asked, trying to change the subject. I could hear my voice shaking slightly as I tried to reach for breath but told myself if I just chilled out it would all be fine.

There began a series of quick walks through long corridors, with Bhavin talking about the different roles, the rotas, then occasionally stopping himself with sentences like 'you probably don't need to worry about that actually', when he remembered I was just being shown the basics in case of a huge emergency. Of course, I have always been very anti-huge-emergency, but that day's training really bumped it up the list of my personal 'Please God Nos', relegating 'accidentally falling in love with a Tory' down to position number three.

When, two hours into the shift, Bhavin handed me an oxygen cylinder to load up onto a transport trolley, the word *Paralympians* flew into my head. If a man can run on blades, I could lift an oxygen tank. Aren't we meant to be Super Humans?

My arms shuddered, and Bhavin started laughing at me. 'Are you still drunk?' he asked, lifting it for me.

'I think I might be,' I whispered, and he laughed even more. He was loving this. If I'd told him I was disabled, his reaction would not have been so warm and welcoming.

At that moment Aiden came over, nodding at Bhavin, who gave him a fist bump.

'Emergency training thing, eh?' he said, looking over at the oxygen cylinder beside me. 'They've got me on surgery this afternoon,' he winked.

I chuckled and stepped forward, hoping Bhavin would finish loading up the trolley.

'How's your day?' Aiden moved forward too, so we ended up swapping places, and he coolly lifted the cylinder on to the trolley. 'I'll take these mate,' he said to Bhavin. 'Hattie can shadow me for a sec if you want a cheeky cig?'

'Yeah? Nice one, I'll be back in five,' Bhavin felt in his pocket for his lighter. 'She's a bit worse for wear though – heavy night wasn't it, Hattie?' He patted me on the shoulder and headed toward the fire escape.

It was much easier for someone to give me a friendly nudge about being hungover than awkwardly leaving me to explain I was disabled, because they didn't know how to say it themselves.

'Bet you're knackered, aren't you?' said Aiden, as he wheeled the trolley slowly in the direction of the lift.

'A bit, yeah.' I tried to laugh it off, but a definite shaking had started in my left hand, my cheeks felt flushed, and I couldn't hide how out of breath I sounded.

'I'm sure it was you, the other week – you skateboard, don't you?'

My stomach swirled and I started to chew on the inside of my cheek. He knew it was me. I could tell from his gorgeous green eyes.

'Well. I think – oh yes, I remember now – yes, I do, I do own a skateboard, but I am not, it's not the type of thing you really talk about, actually.'

'First rule of skateboarding club is?'

'Know the front from the back. Always. But like I say I—' I was talking very, very quickly.

'No, no, I was making a Fight Club joke? It's a film. They say "The first rule of Fight Club is we don't talk about Fight Club".'

I laughed too loudly and winked – yes, I winked – at

Aiden. I would not be winking ever again in my whole entire life.

'So you like films then?' I garbled.

'Yeah, I like making them actually, you know.'

I interrupted too quickly, 'Oh! Well, what you do in your own time, with a consenting adult is . . .'

It was not the best joke I've ever told, I admit. But his face completely fell, and he looked bored.

'Yeah, haha,' he said, after a pause, but it was clear he wasn't really laughing.

'Sorry, I – that was – a joke,' I said.

'Yeah, no I know, people just always seem to go . . .' he let the noise of the lift button finish his sentence.

'What are they really about?' I asked, regretting interrupting him in the first place.

'Just like little short stories. Indie stuff. Bit offbeat. Like, there's one about a tattooist who's scared of commitment.'

It occurred to me, as he muttered the end of his sentence, that maybe he rarely got to tell people what he makes films about because everyone interrupts with the same joke.

'You'll have to show me sometime. I really like the sound of them.'

His eyes brightened a little and he nodded at me with a quiet 'cool' before the lift doors opened. A few people were already in there, but there was enough room for us and the trolley, so we scooted in.

Now Aiden and I were touching, which was incredibly enjoyable for me, but I could have very much done without everyone else. The man in front of me had taken the smallest step back so my nose was just a centimetre away from his jacket. The familiar smell of a heavily scented deodorant hit me when, slowly, it became clear there was something wrong with the lift: we weren't moving. The doors were still closed.

I looked to Aiden as he pressed the door button, as the man in front of me let out an 'Oh Christ' and the woman in the opposite corner gave a 'don't tell me …' as the doors failed to open.

Did anyone know we were even in here? We were trapped in a cavity, dark hollows above and below us. Would they have to cut us out? I couldn't help but think of the sponge in my dad's stomach again.

I became very aware of my own skin, and then of everybody else's skin, and the muscle underneath it, crammed into the small space, shuffling back and forth, and there I was in the lift mirror comparing the bodies, knowing that everyone there was stronger than I was, knowing that I needed to get out of there but not knowing how.

I took a sharp intake of breath and wondered if the floor would suddenly give way and we'd all find ourselves falling. I wondered if I'd shout for Aiden or whether I'd keep to The Plan until the very end.

I wondered if it would feel different if we were all in the same boat, all at risk, all falling through the air, all wishing we could leave. I wondered, if someone miraculously survived, if they would go home and start their very own plan. Do all new beginnings start with a moment when you know, for sure, that the old you has to die?

When the lift jolted, and then seemed to smoothly move downwards, there was a sigh of relief as a nurse rolled his eyes, saying, 'bloody thing.' While everyone else seemed to be relaxing, I tasted blood in my mouth from how hard I'd been biting my cheek.

As we reached our floor and the doors opened without fault, I took a second to look in the mirror again while Aiden wheeled out the trolley. My eyes were failing to hide the look of terror. I hoped I could blink it away before Aiden noticed, hoped it was just strip-lighting making me look so pale, as though I was on the point of fainting, as though I'd just been through something far worse than a lift on the blink.

I looked so ill after that, Bhavin had no complaints when I said I was going to have to go home sick an hour later. Jackie accepted it pretty easily too, although she was obviously frustrated she'd have to book in another half day of porter training for me.

When I got back to the hut, the June sun was beaming, and I moved one of the kitchen chairs outside and tried to breathe in the air. I was just 'hungover'. Hungover people feel sick and go pale and have to go home early. Everything was just as it should be.

After a nap, I tried to go for a walk, back to the woods where I had felt so much possibility. I walked further this time, deeper into the forest. I felt the bark of trees beneath my hands, the rugged beauty that made such a stark contrast to the smooth heat of escalator handrails, the ones I gripped with a clammy palm as commuters rushed past me and I tried to keep my balance. I followed the bark as far as I could, and looked up and up and up at the way the tree grew unsymmetrical, its branches following the path of their own light. But this time, I felt a numbness come over me, despite trying to feel the same excitement I'd felt before. The air had changed and it was time I went back to the hut.

I'd left the light on, and there, against the evening beginning to creep in, the little building looked like an incubator in that field. My incubator, keeping me going in this new life. The warm glow of light gently spilled out onto the grass as a flock of birds flew overhead, swimming in the endless sky. As I made my way up the steps, the windows to the hut rattled in the wind and my incubator suddenly seemed a little unsteady.

Back in the hut, my phone flashed:

> Unfortunately, your application for 'Library Customer Service Assistant: Wales' has been rejected. Please log into your account for more details.

I clearly really needed to hang on to the A&E job and wasn't going to let a bad day stop me.

The Plan was still propped up by the kitchen table, and I realised I could tick off:

> Get Job = Paycheque

Next was 'Get rental = Yearlong lease = SECURITY', which was the last big practical thing to do. I wasn't really giving myself enough credit for how far I'd come. I spent the rest of my time booking in a few appointments with estate agents, and then doodling the dream of a new place to live: a flat of my own in my brand-new life. Somewhere solid, sturdy and made of bricks.

15

#PIG

The first and only comic I ever made was in the summer holidays before Year Eight. Ella and her brother had gone to visit family in Canada for the entirety of the holidays, and I was struggling to fill the time. Sure, I had other friends, and I saw them for shopping trips and the occasional visit to Madame Tussauds – bizarrely, looking back, it was one of my favourite things to do as a young teen – but it wasn't the same as having Ella round for sleepovers and talking to her on the phone almost every day. I had never felt more desperate to stick to our promise to go to the same uni together, because I couldn't imagine spending three whole years away from her.

I had been sorting through my stuff and getting rid of some books that I'd been holding onto for nostalgic reasons. As a very old and mature twelve-year-old, I now deemed 'nostalgia' to be embarrassing and pointless.

'I do not need to keep *The Three Little Pigs,*' I'd announced to Mum, who looked low-key horrified at my decision to get rid of one of my favourite children's books. 'I don't even like the story anymore.'

And as I made that announcement, I decided, that summer, I was going to do a much better job and draw an entire comic all of my own: *The Fourth Little Pig* (working title).

As in the traditional story, the first little pig had a house of straw, and the wolf huffed and puffed and blew her house down. I drew a little pig running, and the wolf was reaching out toward the pig, with a speech bubble saying, 'Please.'

On the second page was the house of sticks. I'd drawn the wolf huffing and puffing, and the pigs running away from their broken home. Again, the wolf was reaching out to them saying, 'Please.'

When the wolf couldn't destroy the house of bricks, she went around the back but found that the pigs had drawn the curtains. They ignored her knocking on the door and windows.

Then I drew the wolf climbing onto the roof and getting ready to jump down the chimney. This was where my comic started to get particularly different, because I drew the wolf saying, 'Don't be afraid, I'm just the same as you.'

She jumped down but got stuck and started to scream for help.

The next page showed the little pigs stoking the fire, their wide, haunted eyes up close, flames and smoke reflected in their irises. After they were satisfied they had killed the wolf who squirmed in the chimney, they blocked it up and tried to forget all about it.

Eventually, when the little pigs died, the house was destroyed by a big bulldozer. This was beyond my drawing capabilities, but I persevered.

The last few pages showed the wolf's skeleton surrounded by

the bricks of the fallen chimney, but the best bit, the big twist was: inside the skeleton of the wolf, was a skeleton of a pig.

I thought this was a moral fable on par with The Bible.

When Ella returned, two days before we were due to start secondary school, I proudly showed her the comic.

'Oh,' she said, 'so the wolf had eaten a pig?'

My expectant eyebrows fell. 'No, no, the wolf was a pig all along.'

'Like, you mean it was a pig dressed up as a wolf? Why did he do that?'

'She, Ella, *she*,' I corrected. 'They thought the wolf was bad because of what was on the outside, but inside . . .' I tapped the bones, smiling, 'it's a pig.'

'Oh. That's horrible. And how was a pig living inside a wolf? I don't understand.'

'Because the pig . . .' I started rubbing the back of my neck. 'Well, you see the—'

'I don't think you should take this into school.'

'I guess, well it makes sense to me.'

'No, no, I like it. Your drawings are amazing. I just think . . . it's a very good thing that I'm back,' she said.

'Yeah,' I agreed, looking at the skeleton of the pig. 'Me too.'

THE NIGHT THAT CHANGED EVERYTHING

01:00

I'm quiet now. Quiet, and cold. The automatic doors keep going; it's getting busier, noisier and more chaotic and the patients that arrive are drunker and drunker. A man is next to me, his legs open wide; I've shuffled to the other side of my seat. I'd leave if I wasn't so worried there was something fractured, something that could cause internal bleeding, get infected, poison me slowly from the inside.

16

#CHAIR

Mum

Martin and I hate all the other couples on this trip

So he's pretended to hurt his knee

But we're actually just going on a walk in the opposite direction

Hahahaha

Well played, very well played

Ella

[Missed Voice Call from Ella]

Pick up your phoooooone

Can't chat doing DIY

Wanking AS WELL as all the sex??

Christ

Oh very funny

Come onnn that was a great one

Hattie?

Here's a little tip for you: when you leave a wooden chair out in the rain, do not decide to blast it with your hairdryer, on its hottest setting, until the wood starts to warp. Definitely don't enter a state of denial and continue to subject it to your screaming Nicky Clarke until the seat of the chair begins to crack. Don't then spend the next two minutes hurriedly putting the hairdryer away, as though you're trying to hide your own behaviour from yourself. There is also no point in rubbing the crack with a lemon.

I had left the chair outside yesterday, and it had rained heavily overnight. I couldn't risk simply leaving the damaged chair for Christian and Nancy to find, as they might have left me a bad review on Airbnb, which would jeopardise me staying anywhere else, and I needed that as a back-up since I hadn't found a flat yet. The thought made me want to roll myself in my duvet; I had been in the hut for two weeks out of the eight and had about a grand of savings left, but I needed most of that for a deposit. If I didn't find a flat before my stay in the hut was up, I'd have to get another Airbnb to stay in, and then things would be very tight.

My only option was to replace the chair. Luckily the chairs

were all mis-matched anyway, and after a few minutes googling I found one that was close enough and ordered it for Click & Collect. Now all I had to do was get rid of the dud. After a quick google, I once again found myself up against an obstacle: the tip asked to see a form of ID at the gate to ensure only local people disposed of their rubbish there. I'd have to keep it in the hut for now, and then go and dump it in the woods before I left the hut for good. Some would call that fly tipping; I would say it was making nature more disability friendly.

Just as my order confirmation came through, a succession of notifications poured in from the group chat. It took me a minute to realise what it was that I was reading, but when I did, I found myself sitting very, very still.

Georgia had messaged asking how everybody felt about a

ROAD TRIP!!

TO WALES SOON

And people had responded

YEAHHHH

And

Can't wait to be reunited with your blue
parking badge

And

What do you reckon Hattie??

I reckoned that I was going to be sick all over my phone.

ELLA: She's not going to reply she's doing DIY

I made a very funny wank joke

That did not get the credit it deserved imho

SAM: Haaaaaa

GEORGIA: Okay well hurry up and finish your drilling Hattie

Because I've got Leave in about three weeks – Friday – Monday? Guys?

PETE: YES that is my weekend off

BEA: Can't wait to finally meet Oliver!!

I still don't know what he looks like!!

SAM: Ella's seen a picture hasn't she?

And then, there it was: the fake picture I had spent so long Photoshopping when I first started talking about this new guy, having decided I needed to enact The Plan.

I had already told Ella that Oliver didn't have social media so she couldn't try and stalk him. But she kept insisting that I must have seen a picture, and how did I know he was real, and she hadn't heard me talking much on the phone? So there came the fake phone calls I pre-recorded, my half of the conversation, laughing along, whispering, chatting. I put them on just loud enough so Ella could hear. Meanwhile, I started to slowly pack my things and decided what needed to go to the charity shop.

And since she kept insisting, I had to create a picture using every Photoshop trick in the book and a dodgy app that created a new face out of two different faces. I went for Nick Cave and the head chef of a local Indian restaurant that I fancied. I had only sent it to her – she wasn't happy with simply seeing it on my phone, apparently – on the condition she did not send it to anyone else. But she had broken that promise, and now the group chat had a photo of a man that didn't exist but were expecting to meet on their impending visit.

ELLA!

You promised

Oh so now you reply

The group chat reacted to the photo, asking for more. I awkwardly kicked the damaged chair to the corner of the room, and opened my laptop in a panic, searching for more pictures of Nick Cave and hoping the Indian restaurant had added another photo of the head chef on their Instagram page. As my phone kept flashing with messages confirming three weeks' time worked for everyone, I tried to combine the two images I'd found on the app, but the only one I could find of the chef was him in front of a flame rising from a pan, sautéing something delicious no doubt, so the combined image had a swirl of fire right in the middle of the face.

I leant back and tried to think straight. The idea of them turning up at the fake address I'd given them gave my stomach another lurch. I'd have to keep them away. Maybe once I'd found a flat, I could say Oliver and I had broken up, but I was locked into the rental and quite enjoying my job? Then they could possibly visit for the weekend. Possibly. But not yet, no way. Lying to them over the group chat was one thing, but in person, all at once, was another. Everything had to feel way more settled before they came. And even then, I'd still have to bluff the dog-walking thing, while actually being at work. Under no circumstances could my friends visit A&E, because I couldn't trust them not to mention my disability, coming in and making jokes about how lucky it was I could park so close to the door. Then everyone would know I was disabled and it would be the end of The Plan.

Until then I'd have to try and tide them over with some more photos. The swirl of flame felt like it was a real fire, causing me to sweat.

Ella and photographs, man. Pissing me off since 2010.

17

#SPILL

Right in the middle of our A-Levels, our school decided it was a good idea to encourage every year group – including the Sixth Formers – to get involved in World Book Day. Ella and I got far too into it and went as characters from our favourite childhood Jacqueline Wilson books. It was weird going from a confirmation of our uni choices – we made sure our first, second and third choices were the same – to opening books written for ten-year-olds and searching for descriptions of the characters. I covered myself in fake tattoos in order to look like the Illustrated Mum, and Ella went full on Lady-Angel-Gabriel-With-Massive-Wings dressed as Vicky, a schoolgirl that comes back as an angel after dying.

'We look wicked,' she said, as we met at the school gates. Wicked was not a usual phrase for Ella, but she had a habit of hearing phrases from other teenagers, or the TV, and becoming obsessed with them. When we both started working in the beauty salon after uni, it was, 'Hey, what else is new?', having picked it up from another girl who worked there. She even found herself doing it at the most inconvenient times, like when she was giving someone a bikini wax: 'Might be a bit sore there, honey, but hey, what else is new?'

That year, the school had arranged for a local photographer to come and set up in the hall. It was my art A-Level exam the next day, and I was keen to spend my time in the art room going over my final sketches, but I had agreed to go with Ella towards the end of the day to get our pictures taken.

She flew into the art room just as I was trying to get the shading right on my sketch of a pelvic bone.

'We're going to miss it,' she said, standing over me.

'Okay, okay,' I said, dropping the pencil and following her out of the room.

'I'm so excited we're going to get a professional picture of us both, you know?'

'Yeah, mate, imagine our profile pics.'

'Wicked.'

We still had a way to go when Ella started to jog.

'Ella – what?' I shouted after her.

'I'm worried we're going to be too late.'

'Yes, but I can't run, can I? It's okay, we'll get there.'

'I don't want to miss this.' She was a good few paces ahead of me now, and I was doing my best to keep up with her, but my legs were starting to burn.

She didn't look back at me when her jog turned into a run and the gap between us widened. Left in the wake of fallen feathers, I called her name, but there was no response.

When I finally made it to the sports hall, Ella was standing in the queue and waved me over. It wasn't half as busy as we'd thought it would be.

'I saved you a place!' she said, clearly trying to ignore the look in my eyes.

'You just left me!' I replied.

'To get in line early.' She shrugged. 'We'd have been way back otherwise.'

'I called after you and you ignored me.' I could feel my cheeks growing red, sweat dripping down my neck. I wanted a cough sweet but didn't want to be photographed with one lodged in my cheek like a hamster.

She went quiet and looked at the floor. 'I just wanted to make sure we got the pictures.'

Others in the queue were looking at us now, and there weren't many people in front of us before we got to the photographer.

'Okay, well, I'd rather we'd got here together.' I was trying to make my voice sound gentler without much success.

'Yeah, no, I'm sorry, I—' The queue moved on and we were only one person away. 'Shall we practise our poses? Because when we're at uni, the club nights always have photographers. So we should get loads of practice in now.'

I could see Ella wanted nothing more than to just move on, and a big part of me wanted to as well, the part of me that wished it hadn't happened at all and was still a bit shocked that it had. I leant into it just enough to agree, and as our picture was taken, I stood there, hand on hip, asking if I should pout or smile.

In the end, I went for something awkwardly in between, but luckily, we did enough different poses that we had the full range from headshot to bodyshot. The headshot is the one that made it onto Ella's pinboard for her 30th, years later; the full costume shot ended up cast aside on the floor.

I said goodbye to Ella at the school gates and immediately complained to Mum when I got in the car.

'Well she saved you a spot in the queue at least.' Mum turned to me, with the indicator noise ticking, as we waited at the traffic lights. I gave a heavy sigh and kicked the glove box.

'Hattie, calm down. We don't do—'

'Anger here,' I mimicked, tears prickling in my eyes.

'Love, honestly, most teenagers run off here, there and everywhere. Come on, she's good to you. Don't hold it against her,' Mum pushed.

By the time the indicator noise had stopped, I reluctantly conceded that it wasn't a big deal.

The next day, I got into school extra early and spent most of the morning pacing outside the art room, going over the plan for my final piece. I was going to do a life-size drawing of a skeleton, with different parts of the body on different canvasses that came together when hung on the wall. But the clever part was, the size of the canvasses varied dramatically, so the body was all out of proportion: it had huge hands and a tiny pelvis.

There's no easy way to say it, but in the final part of the seven-hour exam, as I was laying all the canvasses on the floor to check I was happy, I spilt my coffee on it. And I don't mean a splash, I mean a full mug, all over the chest cavity. I remember the noise of the paper towels being pulled from the holder, my teacher, Mr Sneet, and I trying to soak it up, but it was no good. The pencil had smudged, the canvas was stained. Mr Sneet tried to comfort me, telling me about famous artists that had dropped large glass works of art and it had made the pieces better, even more famous and popular.

'When Duchamp's glass broke, you know what he said? He said, "It is finished",' he offered.

But it wasn't working for me. My detailed, pencil-drawn skeleton had a square of caffeine right in the centre.

'Fucking hands,' I'd said, in what was supposed to be under my breath, but it came out closer to a shout.

Mr Sneet, so focused on trying to make me feel better about the canvas, missed the point of what I was saying. 'What? Hattie, the hands are fine – look, no coffee. No problem.'

'No, I meant my fucking hands and my fucking balance,' this time it was meant to be a shout, but the break in my voice had made it a mess of sound. My throat stung again. 'It's not "no problem" – it is clearly a problem.'

The canvas was still on the floor, and I wanted it gone. I kicked the legs out of the way and stamped on the chest cavity until the brown-stained fabric gave way and ripped a hole.

'There,' I said to Mr Sneet and to the rest of the class watching, 'it is finished.'

Ella had already heard about what happened by the end of the day.

'Oh my God, are you okay? I heard you ripped your canvas?' she asked, buzzing from the drama of it all.

'I didn't rip it, I stood on it,' I said defensively.

'William said your eyes went all dark when it happened, like a serial killer.' She was trying to make me laugh, but it didn't work.

'Well good. Because I wanted that thing dead.'

*

'What do you mean you broke your canvas?' Mum was horrified.

Since the whole school knew about it, and they were due to see my work in a Sixth Form A-Level showing before the summer, I had to tell Mum and Martin what had happened.

'Hattie, this is – this is not like you. This sort of thing – I – I'm baffled, to be honest.'

I found myself biting my cheek throughout the evening. I looked down at my feet, thinking of them stamping through the canvas, silently telling them, 'We need to make sure we don't do anything like that again.' I started to google different breathing techniques as I sat on the sofa. While sceptically reading the benefits of counting to ten, a message from Ella came through:

OMG, just realised the examiners HAVE to give you good marks!!

Or else we might not be able to go to Roehampton together!!!

For the briefest of seconds, I wondered if it was such a bad thing after all.

THE NIGHT THAT CHANGED EVERYTHING

01:20

I think I'm going to pass out. The tiredness and the pain and the tears are too much. I'm not even going to tell anyone. I asked the receptionist how long it was going to be and she said they'd see me when they could. She didn't even look up from her computer screen. I'm just going to let it happen. I hope I hit the floor hard, and I hope everyone who's been ignoring me feels guilty at the sound.

18

#SEEN

'Heyyyy.'

It was 6 a.m. the next morning.

'Heyyyyy.'

I played the sound over and over again. 'Heyyyy.' Practised pressing play. 'Heyyyy.' Made sure you couldn't hear the sound of my laptop. Made sure the recording sounded legit through the mic on my phone. Got the timings just right.

'He's here –' press play – talk over him at the very end so it sounds real – laugh '– there you go.'

Welcome to the world, Oliver. Heyyyy.

Having failed to create another photo, a voice note was my only other option. I'd nicked the sound off a vlogger, then edited it to make it sound a bit deeper.

Take one: I spoke into my phone: 'Hiii fellow parents of Mr Jonathan, the camera on my phone has died because *someone* dropped it in a puddle while trying to take a picture of me on a walk, he's here . . .'

Then I pressed play on my laptop so the pre-recorded voice

of the vlogger would sound like Oliver was in the room with me: '*Heyyyy.*'

I accidentally clicked play twice on my laptop so it made an error 'ding' sound.

I deleted the voice note in a smear of clammy fingers.

Take two. Speaking into my phone: 'Hiii fellow parents of Mr Jonathan, the camera on my phone has died because *someone* dropped it in rainy, puddley gravel while trying to take a picture of me on a walk, he's here . . .'

Clicked play on my laptop: '*Heyyyy* . . .'

Then I laughed, and continued, 'there you go, the camera destroyer' and sent the voice note.

Nailed it. I watched as the replies started coming in.

SAM: Told you he's a murderer! Phone first, then you. Get Out.

BEA: Haa he sounds sexy though

His lack of social media makes him a very difficult man to stalk

GEORGIA: Well we'll just have to come visit won't we – are you free when we said? You never replied!!!

ELLA: Did you get my card btw?

My eyes grew wide with panic. Why would Ella send me a card? She never sent cards. I'd have to drive all the way to the fake address I'd given them and pick it up.

Sorry guys that isn't great timing actually

BEA: Oh mannnn

GEORGIA: But we're all free!!

I know I'm gutted :(

ELLA: Maybe we can find a way

Like we wouldn't have to stay with you

And just see you when you can?

Even if it's just a dinner

GEORGIA: Omg for sure

SAM: We can entertain ourselves

But it's a long way for you to come

ELLA: We don't mind!!

And I've been pretty tired

ELLA: We'll bring you an energy drink haha

Why weren't they listening to me? And, more importantly, what was I going to do now? Muddy up my trousers and fly in for a dinner with them pretending I'd just come from a dog walk? Say Oliver had food poisoning? Actually that wasn't such a bad idea. I made a note of it on the bottom of The Plan, but deep in my gut I could imagine Ella's eyes staring me out over the table.

'And you think it was from some bad chicken, you say? But you're fine?'

For the first time I felt as though I might just need to actually disappear, run away for good. Cut all contact. But the blue lights of police cars edged at the corner of my vision – if I didn't ring my mum for weeks, she'd worry. If I kept in contact with them, but not Ella, Ella would probably message them saying she was concerned.

My legs felt like they were about to buckle, and I made it to my bed just before decking it. While I waited for the blood to return to my head, I got up directions on my phone for the flat I was viewing in an hour. I'd have to leave soon, and my body rebelled as I sat up, filling me with an intense sleepiness that was almost overwhelming.

'No,' I had to say to my body. 'You aren't allowed.'

It felt like my body was sobbing all across the field as I made my way to my car, each bump on the land harsher than before. Where I had once breathed in the dewy moss, now the wet grass was causing me to feel unsteady, without any sense of rich, beautiful air to open up my lungs. As much as I tried to breathe it in and remember how it felt, it wasn't working. If anything, my ribcage felt like it was tightening as the sense of space felt like an extra drag on my tired body; a long way to walk, and then even longer to drive, and then an even longer day to get through.

By the time I arrived at the block of flats, I had hyped myself up to believe this was going to be the one. Things may have felt a little wobbly, what with the visit looming, but if I got a flat, a core part of The Plan had been achieved. Money worries would be off my mind, I'd be closer to work, have more energy and would be able to sort out the visit with a clear head.

My optimism started to wane when the estate agent struggled to get in the door.

'There's a knack to it,' she said, as though it was a positive. When she eventually got in, she took me along a corridor and up five steps.

'I thought it was ground floor?' I asked, gripping the banister.

'Upper ground, we call it,' she said cheerily.

'Bullshit, I call it,' I wanted to say, but didn't.

The flat was very simple, but I liked it. It had a nice amount of light, and an open plan kitchen/living room, albeit with a very worn beige carpet.

'A lot of interest in this one,' she said. 'It's a great find.' She'd positioned herself over the most worn bit of the carpet. 'And such lovely light!' She gestured to the windows.

The bedroom was small, but completely liveable, with the same carpet and what I thought was a wardrobe but was actually the water tank.

'Plenty of space to get your wardrobe in here,' she said, as though I had a spare wardrobe lying around.

I let out a sigh when we saw the bathroom.

'It said on the listing that it had a separate shower, not one over the bath?'

She was quick to speak. 'Ah no, not on this one. Shower and a bath!' She smiled and stepped aside; cue for me to leave the bathroom.

'I really need somewhere with a separate shower.' My throat let out a small contraction.

'What's your budget again?'

When I told her, she breathed out with her lips still closed, blowing the most unjoyful raspberry known to humanity.

'One word, I think: compromise. There's what you want and what you need, yeah?'

'Yeah,' I said quietly. I couldn't bear the thought of having to say, 'it's because I'm disabled, though.'

'I know it'll be snapped up!' she called as I walked toward my car. I pretended I hadn't heard her and made sure I slammed my car door shut.

Jackie

[Missed Voice Call from Jackie]

Need you to come in earlier if you can

Staffing nightmare

Call me when you get this

No problem – not far away will head in now!

Perfect

Thank the Lord for you!

I took some deep breaths. See? I told myself. I am a valued worker at my job. Okay, the flat was annoying. It was annoying they clearly hadn't thought about access when they wrote the listing, and annoying she assumed my need for a separate shower was a high-maintenance desire, rather than the fact I couldn't physically climb in and out of a bath.

But not as annoying as having to explain. My throat was pain free; I didn't need a cough sweet – and hadn't taken one since getting to Wales. I didn't have to deal with her scanning my body as she tried to work out exactly how I was disabled. She also didn't come up with a terrible solution, like how I could get around the problem by hanging onto the sink, and I just needed to be 'inventive', which was what an estate agent had literally told me before.

I got into work to see a very relieved Jackie standing with Melissa by the desk.

'Just you two for now. I can't get anyone else in until later, so you'll be quite stretched I'm afraid, but I'll come and help out where I can.' Jackie had hardly finished her sentence before she raced off toward her office to answer the phone.

I said a quick hello to Melissa and sat down next to her at the desk, looking forward to getting to know her and her whippet a little better. Then Bhavin walked up to us.

'Did you hear this one was struggling on her porter shift?' he said, smiling cheekily at me.

'No? What happened?' Melissa asked, looking between us.

'Wrecked she was. After our drinks in the pub, she went home with someone – did you know that?'

Melissa made an 'ooooh' sound and asked for the details.

'Was nothing really,' I said, smiling.

'Honestly, the next day she was like a zombie, dragging herself through the day, and then tapping out early!'

I winced at the word 'dragging' but tried to console myself

that their tone was friendly. I needed to find a way to speed up in future, though. Just like I needed to sort out the damn office chair that I still couldn't adjust. People had started questioning me: 'think you're above us, do you?' or 'you feeling a bit low today?' depending on what height I was left with.

'I don't think the patients can even see you down there.' Melissa played it off as a joke but looked at me seriously, expecting me to sort out the chair straight away.

'Ah haha, that's the point – I'm hiding!' I laughed.

Melissa didn't laugh back. 'When I was new here, I didn't—' She stopped herself. 'I just don't get it, Hattie.'

I could feel myself growing red, and as she stayed looking at me, I turned around to face her.

'No, you really fu—' I so nearly swore at her. It felt as though my body was taking over, beyond my control.

'Body, what are you doing?' I thought. It was done crying as I dragged it over fields. Now it was in the mood to fight.

Melissa's eyes widened.

'Forget, you really forget what it's like to be new, I think. I've got a lot going on.'

'Oh right, so much that you won't adjust your chair.'

I spun back round to face the computer as my heart rate soared. It didn't seem I'd be invited to meet her whippet any time soon.

This really wasn't the way to make new friends. This also wasn't how I thought the new me in my new life would be acting. What was I thinking? This was not the attitude of a quirky, fun-loving, able-bodied girl. Melissa turned on her heels to go out back without saying another word. I was convinced she was writing an email to Jackie. Then what would I say?

When Daphne came in, she and Melissa had a hushed conversation a few feet away from me. The thought of Melissa telling Daphne about me being snappy made my skin itch. I smiled at Daphne, but she just gave a forced one in response, and went out back, even though she was meant to be helping me at the front desk.

I tried not to overthink it, and when a couple came in, I jumped straight into The Game – Man with Cracked Ribs? – five points. Fell off something? Maybe down the stairs? – Yes! Down the stairs. I still had it. Just.

Aiden came over to the desk and I gave him a little wave, when, from the other side of the waiting room, a voice started: 'Fucking . . .' and the guy kicked the wall, his arm held close to his side.

'Can you sit back down please?' This was all I needed.

'How long's it going to be?' He came to the desk quickly, putting his good wrist down with a thump.

'We're going as quick as we can.'

'Fucking . . .' He pushed one of the plastic signs from the desk, and it clattered onto the ground.

Aiden quickly came round to my side of the desk and started punching in a code on the phone, while I stood there trying to slow my breathing down. Why did this man think he had the right to push something at me? He was going round doing whatever he wanted, moving in whatever way he liked, without thinking about anyone else.

'Okay mate, can you sit back down yeah?' All he had to do was sit and wait.

'No I can't sit back down.'

'Yes you can,' I said.

'You have no idea what it's like to have to sit in a waiting room like this, I bet you—'

'Yes I do, for Christ's sake, so shut up. Just. Shut. Up.' I didn't have any control of it coming out of my mouth. I properly yelled at him, so loud that the waiting room stopped looking at him and started looking at me.

Aiden gave me a quick glance as the man swore even more, telling me I wasn't allowed to speak to him like that, he was in pain, he was a patient.

Daphne appeared, asking Aiden if he'd called for assistance. She looked over to me, asked if I was okay, and I nodded, even though I couldn't quite feel my hands. We only had to suffer one more kick at the wall before security was escorting him out of the building, and all the eyes of the waiting room went back to their own traumas.

'Told you porters come in handy,' Daphne said, smiling at Aiden.

'Do you know the emergency code for security?' he asked, gesturing to the phone, but I could tell that wasn't really the question he wanted to ask. He wanted to know what the hell I thought I was doing get lairy at a patient.

'Yeah, yeah, I just forgot. I might take my break now, if that's okay?'

Daphne and Aiden glanced at each other quickly. I turned around, heading towards the locker room.

'Babe, you sure you're okay?'

I had already turned around, when I shouted back a feeble, 'Yeah.'

Aiden followed me down to the break room just as I was staring at myself intensely in the mirror and muttering about how I needed to sort my shit out.

'Hey . . .' he said gently, standing back a little.

'Hi – sorry – I'll be back up in a minute, I—'

He interrupted me. 'I never went to film school or uni or whatever. To be honest, by the end of college all I wanted to do was get a job so I had enough money to buy a good enough camera and get out of living with my mum. I didn't want to do the freshers thing, the money thing, the studying for three years but you don't really learn anything thing . . .'

I had absolutely no idea where Aiden was going with this but I was glad that I wasn't the one doing the talking, so I carried on standing awkwardly by the sink as he carried on standing awkwardly a few feet away from me, in mid flow.

'But I did have my one mate from college, Wally, we called him, anyway, Wally did psychology, and I would sometimes get these tips from him . . .'

Ah, okay, he was about to therapy me. Brilliant.

'Look, I think maybe I should go back up . . .' I said, moving toward the door.

'And one of the things was, he said, if you've had something bad happen, and you can't stop thinking about it, try to replay it in your head like you're watching it on TV. Like, imagine yourself watching it. The idea is it detaches you.'

I hadn't heard that one before, and I stood still, taking my hand off the door handle.

'Anyway, it helps sometimes. And I realised, when I worked here, I could actually go one better – I could literally watch it back, on CCTV. So, just hypothetically, if I could get the footage, of the guy – shouting – would it help, do you think, for you – just you – to watch it?'

I paused.

'And how, hypothetically speaking, would you do that, exactly?'

'I have my ways,' he said, winking.

He hadn't mentioned me swearing at the guy at all. He'd just come down to offer a way to make me feel better, and even though he absolutely didn't know the extent of the problem, simply him being there, caring, meant that for the first time in a while, I did.

19

#JAMES

In the end, Ella and I did go to the same uni. One of the main nights I remember of that first year was a good couple of months in. Ella and I had gone to some house party and got absolutely twatted within an hour of arriving. It was at about 1 a.m. when I realised I had a presentation to give in my seminar in a matter of hours.

'Ella. Emergency. We have to leave.'

Back in our halls, I got into my room and immediately fell over my washing basket, which made Ella laugh so hard she had to jump over me to use my loo before she wet herself.

I picked myself up by crawling to my bed and opened my laptop while Ella, weeing with the door open, was shouting presentation ideas at me. We had to come up with a marketing campaign and a poster and explain it to the rest of the class.

'Condoms. Seafood. Thrush?' she listed, while pulling up her tights.

'No no no no no.'

'Hedgehogs. The road safety ones. Re-design them.'

'What? I can't beat the hedgehogs.'

'SHAPES. Design a new shape.'

I was on PowerPoint, hastily making my first slide: MARKTING CAMPAIGGN

'Fuck. Ella, I'm too drunk. I need water.'

She ran to the kitchen while I tried to breathe and look at the keyboard. When she came back, she saw my attempts at spelling and took over.

'I'll type. You explain. Is the new shape idea a definite no or . . . ?'

I downed the water and lay on my bed. The ceiling moved ever so slightly. I imagined lying there for hours and trying to entertain myself by looking at the marks on the ceiling, remembering an episode of *Casualty*, playing muted in a bar the other night, as someone lay strapped to a spinal board.

'The sponge. It has to be about the sponge.'

'What?'

'A marketing campaign for surgeons to remember the sponges they leave in patients.'

'Okay . . . but if you did the new shape then—'

'No, this is it. So: "Marketing Campaign". And then the next slide, say about how they left—'

'The sponge in your dad's stomach. I got it.' She diligently typed the story, which took a few slides.

'And then, the poster can be, a surgeon.'

'Okay, but I absolutely can't work Photoshop.'

I moved over and started searching for a copyright-free image of a surgeon.

'Can you look in that folder, there should be a sheet with all the shit I need to do for it.'

Ella started rooting through, found the sheet and began to read.

'Mate, you're going to be fine. It says five to ten minutes. You can absolutely get away with four minutes thirty.'

We did a celebratory high five and carried on with the task, pumped at the idea we were going to nail this.

We woke up half an hour before I was meant to be giving the presentation, both splayed out on my floor, with neither of us, apparently, deciding we should sleep on the bed. I had a glass of water, took a shower, then two paracetamol and another glass of water. I didn't have time to look through the PowerPoint properly, but I had enough slides and enough of an idea of what to say. Ella told me I'd smash it; I told her thank you 1,000 times before leaving and heading off to the seminar room.

I don't think I've ever seen a worse poster in all my life. I only had vague memories of creating it, while Ella did the rest of the typing. I had found a picture of a surgeon, in his scrubs, complete with mask, doing a big thumbs up. Then in a red font that looked as though it had been written in blood, I'd written, 'HE'S REMEMBERED'. At the bottom of the poster, also in red, but this time your classic Arial, I'd decided to go with the catchy slogan: 'Don't leave surgical objects in patients'. I think I have blocked a lot of it out, but I do remember taking a very, very serious tone and very much reminding everyone, about every thirty seconds, that it had happened to my dad, who *died,* even though I'd spent two whole minutes of the presentation going through the story (slides one to four). I also remember using the phrase 'unique' when trying to explain why I decided to target surgeons in particular. For the slide describing the placement of the poster, there was just the one bullet point: 'By the taps.'

The next slide was, for some reason, the second slide again, which I skipped through, then realised, as the screen turned black, that apparently, it was the end.

I went straight to Ella's room after the seminar and filled her in.

'But the main thing is, it is done, and yes, it is a shame beautiful Fred was there, but he is necessary collateral damage.'

Her face fell. 'You did not tell me that it was the seminar group with beautiful Fred.'

I laughed. 'Sadly yes, definitely ruined things there.'

Ella was looking at me very seriously. 'But he fancied you! Just from seeing you in the first seminar. Hattie, this is awful.'

I looked at her quizzically as I brushed biscuit crumbs from my lap. 'Well, yeah, he found me on Facebook after and sent me a flirty message—'

She interrupted, '*And* you were wearing your denim skirt the first time he saw you.'

I was about to absentmindedly agree, but stopped.

'Wait – what?'

She was lost in thought. 'And now you've done a really fucking weird presentation about surgery. Shit. He could have been the one.'

'Ella – what? How did you know I was wearing my denim skirt?'

'I remember, I said – "oooh you must have looked hot, what were you wearing?" because I wondered if he'd seen your legs.'

I sat there staring at her without saying a word.

'Maybe you should explain you'd done the presentation while drunk. Yeah – maybe message him.'

I didn't sleep at all that night. I felt like Ella's words had got stuck on a loop in my head. 'Wondered if he had seen your legs?' 'Wondered if he had seen your legs?' 'Wondered if he had seen your legs?'

Whatever I tried to do, I couldn't shake it. *24 Hours in A&E* played in the background, but I just lay there as it went round and round, until it felt like it was erasing every word I knew.

At 6 a.m., with a headache growing from the base of my skull, I filled out an online form request to see someone from the wellbeing service. In terms of a description of the problem, I put a vague sentence about coping better with other people. In the box that asked for any other information, I wrote:

> ASAP, please.
>
> Think I'm running out of words

I was given a session a week later with a man called James.

'There's only so much we can do in our sessions,' he'd said when we first met. 'Maybe you could start by letting me know what you meant by running out of words? But you're here to cope better with other people?'

'Yes. Sorry. I suppose that's confusing. It's – there's a lot. But I emailed because I couldn't stop thinking about what my friend said to me. And there's been lots of times like that. Where she says something, and it eats away at me.'

'What kind of thing does she say?'

'Well, she asked if I was wearing a skirt—' I stopped mid-sentence. How was I going to explain? How do you talk about the small things, and say that she wanted to know if the boy could see my disabled legs in a skirt rather than being covered by jeans, because in her mind, that would make it even more amazing that he fancied me, because my disabled legs aren't something people find attractive?

I tried a different example: 'Like, a while ago, we were going to this thing, and she went ahead of me, and I can't go as fast as her.'

James wasn't writing any of this down.

'Yes, you have a disability?'

'Yeah, and in my A Levels I was doing this art piece that was a self-portrait and it all went wrong and I broke it on purpose because I was so angry, but she didn't get it, like she didn't understand—'

'I'm not massively following, I'm afraid. Is she mean to you? Is this a bullying thing?'

'No! No, not bullying. But she does these things and I'm like – why are you doing that?'

'And do you tell her how you feel?'

'I sort of try but . . .' I gave out a cough. 'It's very hard.' I paused. 'My dad had a medical sponge left in him and I don't think she gets why I think about that either. I mean, I don't get why I think about it, but I think about it loads—'

'Okay, okay. Let's take it one thing at a time. You didn't answer the question. Do you tell her how you feel?'

'I try.'

'We can only look at you and try to fix you. We can't change Ella, and I mean, we don't all say the most perfect thing perfectly all the time. Do you think you might be a bit sensitive?'

'Hang on, try to fix me? Are you saying you think I'm broken?' My throat gave out a familiar throb of pain.

He paused. 'I think it might be a case of not letting the small things get to you too much.'

I was silent, thinking about my need for a cough sweet.

'Maybe something to think on for next week?' he'd said with an uncomfortable smile.

In our next session, he didn't ask again about anything Ella had said, about my self-portrait, or about the sponge. I could have brought it up again, but he was focused purely on 'resilience'. I decided to be quiet in the session, only ever asking for a drink of cold water. When I left, I found myself purposefully lunging towards a snail. The sound of the shell crunching was more fulfilling than anything James had to say to me, but afterwards, that night, came the uneasy memory of a boy afraid of mermaids, a hotel room floor and silver sandals crushing a shell.

THE NIGHT THAT CHANGED EVERYTHING

01:45

I haven't fainted. Can't even do that. I'm just stuck here, feeling like I'm going to pass out, but it's not happening. The lights are so bright they're making my eyes burn, but closing my eyes isn't helping; it just makes me feel even more on edge. There's no relief and I'm trapped.

20

#SHIFT

Ella

Urgh work is not the same without you

Awwhhh

Gareth was a right nob the other day

I'd tell you but I bet you've gone again

[Missed Voice Call from Ella]

See?

On my first full night shift at the hospital, two weeks after starting the job, I felt like I was staying up late at some sort of weird party for ill people. Maybe like one of those sex parties, you know with the different rooms (I've never been), and I was on the desk letting people in, as people were being called up and led off.

My second night shift was a bit different. I hadn't managed to sleep in the day for as long as I'd hoped, getting into bed at 7 a.m. with a body that felt like it was made with electrical wires sparking. My flushed-cheeked-and-sore-skin tiredness was too driven by the adrenaline that I'd needed to get me home. I was so sure I was going to collapse into the mattress but my eyes were wide open and itchy. 'Come on, body,' I thought, I'm letting you rest now. But for some reason it wasn't having it.

After more failed attempts to rest, I had to get in my car to drive all the way to pick up the card Ella had sent to the fake address.

The lovely eighty-something-year-old lady who lived at the blue pebbledash house with a strange stone elephant in the front garden and a hand-painted sign saying 'Number 52' was surprisingly happy I'd turned up. Although she rather awkwardly admitted she'd opened it, and then realised it wasn't for her. She had carefully put it back in the envelope, and it sat on the table by the front door, neatly tucked behind an ornamental giraffe, in the hope someone would come to collect it.

'Is one of them yours?' she asked, as I thanked her. She realised I was looking a little blank. 'The girls, I mean, in the photo?'

I pulled the card out of the envelope and took in the photo for the first time. There we were, all those years ago, at the piñata party. As the memories flooded back, I was, more presently, trying to hide the horror that she thought I might have an eleven-year-old daughter.

'Oh! No, no, it's me, actually. Well, one of them.' She very obviously tried to take a look at the picture, wanting me to tell her which one I was. I reluctantly turned the card around and pointed.

'Ah yes, should have known with those arms and legs like sticks!'

I smiled politely with my teeth clenched, making sure my body wasn't going to spit out a response I'd regret. I made my way back to the car, slamming the door extra loud as I got into the driver's seat.

At that point, a message came in from Jackie, asking if I could go in early again for the night shift. I groaned. I was so tired. My body was calling out for rest, but I couldn't let it happen. I had to push through.

When I got into work, I sat down on the office chair as six-foot Kieran was just leaving.

I reached down and said to my hands, 'You need to do this.' I pulled and squeezed the lever as hard as I could. My hands screamed out in pain but I ignored them. I carried on, trying to grip the lever harder, trying to be strong enough. A drop of sweat started to run its way down my back, my fingers burned and nausea seeped into my stomach. When my fingers slipped from the lever in surrender, I looked down at my hand and cursed it. Not good enough, I thought. You need to be stronger. I got off the chair and kneeled on the ground, trying to move the lever from underneath, but the chair wouldn't budge without my weight on it. I put my head and chest on the seat of the chair to try and give it the weight it needed, my teeth gritted together, the band of my jeans feeling cold with sweat.

'Hattie?' Jackie's voice was sharp.

I let go of the lever and took my head off the seat.

'I think the chair is broken,' I said, face flushed, muscles burning.

'Can you get up off the floor?' She looked furious.

I jumped up and Jackie sat on the chair, changing its height with ease.

'There is nothing wrong with the chair, Hattie.' She put her emphasis on the word 'chair', and I felt my hands twinge. My legs felt a surge as all I wanted to do was kick the chair over and shout back, 'how about now?' It took all of my energy to stay standing there, still, as she walked back toward her office.

Melissa appeared beside me with a friendly hello, and I told her I was going on my break.

'But haven't you only just got in?' she said.

'I said I'm going,' I snapped, and the regret stung instantly. I took some deep breaths in the locker room and told myself that I needed to pull it together.

'Body, you are ruining the plan. You need to be stronger and you need to stop getting so angry. People will get suspicious and then they will know you are disabled and everything will be as bad as it was before. You are not disabled, okay? You're not. Not in this life.'

When I got back up to Melissa, I apologised, and she said it was fine, but went out back pretty quickly. I sat down at the desk, scanned the room, made my guesses and read over the handover notes. Two out of three. I felt myself slowly calm down.

It wasn't too busy then, just a few people still in the waiting room: one with a suspected broken ankle, another with vision loss, another with a suspected miscarriage. I looked over at the blank, teary stare of the lady with her head on another woman's shoulder. They were holding hands, the first lady had a look of resignation on her face, the second, comforting her, still had a look of hope. The strip lighting was harsh on their faces and, glancing across to the man with his eyes squeezed shut and his leg propped up on another chair, I wondered why the waiting room wasn't filled with lamps and blankets. An older woman came in, her hair tightly knotted back, wearing a purple dress and, bizarrely, one flipper on her foot. The other foot was bare. This meant I lost The Game – no guesses, no points.

'I don't want to cause much trouble. But 111 said I needed to come in, because of what my head was telling me to do,' she looked down at the floor, before quickly adding, 'to myself, I mean. No one else. I'll be no trouble.'

'Hey, you're in the right place,' I said, and booked her in, hoping she'd wait long enough to be seen.

It definitely didn't feel like a weird arty sex club anymore, and I was reminded how boring it is sitting in a waiting room where there's nothing to look at, just a few random A4 frames with shit poetry in them in a font too small to read from the chairs. I absolutely hate poetry, I think it's all a big ruse; I think everyone is pretending they understand it and nobody does, but people just nod and say 'oh wow' like they've got it in one. I later went to look at one of those poems on the wall, and it was pretty depressing. If I had my way, I'd ban all poetry and paper the walls with big pictures of the sky. Give people some space, you know? And also maybe pop the odd mirror in, so if people are thinking they can't be bothered to wait anymore, they might catch a glimpse of themselves and think 'oh hang about, I do look a bit peaky'.

No one came through the doors and I found myself turning to my phone that I'd sneaked up to the desk with me.

Ella

Your card came! The piñata!!

Bloody post

I love it mate thank you so much

VERY weird you only just got it?

Sent it AGES ago

Also did you confirm that weekend for us to come??

Our Son Mr Jonathan

GEORGIA: Hattie this is so weird

Was searching Airbnbs for when we come

And . . . does Oliver do Airbnb?

Georgia then sent an Airbnb link. I sat incredibly still, staring at the messages coming through. I'd dropped the ball, big time. I'd been lazy when I sent them fake pictures of Oliver's place. I'd let the app show me places near to my location and then picked the first nice lounge, and then scrolled down, and the first nice bathroom I'd seen.

GEORGIA: This is the bathroom picture you sent us, but the lounge is different?

BEA: Omg there was a link all this time and you never told us?

SAM: Omg it's soooo fancy

GEORGIA: No guys I don't get it – the lounge picture in this house is different to what you sent us. Is this his house? How is the bathroom the same?

BEA: Oh yeah wtf

SAM: Yeah what's going on

ELLA: Confused

GEORGIA: Hattie??

Realising that even just a quick look at my individual chats with them would show I was online, I snapped out of sitting still, grabbed a sheet of paper from the printer and started mapping out possible answers.

Pretend it is Oliver's Airbnb?
Problems:
The lounge is completely different
= Say it got redecorated? (How?)
= AND the address is different to what you'd told them, but you somehow still got Ella's card?
= ELLA WILL GET SUSPICIOUS
= END OF PLAN

I became aware of a patient at the desk and looked up. They were clutching their hand, clearly a break. Probably fell out the bath in the rental they'd been told had a separate shower.

'Lovely! Take a seat.' I really wasn't concentrating. They'd just told me they thought they might pass out. I wrote up their details and went back to my notes.

Say he doesn't do Airbnb, you sent the wrong photo?

Problems:

– They won't believe you

– Why would you randomly have a bathroom photo on phone?

– They might think you're a bathroom pervert

– They'll get suspicious

= END OF PLAN

Admit you lied

Problems:

– They'll want to know why

Say the bathroom grim and messy? Pants all over floor? So sent Airbnb bathroom?

– Believable

BUT they could still find the other listing of the lounge picture, harder to come back from

– They're suspicious now

– Suspicious = End of Plan

GONNA HAVE TO ADMIT YOU LIED ABOUT THE HOUSE

'Melissa, so sorry, need a break.'

'Another one?' Her tone was stern but I didn't have time to worry about that.

In the staff locker room, Ella picked up after a lot of rings. 'Oh, at long last! A phone call!' she started. 'What's going on with this Airbnb thing? It's so weird.'

'I know, I know, I just felt a weird pressure to make his house look nice because, like, it's fine but it's not amazing and so I sent the fake pictures and—'

'That's a really strange thing to do?'

'I know, I know, can you help me out? Like pretend it was some in-joke between us or something?'

'Well that doesn't make sense, does it? What would the joke be? Honestly this isn't particularly cool of you, to ring me when you need me to cover for you, and I don't even get what I'm covering for?'

'I'm so sorry, I know it's all got a bit messed up. I—'

'What's going on, Hattie? Something isn't right.'

Her suspicious tone made my legs go wobbly. I thought back to The Plan:

> **WITHOUT** ANYONE KNOWING THE REAL REASON

She couldn't find out. If she found out she'd want to talk about it. I couldn't do that. I couldn't have her trying to convince me to come back. I couldn't go back.

'No, it's all good, just please can you help me out with this?'

'Only if you stop being so weird about us coming, okay? Like, for God's sake, we're all making an effort to come see you and you're being a bit off about it.'

'Yeah, no, sorry, of course, of course, I can't wait to see you all.'

She paused.

'Okay. Okay, I'll write it now. I'll put "hahahaaa we got you. Bit of an in joke between me and Hattie". Okay. Done.'

For the first time on the call my vision started to return to normal.

'… And Sam's replied saying "that's weird",' she said. 'And Georgia – Georgia is now asking if you work in A&E at Fallowfield Hospital in Wales?'

'What?' I could have screamed.

'Yeah, she says her old roommate, Millie, from uni came in with her boyfriend the other day, thought she recognised you, said some guy was getting all shouty? But you dog walk, don't you?'

'I need to go.'

'What? You can't—'

I hung up the phone and, without thought, threw it across the room. It clattered on the ground and I could see the screen had smashed.

'Hattie, who are you talking to?' I hadn't heard Melissa come in.

'Phone screen broke,' I gushed, picking it up and quickly checking it still worked. When the light came on as normal, I chucked it back in my locker and left, without letting Melissa respond.

I raced back upstairs to the desk to find Daphne sitting there, having just got in. The edges of my vision were going blurry again, my hands not feeling like they were my own.

'There you are! Thought you were MIA, Aiden here was just saying about the …' she started to whisper, turning her face away from the waiting room, '… lady with the flipper.

Thinks we should keep an eye? She was getting a bit teary. But I couldn't leave the desk.'

'Oh right, yes, sorry, is she okay?'

My arms didn't feel like my own either. Soon the feeling would spread into my chest.

'Yeah, I just went over to check,' said Aiden. 'She says she wears the flipper on days she feels like she's going round in circles.'

21

#TEST

In November of my first year at uni, I went to my annual neurology appointment in London. Ideally, this would have involved me sitting in the waiting room, alone, with a box television on the wall playing strongest men and women competitions from the early nineties.

Then a nurse would have come in, holding a blue hospital leotard with optional white leggings. I'd have got changed in a dressing room with two doors, and then the nurse would've led me into a long corridor, and I'd have found myself standing in a circular space. The nurse would have taken her place next to six other medical professionals, all stood with their backs against the wall, looking at me. But I wouldn't have been looking at them. I'd have been focused on the red-and-gold high-striker strength machine right in the middle of the space.

The hype would have started quietly at first. There'd have been the occasional, 'you can do this', 'here we go' interspersed with a low drum of rhythmic clapping. The nurse would've told me I could go ahead whenever I was ready.

'Feel free to take a run up.'

I'd have taken her advice and the clapping would've sped up, like it was match point at Wimbledon. That's right, motherfuckers, I was about to serve.

With all eyes on me, I'd have sprung forward, the mallet swooping through the air and down, meeting the metal hard, dead centre. The room would have fallen silent and then, as the bell rang out, the doctors would've jumped in the air, throwing off their white coats and waving their stethoscopes around their heads like lassos. We would have pooled in that circular room, a chaos of hugs and tears, enthralled by the knowledge that for another year, at least, the progression was not severe enough to stop me. Defying dead nerve endings year on year since '92.

Like I said, ideally. Because ideally, I wouldn't have had to wait in the neurologist's crowded waiting room that was so hot I felt like I was going to pass out. I wouldn't have had to sit in a room full of doctors who stared at me but did not smile. They were 'part of the team', I was told. No one ever told me whether I was, too.

I wouldn't have had to lie in my pants and t-shirt while a doctor asked me to push against him with my legs as he gripped onto my feet, feeling overwhelming shame about how long my toenails were. I wouldn't have had to listen to him call out 'four . . . four plus . . . four – hang on, let's try again?' as someone noted down the progression of my muscle weakness. I knew the higher the number, the better, but I didn't know who invented the number system.

Ideally, they wouldn't have asked me to do nerve conduction tests, where they wired me up to a machine and put an electric current through my muscles to see how quickly my nervous system reacted, strengthening the current every few seconds until they finally got a reading. Ideally, they wouldn't have tested how much sensation I was losing in my hands and feet by asking me to close my eyes and say yes when I felt a sharp pin touching me. Ideally, I wouldn't have had to lie and say yes when I felt nothing at all, and they wouldn't have worked out what I was doing and ratted me out, saying they'd have to start the experiment all over again, which meant I opened my eyes to a room full of people looking at me like it was all my fault. Like I'm the one to blame.

To distract myself on the train home from my appointment, I texted the guy I'd slept with the night before. It was the first time I'd had sex, and I had given myself a solid six out of ten for my performance.

Wanna come over again tonight?

Do you think you can go on top?

I genuinely didn't know. I had practised on my bed with a pillow underneath me but the pain in my legs was searing.

It hurts a bit, but . . . You could sit on a chair and I could cowgirl? ;-)

He didn't reply.

So . . . shall I put on my cowgirl boots or . . .?

Hey sorry Hattie I don't think it's going to work.
I just like it kinda freaky

I can be a freak

I mean very physical.

I wanted to try a disabled girl but not for me x

I forwarded the message to Ella and waited, as I watched her type and then stop typing and then start again.

Oh god

And that was it. No follow up. No call. Just 'oh god'.

It's a shame when you break your phone because of a text; I'll never forget the sound it made when I chucked it on the ground and stamped on it, right there on the train.

The next day I had another session with James. I put the broken phone down on the little table between us, next to the tissues.

'I need to find a way to stop doing things like this.' I looked at him, pleading.

'Why do you think you do it?'

'You were right in our first session. It is me. It's all me. Overreacting. And I asked if you thought I was broken, and you didn't say no. I think that's what it is. I'm broken so I break something else.'

'So when you look at the broken thing, do you feel less alone? Because there is something else broken too?'

I paused. He wasn't denying the idea I was broken, and he was the expert.

'I think that must be it.'

'So what do we do now?' He smiled.

'We need to find a way to fix me.'

THE NIGHT THAT CHANGED EVERYTHING

02:00

Dropped my phone on the floor a while ago. I bent to pick it up but the pain seared through my ribs. The man next to me bent down to get it instead.

'There you are darlin',' he slurred. 'I'm fucking out of here now. This is some sort of joke.'

He hobbled out of the waiting room, and in spite of myself, I found myself feeling sad that he'd left.

22

#TEA

It was the same night that the group chat had found out I worked at the hospital. I was, for the rest of the shift, existing in another liminal space. Between The Plan being intact and it falling to pieces. They knew where I worked now, and they could come in at any time, with their jokes and their knowledge, and ruin everything. I didn't know what I was going to do, or say, but I knew I had to focus minute by minute on my job, on that night, with my phone in my locker. I could not fall apart. For the moment, the very present moment, I still had time.

I popped to meet Daphne out back to see how busy things were as she worked on admissions to the wards. She tried to get me involved in some office gossip about Anne's new haircut. As she told me the history of every haircut Anne had ever had, and how they were all, in her opinion, a different type of terrible, I glanced back at the desk to see a flash of orange, a flash of orange that was now static and appeared to be sitting at my desk. Not wanting to alert Daphne to the fact I'd managed to let some opportunist jump on the desk, I casually said I'd better get back, then raced over, suddenly realising it was Aiden.

'Oh, hey,' he said, taking his hands off the keyboard.

'I think you're still on my account there,' I pointed to my login signature at the top of the screen. He rolled the chair back and stood up. He was tall enough that if he hugged me, I'd be out of sight from anyone looking at us from behind. That would be lovely. To be held by someone, hidden from the world, but not alone.

'Ah yeah, right you are.' He went round the other side of the desk as I sat down. 'Was just trying to check my shifts on the main hub,' he continued. 'What do I have to do to keep you from ratting me out to the boss, eh? Cuppa tea?'

I glanced up to see a cheeky grin.

'Go on then,' I said. 'I am pretty exhausted.'

He went off in the direction of the break room.

'Here you go, body,' I thought, 'some tea to wake you up.'

He came back with two mugs and put mine down on the desk. He stood by me and drank his while I put my hands around the warmth of the ceramic.

'Ah, I'm just so tired,' I said, unable to think of much else to say. Minute by minute it felt like I was heading closer to my phone vibrating in my locker.

'No need to chat, it's okay. Get that down you. Let the caffeine do its job.'

I nodded and took a sip, so relieved by the gentle company of someone who didn't expect me to speak. I decided then that he was going to let me off the skateboarder thing. And he didn't seem bothered by me freaking out in the lift, or unlike Bhavin, about how slow I was. He wasn't wondering why I was always too high or low on the chair, or late, or snappy. When people suspect something is different about my body, occasionally, they go ahead and ask, but more often they just wait for me to bring up the subject, and then go really, really quiet once I've told them. Maybe they'll add in a question like, 'Ah yeah. Do you get tired a lot?' and then go back to being deathly silent, staring at me for an answer. You can silence a whole group of people that way, just by saying, 'my body . . .' It's the most annoying magic trick. But Aiden wasn't looking for me to say anything, he just wanted me to drink my tea.

'We can go up and watch that CCTV after your shift, if you like, by the way?'

'And how are we going to manage that? You might be allowed, but I'm definitely not.'

'Wally did not complete his psychology degree. In fact, he completely and utterly flunked it, became a gi-norm-ous alcoholic, went to rehab, found Buddhism, now he lives a life of solitude with few possessions or desire to do anything other than sleep and meditate. But what he does do, because one still needs to pay rent, is work here, on security.' He grinned at me as he took another gulp of his tea.

I laughed, and then, for a moment, imagined us up in the room, in the dark together, as the screens played, his hand reaching out to mine . . .

But I didn't have time. Things were bad. Really bad. I had to fix the situation on the group chat or before I knew it, I'd be confronted by them all, asking me why, why, why, and Ella telling me I needed to come back.

'I'm actually pretty over the whole thing, so I'm all good.

But thanks, by the way. And for the tip, about imagining you watching it back? I like that idea.'

He said it was 'no worries' and had to get back to work. Pretty soon after Daphne came out and continued with the history of Anne's hair: '. . . and then in 2009 she went box dye black. Like a goth, but one that shops in Debenhams . . .'

I looked over to the waiting room; the woman with the flipper had been called, as had the man with the loss of vision. The man with the broken ankle was still waiting, and so were the two women. I wondered how many of them were waiting for confirmation of what they already knew. When people come to A&E, they come to get fixed, but if they can't fix you, where do you go next? You cross a line when the people who are meant to fix you can't. You start to see the cracks in all things, all places, all people.

At about 5 a.m., Aiden came back to the desk, looking exhausted.

'My turn to get you a drink,' I said, just about to go on my last five-minute break. 'Tea?'

'Can I have a coffee actually?' he said, rubbing his eyes. 'You're the best.'

I was still running on adrenaline, and my hands had started to go a bit shaky. I was focusing on work until I didn't have to. Then I'd have to go home and look at my phone.

I couldn't carry two mugs up the stairs at the same time, so I just went about making Aiden his coffee. There wasn't enough in the open jar, so I had to root around and find a new one while the kettle boiled. I gripped the lid with my hands and felt a familiar sinking feeling when it wouldn't turn.

'Shit,' I muttered. 'Shitting hands.'

I really wanted to make him a coffee. I'd felt a genuine relief when he brought me up that cup of tea, and I hoped I could repay the favour. I wanted another moment where we could just sit together without talking. I wanted to feel the comfort of being with someone who didn't seem to want to talk about someone's bad haircut.

I tried. I really tried. The same pain on my skin, the same sweat on my forehead. When Aiden appeared, I had the coffee jar clamped between my thighs as I tried to twist the lid.

He laughed gently.

'Did you want a hand or is this a secret trick to make the coffee extra good?'

I smiled and put the jar in his outstretched hand. He twisted the lid without commenting on how easy it was.

'Hey, you might wanna go back up – Daphne's getting a bit funny about you going over your five-minute break.' My heart sunk.

'Oh, right, yeah. I'm sorry I couldn't do your coffee.'

He shrugged. 'No trouble. Next time, eh? I liked our little hot drink break earlier.'

'Yeah,' I said. 'Next time.' I paused, wondering if I should ask him not to tell anyone I couldn't open the lid. But I worried that that in itself would sound suspicious. And as much as I wanted a next time, I was aware that I'd always only be able to bring one mug up to the desk at a time.

Getting to know Aiden was both a brilliant part of my new life and a rising risk. I was too exhausted to think about it any more than that. I figured I'd just have to be careful. I turned around without saying anything and returned to the desk to Daphne asking what had taken me so long.

As much as I didn't want it to, the sun rose and my shift was over. I removed my phone from my locker like a murderer removing a body. Forensic. Detached. I didn't look at any more messages. I drove home but I didn't remember the journey. The sun was surrounded by a watercolour blue, but it only registered briefly before I felt frustrated at the brightness in my eyes. The warmth wasn't comforting, either. It made me feel itchy.

I got home and started to make a cup of tea in a calm, methodical way, placing the mug gently down, switching on the kettle, removing a tea bag from the box. I opened the fridge, got out a bottle of fresh milk, untwisted the lid and pulled on the foil seal. I don't know how many times I tried, maybe three, possibly four. The foil wasn't coming off. The need to keep it together at work, pushing down the feelings, the fear of it all falling apart, finally erupted.

I don't know if the WhatsApp group thought I was purposefully not replying, or just busy, but I doubt they thought I was smashing up the already damaged wooden chair, letting the pieces fly in all directions. I doubt they thought I was hurling it against the floor until the back came away from the seat, two of the legs breaking off. I doubt they thought that everything from that day was coming out in one long, grieving scream.

I didn't realise I'd done my foot in until I saw my sock change colour. I carried on kicking despite the blood. I saw the red patches on the floor and felt nothing. I continued, hurling it apart. When a piece of wood flew up and hit me in the face, I deemed the nosebleed to be too mild for attention.

I bashed one of the legs against the floor over and over again. My arms felt as though they were on fire, and there was no way the chair leg was going to snap in half, but I just kept going: I liked the sound it made as it hit against the floor, feeling the shudder up my arm and into my shoulders. I licked the nose-bleed and swallowed the taste of metal. I could feel the blood continue to run down my face and eventually let it seep into my mouth. My damp sock made prints as I walked around in circles, kicking the pile of wood until I slumped down on the floor and lay there, staring at the broken body of the chair.

When I started to pick up the wood all over the floor, my foot was still bleeding and making marks on the parts I was trying to clean. I sat down with cold, wet kitchen paper against my skin and whispered gently to myself.

'It's okay. It's okay. It is finished.'

23

#FALL

The first proper Eco Society social I went to was on the first of December, at a Winter Wonderland fun fair. The only trouble was, I hadn't told any of them about my disability. I needed them to know I was going to be slower as we moved around the fun fair, but I still hadn't found the words. It was too much of a monologue to say: 'My muscles are weak, and my balance isn't good, but I've never quite understood where it comes from. You can't point to it; it's not a part of the body. There's not a little window at the back of your head that the doctor can look through and see a little red and pink spirit level and say, "Oh yeah, it's way off". Sure, ears and brains and eyes and feet are part of it, but it seems to just float along and then, in my case, suddenly lifts off up into the ether like a skydiver inflating their parachute and I'm the one left falling.'

On the day of the social, I texted Pearl, since we'd swapped numbers, and the group chat wasn't a thing yet.

Hey Pearl! You still on for the Christmas social tomorrow night? Just a heads up I have a disability that results in muscle weakness, I wanted to let you know as sometimes I can be a bit slower on the stairs etc, and the rest of the group don't know, and I –

I wrote out so many different versions, sucking on a cough sweet throughout. In the end I decided to take it in stages.

Hey Pearl! You still on for tonight?

Hey Hattie, sadly can't make it. Have a great time though!

I was surprised by how physical the disappointment felt.

'Ella,' I asked, having gone over to her halls, 'do you think it's weird if I do a big Facebook post about my disability and tag people? That way everyone will know?'

She paused as she got some mugs out of the cupboard. 'I think that might be a bad idea. I think you should just tell them tonight. I'll be with you remember? I'm going to pretend I've wanted to join Eco Society for ages.'

'Yeah. Yeah okay. Thanks. Just don't mention the fact you don't recycle.'

She smirked and sniffed the milk.

'Sure. Anything else you'd rather I didn't say?' she asked sarcastically.

It was hard to find the right time to do it. I kept losing people in the crowds, and we all ended up separating fairly quickly after agreeing to meet back at the drinks area in an hour.

Ella and I wandered around before shuffling into the hall of mirrors.

As we stood together in front of a mirror that made our bodies merge, I said, 'There's this thing we're learning about called The Golden Ratio, which is a ratio that artists have been using for ages. It's even found in nature, like in the proportions of a snail's shell. It's meant to make things look perfect to the human eye.'

Ella wasn't listening properly.

'I wish I was taller,' she said, going over to another mirror.

'Hey, what would you do if for your whole life you had a funhouse mirror in your house, and the whole time you didn't know, until eventually, you found out – would you get rid? Or would you keep it, because you were used to the distortion?' I was looking straight at her, as she carried on making her body wobble in the mirror.

'Obviously get rid,' she laughed, 'and celebrate you're not a troll. Where're Sam and Pearl? Are they in here?'

She turned the corner and left me looking at my body, stock still and deep in thought.

In the end, I told them when we all met up again in the drinks area.

'Oh, guys, just so you know, I should probably mention, I have a disability, which makes me a bit wobbly, and affects my muscles, so I'm a bit slower on the stairs and stuff,' I gushed out before taking a large gulp of wine, which only maximised the burning in my throat. The silence was heavy, and I saw them all reframe me, recalculate who I was, who I'd been all this time.

'Oh, I had no idea,' said Sam, which was followed by a few nods.

'Yeah, you wouldn't know,' said Ella to the ground. 'But sometimes you can tell.' And then, turning to me, she said, 'I've known you so long I think I know you better than you do sometimes!' She laughed, giving me a nudge. 'Did you guys know we've been friends since primary school?'

My throat was in so much pain, but I knew there was so much more to say. All the different ways it affected me, how my fatigue meant sometimes I could do things and sometimes I couldn't, how I needed a lot of help if I fell over. But I also wanted to break out of the new way they saw me, I wanted to fight against the stereotypes. That felt like the priority.

'We can laugh about it though, okay? Like there's a lot of benefits, my blue badge, for example.'

'Absolutely, it doesn't need to be a big deal,' said Ella. 'Now, should I have another one of these hot toddy things before we go on the ice rink, or is that a bad idea?'

It was like I had been kicked in my ribcage. I felt like such a hypocrite, knowing I found it painful to say the words, but it was painful to have someone else say them for me, especially when they were saying it all wrong. It was clear then that my therapy with James still wasn't helping. I couldn't carry on like this – I needed to find a way to sort myself out, and fix what was broken in me, even though I couldn't even really pinpoint what it was. I needed to find another therapist, one that could understand and help me find the problem, help me find a way to change.

Later, I sucked on two cough sweets on the edge of the ice rink, watching as people tried to keep their balance and stay steady on the ice, feeling every single wobble, trip and fall.

THE NIGHT THAT CHANGED EVERYTHING

02:03

Finally get to see the nurse. I tell her something feels broken inside, but she doesn't seem to be listening or acting particularly concerned that I've been crying so much for so long that my eyes are a bright, painful red, and my voice is raspy, about to give out entirely.

24

#SCREAM

I rolled over and stared at the pile of wood from the smashed-up chair. Then I looked over at The Plan, my resolve refreshed anew.

The epicentre of The Plan – the You Are Not Disabled part – was feeling too wobbly. It felt like it was getting kicked from both sides, my old life and my new. My hands were under scrutiny at work. They were not up to the job and needed fixing. I walked over to The Plan and added a line:

> GET STRONGER SO YOU ARE LESS OBVIOUS AT WORK. NEED TO DO OFFICE CHAIR, CARRY DRINKS, OPEN JARS ETC.

This wasn't going to be that easy, but I was determined.

I got out of bed and picked up one of the wooden chair legs that had been abandoned on the floor. I squeezed it tightly and felt the strain in my fingers. It wasn't quite right though, not enough of an exercise. I wandered round the hut with it, feeling as though I was on to something. When I saw the sharp points of the kitchen scissors, I gave a small shout of delight.

I used the scissors to try and cut into the wood. I was gaining strength from the squeezing motion, and the wood had good resistance and was never going to break. It also, if I squeezed hard enough and for long enough, left a satisfying mark on the wood, a little line that marked my progress.

My old life was putting The Plan under threat too, and I needed to fix that. They knew I worked at the hospital, which put me at risk of being found, and which could, one, reveal my disability if they came in making jokes, and two, mean Ella asking loads of questions and finding out the Real Reason I left. I scrolled back through the group chat and began to write a message.

Our Son Mr Jonathan

Guys I'm so sorry I know this all is seeming really weird

Basically Oliver and I have been drinking way too much

And it's made me be a bit all over the place

But I knew it couldn't last forever so yeah I'm part-timing as A&E reception

Bit more secure than the dog walking

It wasn't a perfect solution, but it didn't need to be. I just needed time. I got the idea of blaming being drunk from how much Bhavin seemed to find it funny I was hungover. I don't understand why society finds it so acceptable, but I wasn't going to question it now.

SAM: Hahahaaa Hattie's been half cut this whole time

LEGEND

GEORGIA: Please don't go tee-total before we get there

I am once again appalled you can't come to Ella's party

BEA: I know isn't it like the first one you've ever missed?? Since primary school!!

I know I'm so gutted, honestly

ELLA: We can make up for it when we come to visit

Yeah that'd be SO nice if it works out

ELLA: Oh, it's happening

Haha YAY

Trust me, I was *not* laughing. Or celebrating.

However, not only had Ella now gotten so suspicious that I really did have to keep my promise of letting them come, it was also in my best interests to have control over their visit. Now they knew where I worked, there was nothing to stop them 'turning up' as a surprise.

Ella

I don't know what's going on but I'm not buying the drinking thing

We ARE coming to visit

Because you owe me and you promised

And you and I will have a chat

Just the two of us

About what on earth is up with you

Hey what else is new

I'm serious

With this in mind, the search for a flat was more important than ever. They were under the impression that living with Oliver was a short-term thing anyway, until I got my own place, and then I would just need to say that we were going through a rough patch or something. We'd spend the least amount of time in my flat as possible so they couldn't start snooping, thinking it was weird I had no pictures of Oliver or wondering why I had a wooden chair leg with incision marks in it. Dinner. A film. Coffee. The aquarium? And I'd have to make sure, under no circumstances would they visit the hospital. I was so annoyed I had all this to worry about when I was meant to be living my best new life.

Later, in the hospital's car park, I rang the numbers I'd listed after my Rightmove scroll. Only one estate agent picked up, and that was to tell me the flat had already gone. My heart, which had felt fluttery with hope when my call was answered, sank at the news.

'But we do have a top floor flat nearby?'

'Is there a lift?'

'There is . . . but it has been out of order for a while now . . .'

I ended the call before my body could spit a response.

Inside the hospital, Jackie said I'd be working reception for the first half of the day, then after lunch I'd do my second shift shadowing a porter. My heart was about to sink before she told me it was with Aiden. Finally, some good luck. At lunch, I sat in my car and got out my scissors. I'd brought the wooden stick into work with me and was going to practise getting stronger every lunch break. I spent so long cutting into the wood I almost forgot to eat my sandwich. As well as the strength exercise, it was calming me down. I imagined the chair leg was each of my friends back home and funnelled my anger into squeezing the scissors. I made the deepest mark when I thought of Ella.

'So, where are we going?' I asked Aiden as we made our way down the corridor.

'Stock cupboard,' he said, his smile making my legs go a little wobbly for a nice reason, for once.

'Hey, you know the other day – when you were at the desk,

on my login, was that really to check your rota? 'Cos, you know, I noticed you porters have it on the board in the staff room.'

'Ahh yeah, well, it's a bit of a story, but I was just wondering about a patient really, and thought I might be able to see on your screen.'

I laughed a little, mainly in shock at how honest he'd been.

'That's very illegal,' I said.

He paused. 'Sometimes I wonder about patients I'm taking round, you know. They don't always tell me what's up, obviously, so I come up with a story in my head, and yeah it gets the better of me sometimes and I want to know if I'm right.'

'I PLAY THE SAME GAME.' It was the least chill I have ever been. 'I thought I was the only player.'

'Well I wouldn't call it a GAME,' he said, putting on an overly serious, moral voice.

I laughed, and a little bounce of energy came from my chest. 'How long you been working here then?' I asked, grabbing the banister as we went up the stairs. I wasn't having to rush this time though, like with Bhavin. We seemed to be going at the same pace.

'A year or so?'

'Nice one, what were you doing before?'

'Astronaut.' He smiled. 'But I needed something more down to earth.' He put out his hand for a high-five in jokey enthusiasm for his clearly terrible joke. I quickly slapped his hand and turned to go up the second set of stairs. 'You know how it is, I'm on the moon, having a mosey around, and I'm thinking, you know what I need? I need to wear a shocking orange t-shirt in a hospital while I push patients around.'

'And what a lovely orange t-shirt it is,' I said, planning my next question. 'And you live near here? Easier commute than going to the moon?'

He gave a small laugh and agreed, saying he was really close to the hospital. Before that he was sharing a room in a five-bedroom place, and it was all a bit too crowded for him.

'Do you keep in touch with any of them?'

'Nah, not really,' he said quickly. 'We kind of have different interests. Bit like here actually, it's been hard to . . .' He stopped himself. 'Hard sometimes, isn't it?' he finished, vaguely.

'Yeah,' I said. 'It really can be.'

We got to the stock cupboard and Aiden opened the door. It was like a walk-in larder full of supplies, and I wanted to take a closer look.

I'm not sure if Aiden had even registered I'd fallen before he heard me shriek. I'd missed the fact there was a tiny step up into the cupboard and tripped, tumbling hard on the floor, my knee instantly stinging and my wrist feeling bruised.

'Oh shit!' he said. I was still lying on my stomach, facing the ground, not wanting to look him in the eye. 'You okay?'

I rolled onto my side and said I was fine, still not looking at him, but he clocked the dark blood staining on the knee of my light blue trousers.

'Should I get someone?'

'No, no, I can sort it.' My tone was stern, the same tone I was using to speak silently to my body: 'What was that? You can't do that. You can't fall here. Not now.'

He stepped into the cupboard and I shuffled up to make space, as he threw me down a few plasters and dressings, rather haphazardly.

Now sitting up, and looking at the blood stain blossoming,

I needed to get him away from me, away from me rolling up my trousers and looking at my muscle-wasted leg under the strip light.

'Can you just, step out, and make sure no one comes in? I need to take these off.'

'Sure, sure.' He immediately turned his back. 'But I really can get someone?'

'I really don't want you to do that,' I said. I did not need this turning into a 'thing'. I did not need this to be news. I needed this to stay in the cupboard.

I rolled up my trouser leg and inspected the wound. Only superficial, taking the top layer of skin off. I looked at the random assortment of things he'd thrown down to me and found a spongy plaster that would do. I ripped the backing off with my teeth and pressed the plaster on to my skin, then went to gather up the other bandage and antiseptic wipe and – I had to read the words on the plastic twice before it sunk in. In small writing, across the side: *Surgical Sponge*.

I'd never actually seen what one looked like before. I was desperate to unwrap it there and then, but instead I shoved it up my sleeve, and tried to get up. I tried really, really hard, but the cupboard was too small – I needed to get into a kneeling position, and then push on the shelves to get up, but my knee was stinging too much, and the shelves were too full for me to be able to properly lean on them, and as much as I tried, I just didn't have the strength.

I needed Aiden. He was going to have to help me up, but the closer I got to people, the more they saw of me, the more difficult it was to hide my disability. Was I really going to be able to keep hiding the disabled girl staring back at me? Had I ever left the grey zone of those service station toilets, my New Life close, but in reality, forever out of reach?

Aiden gingerly knocked on the door.

'All good?'

'Come in here a sec,' I said, and he stepped in slowly.

'You can't tell anyone about this.' We were inches away from each other.

'What? No, no, it's cool. Are you . . .' he looked down at me, still on the floor.

'I mean it.' I sounded half furious, half desperate.

Aiden shrank back a little. 'I won't.'

'I need you to help me up.'

He put out his hand, but my heart sank. I needed him to properly lift me. Like a child.

'I need more help than that. I need you to put your arms under my arms and lift.'

'Oh my God – how hurt are you? Hattie, is something broken?'

The words made my eyes and throat and stomach sting like I'd downed a mug of bleach.

'Please. Just—' The wobble in my voice, my throat giving out, tears on the brink of falling.

He didn't say another word and went to lift me as I had told him to, getting so close I couldn't help but notice how great he smelled, but this was not a move. This was not a sexy, intimate moment, this was a fully grown, able-bodied man, picking up a small girl who had hurt her knee pretending she could catch balloons like the other kids.

And just as I was up, and we were standing so close to each other, the door opened. Jackie.

'What on earth? Aiden?'

'No – no – I – her knee – see . . .' Aiden stepped out of the way and pointed to the blood blooming on my trousers.

'Ah – okay – Hattie, what— actually, can you both come out of the cupboard?'

We stepped out and I refused to look at anything but the floor.

'What happened? Are you hurt?'

'I tripped and he helped me up.'

Jackie took a long pause.

'Can you be more careful in future, then? And perhaps – well – that didn't look good, what I saw.'

Aiden stepped in again. 'Honestly, I can imagine – but I was just helping—'

'It was a very close way to help someone.'

Another pause. The sounds of wheels on lino, doors swinging open and closed, machines beeping and pens clicking seemed to get louder and louder in my ears, disrupting my thoughts. I could only carry on looking at the floor.

'I don't want to see anything like that again. I was looking for you to see how it was going. I couldn't find you anywhere.'

Another pause.

'I don't have time today but we might have to have a meeting about this. Hattie – are you okay?' She clenched her jaw as she waited for my response.

'Yes, yeah, honestly, I'm fine.'

'You tripped?'

'Yep.'

'And he was helping you up?'

'Yep.'

I knew how it sounded. But I couldn't give more details. She gave me a searching look and walked away, telling Aiden to get on with the training.

The words came out before I could think. 'You told her. You promised me you wouldn't tell anyone and then—'

'She thought we were – and you're basically crying – do you realise how that would have looked? Hattie, I had to say.'

He was right, of course, but inside I was in chaos.

'No one else. You tell no one else.'

'Hattie, if she calls you into a meeting, you have to tell her you told me to lift you like that, right?' I'd never seen him look so worried.

'I'll make it clear you weren't doing anything inappropriate.'

Aiden nodded, but was quiet and said little else to me for the rest of the shift, apart from when he had to show me something. The silence between us was agony.

'You live on your own, don't you?' he said at the end of the shift.

When I nodded, he told me he wanted to make sure I was okay, and could I text him later, just to say I'd got home all right?

'You don't have to,' he said, as he gave over his number. He was acting distant, with hardly any emotion in his voice.

I walked away from him, heart pumping in my chest, tears desperate to fall. I took the surgical sponge from my sleeve as soon as I got to my locker. I was going to inspect every inch of what had been missed and left to fester.

25

#WRITE

In my first session with Catherine from Wellbeing, I sat down and immediately announced I wanted to talk about my childhood. She seemed a little taken aback but there was no time to waste, and I launched into it.

'... So the vicar burnt a hoard of sage and the smoke filled my tiny bedroom until I gagged, at which point he encouraged me to force a wooden crucifix down my throat so I would expel the badness in me. I was sick all over the carpet and the only thing that was expelled was a watery pink blancmange. Then he poured water over my head while speaking in a language I didn't recognise – it had a lot of throat to it though – I actually thought he was going to be sick, at one point, and I was quite interested to see if he ate Angel Delight, too.'

Catherine was enraptured. 'And you say it was your mother who asked the priest to do this?'

'Yes, Mother said it would make me better. But it's just meant I have to suck a strawberry soother whenever I go past a church, because –' I took a packet of cough sweets from my pocket and made the sign of the Holy Trinity '– the memory of it gives me a sore throat.'

Of course, none of that actually happened: I made it all up. No exorcism. I was keen to see Catherine with a pre-prepared plan. It was a lot of work for me to construct all this, but I had learnt from James that if you're really going to open up to somebody, you need to know they're the right person to open up to. I wouldn't tell her the truth until I could see how she dealt with my lies.

In session two, I sat in her very grey office with her big windows and fake Kentia Palms, and said, 'Well this week, Catherine, I've been having the weirdest dreams about my left elbow,' and I talked at length about the specifics, how it's always on a grey day, late afternoon before bonfire night, and by the end of the dream I'm screaming as a Catherine wheel fizzes in the distance, my left arm uncannily hot and swelling.

She did manage to correctly work out that the Catherine wheel was in reference to her, and maybe the dream was about therapy. 'There is something wanting to come out, underneath the surface?' she questioned, about the broken arm.

Due to her good work in the third session, in our fourth, I started to tentatively bring up some truth.

'I sometimes feel like . . .' I coughed. 'I find myself getting angry with my best friend sometimes. It seems she doesn't really listen to me or – I don't know, like she doesn't "get" the disability stuff.'

I was distracted by the image of the surgical sponge in my dad's stomach once again. It was always there, at the bottom of everything, and sometimes I could hide it with a river of other thoughts, but before long, that river would run dry, and there it would be, waiting on the bed. It was not in my plan to bring up the sponge yet, Catherine had not really made enough progress. But the image was so clear to me, it seemed impossible to hide. I went slowly.

'And then, I don't know, there's this thing I can't stop thinking about. So, my dad, well he had this operation—' She interrupted me for the first time in ever. She was usually so happy to let me carry on talking.

'Hold on. Let's stay on the disability thing.' And that was when she very randomly asked me to write a letter to the non-disabled version of myself: a parallel-universe me, she said. I was disappointed she didn't like my question, 'What would I put on the envelope?' – but I meant it. Where would I be living?

Catherine never brought up my dad again, so I didn't even get to mention that he died, or talk about the sponge. She spent our fifth session obsessed with the letter-writing.

'Today I want the non-disabled Hattie to write back to you. What kind of person do you think the other Hattie is? Is there anything she wants to say, do you think? We need to give her space to talk.'

She talked about this other Hattie like she cared for her more than me.

I told her the other Hattie was actually quite boring. 'LOVES geography, she does. It's all sediments, sediments, sediments with that girl.'

Catherine didn't have a sense of humour – she wasn't having it.

The more Catherine started to talk about the other Hattie, the more I started to picture her in my head. Even after our sessions ended, I couldn't stop thinking about this other version of me. As the years went by, I wanted this idea to come into reality. All the stuff she didn't have to deal with, the life she would be leading. This was the fix I'd been searching for. And that was when I didn't just want to think about her anymore, I wanted to *be* her.

THE NIGHT THAT CHANGED EVERYTHING

02:07

'Why can't I have an X-Ray?' I ask.

The nurse says she doesn't think there's any need.

'But it hurts. Inside.' My eyes fill with tears again, but her expression remains clinical. 'No, there isn't any one I can call,' I say, my voice shaking and ready to break.

26

#CHAT

Mum

Hope all going okay love? x

All good. Sorry not been in touch. Just busy x

Aiden

Hi it's Hattie

Just to say all good!

Heyy

Glad to hear it

And you will talk to Jackie?

Hopefully she won't ask for a meeting

But if she does??

Yeah, of course

Okay thank you

Was good to hang out today

Yeah, it really was

I knew I couldn't make it seem like Aiden had done anything inappropriate. I just hoped I wouldn't be questioned too much on why he needed to pick me up. And I hoped Aiden wouldn't start to question that either.

Our Son Mr Jonathan

SAM: Countdown to partaaaaaay

BEA: Ella's funeral for her twenties

SAM: Can't wait mate.

Pearl you coming?

ELLA: Nah she's working nights

GEORGIA: Awh pull a sickie Pearl!

SAM: Not sure you can as a nurse

GEORGIA: Yeahhh you can

SAM: Haahahaa

Ella

Happy Birthdaaay!

[Missed Voice Call from Ella]

We are coming in less than 2 weeks

Is that the first time we're actually going to have a conversation?

Rest-Assured Rentals

Hi Hattie thanks for your enquiry about the three properties on our website. Unfortunately, our list is full for two of them, and based on your earnings, the third is unlikely to work as you wouldn't pass the landlord's threshold. We do have a top floor flat coming on that may be of interest? Details attached.

I swiped away all other messages and replied to the one from the letting agent.

Hi there,

Thanks for letting me know. I need to move into a property within 10 days. Top floor is no good. Please send me anything else you have.

If I didn't have a place by then, I'd just have to say I was ill and they couldn't come. But I knew, deep down, this wouldn't wash with Ella. The chances of them coming anyway, since everything was booked, were high. And the chances of Ella being so suspicious that she just turned up at A&E were even higher. I would have to ask for last-minute leave from Jackie to make sure I wasn't there. Or pretend to be sick? But we were only allowed three sicknesses in six months before being called into a meeting about our attendance. I kind of needed to save them for when I got a cold and couldn't get out of bed.

I felt like everything was falling from my grasp, so I put on an episode of *24 Hours in A&E* to play The Game and calm me down while I got ready for work, but I didn't have time to get out my notebook to make notes. As the show played on, everything looked like a break. Broken, Broken, Broken. It wasn't calming me down at all.

As I reached for my keys on the side, I looked again at the surgical sponge I'd taken from the cupboard. I had spent a lot of the evening staring at it. It took me ages to work out what the little blue string on it was until I googled it and realised it was literally to stop it getting left in people's bodies. And yet, the article admitted, they were still too many occurrences of them being missed. The image of it flooded my mind again, sewn up, in the dark, inside a body. I felt nauseous at the thought of it, but the image wouldn't leave my mind. I had no choice but to leave it there, festering, as I got ready to go to work.

I double checked I had the chair leg and scissors with me, and made my way out of the hut, out to a drain grey, cloudy morning with a breeze that seemed too cold for June. The walk to my car seemed longer than ever, and the ground harder and more uneven. Even the birdsong seemed a little out of sync, like things were not quite matching up as they should; beaks opening and closing at the wrong moments, feathers itching in the disharmony.

I parked in the hospital car park and got out my scissors and the stick, pressing hard, thinking of how I'd fallen over yesterday, how I had to be alert today. It was the deepest mark I'd ever made. If my hand didn't burn, I wasn't doing it hard enough. Then I got all my things together, locked the car, and heard Daphne's voice.

'Okay, babe?' she said, and I smiled, before I noticed her furrowed brow as she looked at my car. 'Eh, not being funny but it's not really fair to park there, you know?' It took me a minute to work out what she meant. When it hit me, she was already ahead of me. 'I'd move it, if I were you.'

I'd been so distracted that I'd gone on autopilot, parking right in the blue badge space.

'I didn't notice!' I called back, too late. She didn't turn around.

I moved the car and it made me late for work. By the time I got up to the desk, Melissa and Daphne were talking, but stopped when I appeared. Then Jackie called me in for a chat and I felt like I'd been kicked in the chest.

When she started off by saying how well I was doing, I smiled uneasily, convinced there was more to come.

'I do need to check about yesterday, though. Can you go through what happened? You looked very upset.'

'I know how it must have looked, but I need to just make it very clear – Aiden – he's a good egg. Nothing inappropriate. He did nothing wrong. He was helping me as I asked. I literally . . .' I felt my throat start to burn. 'I literally tripped into the cupboard and I was upset because I'd got blood all over my trousers and my knee stung and—' This wasn't going to make any sense to her. Why would a grown woman cry at a scraped knee?

'I was just – it seemed odd to me you couldn't get up by yourself? That would be an easier solution?'

'I asked him, though, I promise, like I said, good egg. He didn't do a thing wrong.'

'Okay, okay, I believe you, and I'm glad, of course, but – next time, well look, I hope there's not a next time, but watch where you're going, and be aware of how things look to other people. He really could have got in a lot of trouble – because of how it looked to me – when it would have been a lot better to just get up or ask for his hand. Do you see what I'm saying?'

I nodded as my cheeks blushed red. 'I didn't think.'

'Okay. Well we shall leave that there. There's just a couple of other things I wanted to raise with you. Firstly, there was a bit of a discrepancy the other day on one of your notes about a patient that got flagged to me by the triage team. You wrote chest pains and abdominal pains, and the chest pains meant he got bumped up the list a bit, but when he was seen he said he didn't have chest pains at all – it was just the stomach stuff? It was a good few days ago now and he may well have told you otherwise: people have learnt tricks in the system, but it's important to make sure you record the details accurately.'

I apologised, trying to remember who it could have been, saying I'm always pretty careful and I did remember someone telling me about chest and stomach pains. Although, I thought, did I guess chest pains and it was actually stomach? My memory of patients started to merge and words flew in front of my eyes, confusing the notes I had made and the ones

I had secretly looked up afterwards, confusing my guesses with what they'd told me.

'Secondly, I've had a bit of feedback from a few people that you have been a few minutes late to your shift, and to put it bluntly, you don't seem to be running up the stairs when you're tight on time. After putting your stuff away in your locker, if you're late as it is, you really need to be quick as you can, please. I couldn't help but notice you were late today? It's really not on.'

It was another moment where I was sure Jackie could hear the sound of my heart thudding. I nodded, eyes wide, waiting for her to carry on. Once I got a flat I'd be so much closer. But I was running out of time.

'And it'll make it easy for you anyway, not rushing in and plonking down on a low chair that you can't be bothered to sort.' She said it like a joke, but she wasn't laughing. I needed my hands to be stronger, faster.

'Yeah, of course, no problem,' I said, trying to sound relaxed.

'Apart from the obvious, how did the porter training go?'

My heart plummeted.

'Great!' I smiled, far too enthusiastically. Aside from my dentist, I don't think I've ever shown anyone more of my teeth in one go.

Jackie recoiled slightly at the smile. 'You sure?'

'Very sure.'

There was a pause. She looked at me intensely. 'I have to remind you that you're still on probation, and I need you here firing on all cylinders. You need to be on top form or else we're going to have to have another conversation and that's when things start getting serious. So for your next shift, it'll be *on time* – yes?'

'Yeah, absolutely,' I nodded, and left her office as she kept her eyes on me. I wouldn't be able to ask for some last-minute leave anytime soon. I had to find a flat.

As I turned the corner and went back to the desk, Aiden and Daphne were standing close to each other, talking quietly. When they saw me, they very obviously stopped chatting, and stepped apart. My cheeks started to flush. Were they talking about me? Did Daphne say I parked in a blue badge space, and how out of order that was? Was Aiden saying I decked it in a cupboard? I was in trouble, people had noticed things, if not the big stuff, then tiny stuff, but the tiny stuff would eventually add up. It always did. The more I got to know them, the more dangerous everything felt.

'All okay, mate?' asked Aiden, looking over at me, concerned.

'Fine – all sorted. Nothing to worry about.'

He leant in closer to me, eyeing up Jackie's office.

'So she's not . . . she knows I was just helping—'

'I promise, you don't need to worry.'

'Cool,' he said with a relieved sigh. And then, looking at me again, 'You don't seem – did she say something else?'

It was all I could do not to burst into tears right in front of him. I only just got by with a quiet shake of my head. He bought me a tea unprompted later that afternoon and tried to distract me with his idea for a dark comedy about train-spotter spotters.

'It will be about a guy who spots trainspotters as a hobby, from the train, you see, so the trainspotters are out in the fields waiting for the train and the trainspotter spotter is on the train, looking out for the trainspotters—'

'Are you coming for drinks later?' I interrupted, distracted by racing thoughts, trying to plan for all eventualities. We were meant to be having after-work drinks later on.

'What? Ah ... no, probably not.'

A part of me wished he was coming, but at the same time I felt worried that, in a quiet moment, when everyone else was talking amongst themselves, he would ask about the cupboard, and why I needed so much help getting up off the ground.

I drove to the pub to be the first one there, to avoid getting the first round in, and stick to drinking orange juice. I sat at the dark wood table and tried to avoid my reflection in the rectangle mirror that stretched the length of the table, pretending instead to take an interest in the watercolours of hills and lakes dotted around the walls. They were at odds with the darkness of the pub, and the paint seemed to have faded, like the place itself had sucked the life out of them.

The group arrived about five minutes after I'd sat down, full of energy even after a long shift. How did their bodies have so much to give? Mine felt worn and hot with exhaustion. I smiled at them all, waving over enthusiastically to try and match their energy.

'Orange juice?' said Neil, seeing mine. 'Nah nah, we can't be having that.'

Bhavin interrupted. 'This one's a lightweight though, should have seen her on our porter shift. Dragging yourself up those stairs, you were!'

'She does that when she's not hungover and all!' quipped Anne, and I did my best to laugh, as everybody did, before she said, 'I'm only messing, love.'

But I knew she wasn't messing. I was being talked about in

the wrong way. I was trying to think of a reason for being slow on the stairs when Daphne started talking again.

'Guess who we had in today, guys?' She started speaking again before anyone could answer. 'Quasimodo!'

The table erupted with cheers before Neil looked over at me, not joining in.

'Not met the quad-meister yet?' he asked.

I shook my head.

'Ah, you must have been on break – although, you'd have seen him in the waiting room, he's the most annoying guy – we swear he just comes in to flirt with Anne,' Neil said, looking round the table as they nodded in agreement.

I was confused.

'Is he a patient? I mean, why does he say he's coming in?'

'Headaches. Always got a headache.'

'Oh, like a migraine?' I asked.

'God knows. But he is so frustrating, in all the time for the same reason, and always being extra nice to Anne.'

'Clearly like, a what? Fifty-year-old virgin,' added Bhavin.

Zoe started humming the theme tune from *Beauty and the Beast* while they all laughed. I figured the man they were talking about had a hunched back, and as far as I could tell, was just sitting quietly in the waiting room clutching his head. And maybe he flirted with Anne inappropriately, but that had nothing to do with his spine.

'Oh come on, Hattie, we're only having a joke,' nudged Daphne, seeing that I wasn't joining in at all. I took another gulp of orange juice and scrabbled in my bag, pretending to look at my phone.

Our Son Mr Jonathan

ELLA: Hattie I misss youuuu at my partyyyy

Big time

Cn't wait to c u

And if you're at work in A&E we hang on lunch break

SAM: Yeah We Fltt wuth yo

ELLA: Sam drunk already lol

I couldn't feel my hands again. I refreshed my emails to see if the letting agent had replied.

> Rest-Assured Rentals
>
> Hi Hattie, that is a tight turnaround. I will send you details of what we have, but I would suggest you do look at that top floor flat? With such a time limit, it's a case of working with what is available.

I could have thrown my phone at the wall, but I'd already done that, hadn't I? I'd done it the other day in the locker room and I'd done it when I saw James, and we'd both agreed I needed to be fixed. This was meant to be it. *This* was meant to be the fix, to be not-disabled. And here I was, back again, phone with a cracked screen in hand, wanting to smash it up even more. It was like I was in a time loop of things falling apart.

'Hey, come on, let's do characters from cartoons. Which would we all be? Zoe's Ariel, cos of her hair . . .' Zoe swished her red hair in recognition. 'Hattie's – who's Hattie, guys?' I looked up from staring at my phone, eyes glazed over. 'Jessie! From *Toy Story*! The cowgirl.'

It was better than it could have been, but my body was out of my control again. I should have been laughing, but I wasn't.

'Cos you're very sweet, and you're tiiiiiny like a doll.'

All I could do was give a half smile, and start, again, to bite the inside of my cheek.

Neil looked at my arms intensely for a minute. 'Oh my God, you're actually so small.'

'Stronger than I look!' I said, in raspy breaths, trying to sound like I was having a good time. But I'd pushed myself too far; my body was heavy, flushed, prickling with tears.

When he put his arm on the table asking for an arm wrestle, I tried to just laugh it off again, but the laugh came out in uncomfortable, high-pitched bursts.

There was no use trying to get away from it. I put my arm on the table but didn't roll down my sleeve. I gripped his hand and he repeated, 'So small!'

'One!' the group shouted. 'Two!'

My knuckles hit the table with a bump, as heavy as when that llama piñata hit the ground. I recoiled my arm. The closer I got to them, the more they saw of me.

'You win,' I said, aware my face was growing red. My voice couldn't hide how upset I was, and there was an awkward pause around the table.

'Come on, you can't have been trying. Round two.'

'No, someone else.'

I was not going to let them see the tears forming behind my eyes, but the atmosphere in the room had already changed.

People were looking at me intensely, that same look that came from the woman in the service station toilets, that had followed me all my life, and was now staring back at me: 'What the hell were you thinking? Look at you, compared to them. This was never going to work for long.'

'I actually think I'm going to go home,' I said, and divided the table between people thinking I was just a sore loser and people telling me to stay. I ignored them all and walked outside to my car, setting off immediately, but after about five minutes I had to turn into a university campus, pulling up on the side of the road, because I couldn't concentrate properly.

I screamed the loudest and longest I have ever screamed in my life, hitting the steering wheel with my fists, kicking my legs, with my eyes squeezed shut. When I opened them again, two girls were standing in front of my headlights, peering into the windscreen, looking concerned. They could have been me and Ella on the way to a party, all those years ago. I beeped my horn and flicked my lights on and off, shouting at them in the strobe: 'GO!'

They gave each other a look and started to walk away quickly.

'Why can't I do it?' I screamed. 'Why can't I be who I want to be?'

I ignored the flashing coming from my phone, knowing it would be the group chat, knowing I was going to have to go and see a top floor flat because it was the only thing left to do. I was tired of the lying, but I knew that the other option – the option to go back – would kill me. I couldn't live the life of explaining, of cough sweets, of glances, of the looks I got when people reframed me. I had lived that life and reached an end point. The only thing to do was to start again.

I sat in the dark for a long time after my screaming had stopped. My mascara left trails down my cheeks; snot was pooling on my top lip. I tried to think rationally.

It was getting too dangerous. People were going to start asking questions. I wasn't going to be able to keep brushing things off and getting away with it. Sitting in that car, I felt utterly stupid for thinking I could make new friends and start again without them knowing I was disabled.

I got back to the hut and scrawled my new objectives at the bottom of The Plan.

> NEW PLAN
>
> NO NEW FRIENDS, JUST ACQUAINTANCES
>
> YOU HAVE TO KEEP YOURSELF TO YOURSELF
>
> OR ELSE THEY WILL FIND OUT YOU'RE DISABLED
>
> AND THEN YOU WON'T BE FREE

It was the only way. It was the closeness that was making it all too risky. I could still save things at work; I just needed to back away now. That would cut my risk in half. I would keep from getting into conversations, stop people noticing things. Keep things purely at a surface level. If I didn't get too close, didn't go for drinks, didn't make friends, then I could keep the plan going. I could still be not-disabled. I could still avoid having to go back to London. I could still be free.

THE NIGHT THAT CHANGED EVERYTHING

02:11

I say, 'Yes, of course I've tried calling.' Tone heavy and eyes squinted. 'I've left her so many messages but she won't pick up.'

I dial the number again. 'See – look – it's just ringing out?' I show the nurse the phone screen, the noise of the rings, going so slowly. I'm staring at the screen, saying, 'See? See?' as we look at the name in white writing, above the little icon of the phone – ELLA.

27

#CAR

Rest-Assured Rentals

Hi, understood. I would like to see the top floor flat asap please

The letting agent rang me and we arranged a viewing for later that day.

Our Son Mr Jonathan

SAM: Oliver is 52 Beaumont Road?

Sorry, yes yes that's his address

But actually, I might be in my new place by then!

Ella

Mate I'm so hungover

If I have to massage a gross body today I might be sick on it

Wait, you've found a new place??

Where? When? We need to know for when we come!

None of our clients were gross

Where's the new place?

I walked into work with a clear focus: I would brush off any mention of me leaving the drinks early, not get involved in too much chat and keep completely dedicated to the patients.

Melissa came in and I was polite but curt to her, trying to hide my legs under the desk so she couldn't see how high off the ground I was.

'Okay?' she asked.

'Yeah, thanks, you?'

I turned toward the computer screen and pretended to look through emails.

'Yeah, I'm okay lovey. Hey, was everything okay – what with Neil and the pub?'

'Ah yeah, sorry about that. I used to arm wrestle like that with my ex. Just sort of brought back memories.'

'Ah no,' she said, and I could see out the corner of my eye that she was staring at me, wondering why I wasn't turning round to look at her. 'What happened between you two?'

I stayed focused on my inbox. 'I don't want to talk about it.'

'Are you sure everything's okay?'

It would have been so nice to get to know her properly, but that door had closed. I hoped she would take the hint.

A patient came in and saved me from answering her.

Patient 1: Back injury – Gonna say fell off a ladder? Possible cracked vertebrae? Will monitor.

It turned out to be a busy morning, and a queue seemed to materialise from nowhere.

Patient 2: Chest pains – Recently out of heart surgery? – Panic attack? Yes! A panic attack. Into the waiting room he goes with his mate trying to calm him down.

Patient 3: Christ there's blood everywhere. My God. Jesus. He looks like he should have come by ambulance. I can literally hear it dripping onto the floor, he looks very— Fuck.

As predicted, all my training went out the window when a patient came in with a major life-threatening injury. I didn't clear the area, didn't make a note of the time, didn't press the emergency alarm.

I just stood up the minute he collapsed on the floor and shouted, 'Can I have some here in help please?', when I had meant to say, 'Can I have some help in here please?'

Luckily Melissa knew what to do. The guy was whisked away before I'd even had the chance to move, and I was promptly reminded that I needed to call urgently for a cleaner. The blood had pooled on the floor and smeared as the resus team had got him onto a stretcher and applied another dressing; the kitchen paper he'd been using had surrendered long ago.

After the cleaners had left, Aiden turned up and commented on the drama. He started off leaning a little on the desk but quickly retracted and stood upright.

'So, was that your first fainter?' he asked.

'Yeah – well – it might have been a bit more than a faint,' I said, peering at the spot.

Anne appeared from out back and started talking to Aiden, asking about his new flat. I wanted to join in, but this sort of chat had to be off limits now, I reminded myself. I sat back down and returned to my emails, thinking about the fact I had the flat-viewing later that afternoon.

'Now let me guess – it's a mess already, bachelor life-style and all?'

'Ha, yeah, something like that.'

I glanced up and noticed he put his hands in his pockets and started to rock gently on his heels.

'So Hattie—' he started.

Anne interrupted him before he could finish. 'Nice young lad like you, surprised you aren't moving in with a partner!'

'Ah haha, yeah, no, just by myself.'

It was impossible for me not to glance up at him. He took his hands out of his pockets, flexed his fingers and put them back again, digging even deeper.

'Well I'm serious, keep it looking spick and span or you won't get anyone coming back.' She winked. Aiden took the tiniest step back.

'I actually do a minimalist thing,' Aiden said, shrugging.

'Ooooh! Get you!' Anne dived into a story about how apparently Zoe had gotten into trouble for slacking on her cleaning shifts, when Aiden looked down the corridor and said he was needed. He didn't seem to be into gossip the way everyone else was, and maybe that was why he hadn't come to the pub. I was starting to trust that he really hadn't told anyone about me decking it in the cupboard – no one had brought it up at the pub – but I expected that people had been gossiping about me. I just hoped it didn't go any further than that.

I bumped into him again just as I was coming off my shift for my lunch break. Distancing myself from him felt almost impossible.

'You know that guy who collapsed?' he asked. I was excited at the look of a story behind his eyes. 'Well apparently, he drove himself here. Can you believe that? Fell from the loft hatch, lives alone, said he couldn't remember the number for an ambulance but he seemed to know how to work his car. I mean he only lives five minutes away and abandoned his car in a no-parking zone, but still, can you imagine it?'

I recalled how pale he looked and the sheer amount of blood.

'You sure there were no other patients brought in by ambulance after a hit and run?' I laughed, imagining him swerving down the road trying to keep the kitchen paper from falling to pieces with one hand, the other on the wheel while trying to blink the blood out of his eyes so he could stay on the right side of the road.

We both had the same idea at the same time. Five minutes later, we were out in the car park looking for his car, as I convinced myself this type of activity was just – just – on the right side of the line between acquaintance-colleague and something more. But, to be honest, I was genuinely desperate to see the relic of a bleeding man who thought it easier to forgo the ambulance and drive himself, rather than pick up the phone and try to convince someone that he needed to be seen.

As legend had foretold, the car was abandoned on a pavement near the main entrance of the hospital. He had managed to be pretty skilful to not cause complete mayhem, getting himself so far on the pavement that he wasn't blocking any of the major exits or entrances. A sobering stain of blood marked the tarmac near the driver's side door, and looking into the car, we could see similar marks on the steering wheel and seat.

Aiden reached over in the direction of the car, and I found myself staring again at his forearm, imagining it wrapped around me, with all that rain and thunder – before I realised he had opened the door and was standing with his eyebrows raised, waiting for me to react.

'Christ – must be –' I peered into the car, seats soaked in a dark crimson, and saw the remote key sitting in the cup holder by the handbrake. 'Yeah, well you wouldn't think of grabbing your keys and locking it, would you?'

'In you get then,' said Aiden, beaming.

I laughed but he kept the door open.

'I'm not getting in there.' I took a step back.

'Suit yourself. I'm going to move it before it gets clamped.' He was in the driver's seat before I could say another word.

'Wait –' I said, holding the door open. 'Can't we just explain to the – the – parking people whoever they are – and then they can move it?'

'Parking are bastards, Hattie.'

He pressed the button to start the engine.

'Well okay, hold on then.'

'Buckle up,' he smiled.

'Thought we were just parking?' My hands were clasped on my lap, I was leaning forward slightly and my feet were to the edge of the footwell.

Aiden rolled his eyes and put the automatic car into drive,

moving it off the pavement and heading towards the main car park. Not ten seconds later, an alarm started.

'Well, that's a very annoying noise,' I said.

'Yeah, some annoying person didn't put their seatbelt on.' He grinned.

The little belt symbol was flashing on the dashboard.

'It's not even working,' I said, tugging at the black clip.

We joined a queue and Aiden looked over to me.

'Do you want me to give you a hand?'

I nodded, admitting defeat.

He seemed to have an intuitive sense of what I needed. Unlike my friends on the group chat, if he had asked to come and stay, and I had said I was tired and it wasn't a great time, he'd had left it. He wouldn't send me messages with question marks and chase me for not responding to him sending a card. He'd just be happy to see me whenever I wanted, whenever was right. Despite the very real, ever-present fear of him finding out and telling everybody I was disabled, I had these moments where all of that cleared and I felt lighter being with him than I'd felt around anyone in such a long time.

As he reached across me, I turned my head to the side and held my breath. I tensed my body, gritted my teeth, pressed my lips together, tried to think of the man in A&E, pictured his dry mouth, his hands clinging onto a soaking sick bowl. But it was no good, as Aiden struggled with the seatbelt too, and his neck was so close to me, I couldn't help but breathe in. He smelled earthy, almost woody, like birch broken open and oozing with sap. I edged closer as I felt his hand brush past my face. Pulling the belt slowly past me, he took a sharp intake of breath.

'You okay?' I asked, my body tense again.

'Yeah, yeah.' He breathed out a sigh as the belt came across me. 'Got this new tattoo,' he said, gesturing to his side. 'I just keep forgetting it's not healed yet.'

As he pulled away, I closed my eyes for a few seconds, keen to remember how it felt to be so close to another person. Aiden was back in his seat, and I ran my hand over the black strap, telling him 'cheers' and looking intently out of the window for an empty space.

'Aiden,' I said, tentatively. 'I'm really glad you work at the hospital. I mean, I'm really glad we both do.' I let out a small laugh. 'I mean, I'm glad we met.'

'Me too,' he said, looking at me straight in the eyes, and I looked back into the radiant green of his. All I wanted to do was get closer and breathe him in again. When he pulled up the handbrake, I found myself looking at his tattooed forearm and thinking it looked so good that I literally wanted to lick it.

He parked the car and picked up the keys, spinning them around his fingers, saying he'd get them to the guy. Once we were both out of the car, we stood next to each other at the boot and I tried to act normal, wondering if my cheeks had gone all red.

'Did you see where they took him?' I asked.

'Resus for a bit to sort out his stats but I'm not sure after that. I'll ask around, see if anybody took him. Reckon he'll need a blood transfusion.'

'Just can't believe he drove here,' I garbled, before saying I better be getting off – I was owed an hour's time off in lieu that I wanted to take on top of my lunch, and needed to go to meet the estate agent.

'Sure, sure. I'm over time for this "quick break" and all. Catch you later, yeah?'

He tapped the boot of the car gently with his hand and I headed off in the direction of my car, only to hear him call my name again.

'Sorry – keep meaning to ask – do you need a hand with that office chair?'

I froze. 'What? Oh, no, I mean, it's fine.'

'Didn't want to make a big thing of it but I can sort it for you if you need a hand?'

'It's just . . .' my voice shrivelled into a croak and a familiar pain started to grow.

'Hey, it's okay – I got ya.' He put out his hand for a fist bump and I reciprocated, tentatively, as he ran off in the direction of the hospital.

There was a relief in not having to explain, and a feeling of wanting to be closer to him. But there was a sharp warning coming from deep down, knowing that he had noticed the chair, that I still wasn't strong enough, that I was treading an uneasy line and not being strict enough with myself in the New Version of The Plan. Everyone else I was comfortable with backing away from, but Aiden, the one who never asked for an explanation? Aiden, with his kind eyes and gentle gestures? Aiden, who had the world's best, most beautiful forearms? I knew that I had to, but I just couldn't bring myself to cut him off entirely.

As I met the estate agent outside of the building, I felt drained at the prospect of having to climb all the way up to the top floor. I was so much slower than him and he waited awkwardly by the front door. It was four flights. I was exhausted. But if this was the only one I could move into before the visit from the group, it was my only option. It was small and hot, without a separate shower. I just couldn't say the words. I couldn't tell him I liked it, even though it's what I needed to do.

'I was going to mention,' said the estate agent, as I stared gloomily at the damp-stained bedroom walls, 'there is another one that's just come up on the opposite street. It's ground floor, but did you want to take a look?'

I could have kissed him. 'That would be very nice,' I said, 'because this is great, but I see the damp, and unfortunately I don't own a dehumidifier.'

When we arrived at the flat that was actually on the ground floor, with a door that seemed easy to manage, I let out a grin. It was small, with an unfortunate grey carpet that really dominated the lounge area, but it was light, with sunshine beaming into the kitchen, and the bedroom felt warm, with a built-in wardrobe and room enough for a double bed. Yes, Hattie, in the final hour, you're on the brink of working this out. If I moved in here, the group could visit, and I could keep the lie going. And they would leave, and I would, just about, have my new life intact.

28

#CLIMB

My life in London was filled with stairs.

Ella and I ended up living in separate student houses throughout uni but had always planned to try and find a two-bed place as soon as we graduated. Ella had been working at the salon while studying and basically got me the reception job by ensuring I knew every single thing about the place, so that when the job came up and they interviewed me, it was like I already worked there. The rush to find a flat was stressful, and our budget was pretty tight. The morning we were meant to view a two-bed in Walthamstow, I'd gone to bed with the slightest sore throat and woken up with a raging fever.

Ella

Love I'm so ill

What? Noooo

Mega fever, you'll have to go on your own, sooo sorry

It's not till 4 p.m.? You might rally

Have you got any Lucozade?

I'll keep you in the loop x

Ella knew I normally needed to down a lot of Lucozade after an illness to try and get my strength back, but I was not 'after' the illness, I was very much in it, so surprise surprise, I did not rally. What I did do was pass out on the loo because the fever had sapped my energy so much I literally didn't have the strength to stay upright for more than about a minute. I was used to this. The most mundane of bugs can wipe me out for days, with a temperature sending my body over the edge as I struggle to muster the energy to fulfil my most basic needs. My balance is off more than ever and I feel too dizzy to even make it to the tap to get myself some water, so I get dehydrated and even more dizzy. It's a cycle often only broken by someone helping me out.

On the day of the Walthamstow viewing, two of my housemates had already left for home and the only one left, Sam, wasn't going to be in until lunchtime. I could have cried when he finally got back and brought me a glass of water.

Ella

No rally. Sorry mate. Let me know how it goes

What shall we do if I like it?

I hear places are being snapped up

You can go for it. Can transfer deposit, just message/call

Ok great xx

At about half four, I got a phone call from Ella. It woke me up mid-dream about a leisure centre that released a crocodile into the pool ten minutes before closing. The vending machines in the lobby had snacks for the crocodile; I had just pressed the button for a packet of raw bacon when an alarm sounded, which turned out to be my ringtone.

'Hey, how did it go?'

'Hi, so I'm here now. The one they just showed me actually went this afternoon, but there's another one in the same building that I can get now if I pay the holding fee?'

'Have you seen it?'

'No, it's the same layout though. On the first floor, same price.'

'Ah okay, is there a lift?' I could manage one flight of stairs, as long as there was a handrail. I was just a lot slower than most people and had to be careful not to fall, especially when carrying bags of shopping.

'No lift, but the stairs are pretty good, banister and everything.'

I could make it work.

'Yeah, okay cool. That's okay. Yeah, if you think we should go for it I trust you.'

'Yeah, I really think so. It's really nice and places are going so fast.'

'Yeah, I know. Okay, I'll send you the money now.'

'Amazing – thank you!'

I ended the call and sent her the money from my phone, drifting back to the swimming pool, where a lifeguard was asking why I was throwing a ham sandwich into the water. I tried to point out the crocodile but it was nowhere to be seen.

'Hattie, I promise you she said first floor, but this will be okay, okay?'

We were standing in the empty Walthamstow flat having just got the keys. Moving men were on their way with all our stuff.

'Can you call them? Can you call them and say?' I asked.

'I don't know what that will do. Everything's signed and we've got the keys and I know they've fucked up and that's really shit of them but we're in now,' Ella said.

'I would never have agreed to it if I'd known it was second floor.'

'I know, but it is just one more flight of stairs, okay? I know it's really not ideal but you can do the stairs, you know? Do you want to call them? Would that make you feel better?'

'Ella, genuinely, I . . .' I couldn't order the words properly in my head, 'need a minute.'

I went into my room and grabbed onto the windowsill to help me onto the floor. I lay down and stared at the ceiling, cough sweet in my mouth. I didn't want to let this go. I don't think she lied about it being on the first floor. I think the agent got it wrong and never corrected herself. But clearly, Ella and the agent thought there wasn't much difference in one flight of stairs. Neither of them seemed to think it was a big deal. How could she know me so well and not get that another flight of stairs makes a big difference? That having to carry shopping up there, and go up and down for work every day was going to be exhausting? That the chances of me falling were so much higher? That one flight of stairs would have been a difficult compromise as it was, but two? No way. Why did she keep doing these things?

'Ella,' I told myself I would begin. 'Please can you call the letting agent and ask them why they told you it was first floor? I understand it very likely won't change where we are physically, but it will definitely change where we, or at least I am emotionally about this. They shouldn't be allowed to do this, and I want answers. I don't know how I feel about living here at the moment. This is the first step in trying to work out what we do now.'

I got myself up from the floor and walked down the hall toward the living room. I replayed the sentences over and over in my head. They shouldn't be allowed to do this. I want answers. I found her looking at the fridge.

'Ella, please can—' The doorbell buzzed.

'That'll be our stuff!' she said, running toward the front door. And as each piece of furniture was carried into the flat, each box of our things, the microwave, the house plant, the washing machine tablets, our duvets and our hangers, the more ridiculous it seemed to try and argue that we should never have been here in the first place.

'Don't you love it, eh?' asked Ella, after all our things were in the flat and she was gladly unpacking boxes.

'I just don't know if I'm going to manage,' I said, hesitating over the open box.

Ella was busy plugging in the microwave. 'Can't you just give it a try?'

I turned and walked slowly back to my room to get another cough sweet and rammed it in my mouth too quickly. I nearly swallowed it whole. As I choked it out, Ella came to my door, assuming the tears streaming from my eyes were from the coughing.

'Oh my God, don't choke to death on day one of moving in!' she said gently, her hand on my back.

As the sweet stuck to the lino of my bedroom floor, two flights of stairs above the ground, I had never felt more trapped. And when you are trapped, you need to find a way to free yourself.

If only I had got out of there then, maybe I wouldn't have found myself alone in a hospital one New Year's Eve, desperately trying to get hold of Ella, getting angrier every time she didn't answer, feeling like I wanted to scream down the line – 'But, Ella! This – all of this – is your fault!'

29

#SICK

The estate agent said he was going to email me at the end of the day with all the forms to fill out for the ground-floor flat, and I'd be able to move in in a few days. My savings would see me through the deposit and my job would mean I passed the reference checks. When I got back to my desk, the chair was somehow at exactly the right height, and I tentatively sat down, paranoid someone was going to mention that Aiden had done it for me. But that comment never came, and I settled into work, keeping my head down.

'God, you are quiet today,' said Anne, after I'd not joined in while she was going on about Daphne's bad lipstick choices. Why was everyone here so bitchy? So often places where you think literally anyone is welcome, you find, if you just scratch the surface a little, that that isn't the case at all.

'I'm just really busy,' I replied, a little too sternly. I'd need to get the tone of my voice right. Detached but not angry. This was how I was going to play it now.

'Suit yourself,' she said, with a sharp tone, as another patient came to the desk.

'I think I'm going to die,' said the woman suddenly before me, gripping the desk. 'Please please help, I'm really— I think I'm going.'

The words rattled inside me, the words Mum told me Dad had said, as a bed crowded with giraffes and a doctor saying 'sepsis' floated into my head.

'Do you know of any infections you might have?' That wasn't the script. But I knew what I was doing.

'I had a bladder infection but I thought it had cleared up – I don't know.'

I took scant details of her name and told her to sit down, that I would make sure she was seen ASAP.

I copied down all the symptoms of sepsis that I knew: *URGENT: Ongoing bladder infection, sense she will die, high fever, extreme pain, shortness of breath and discolouration to the skin. Sepsis?*

I wasn't strictly meant to write my own diagnosis, but I decided the question mark and the severity of the illness made it excusable. Within a few minutes the triage nurse came through the doors and ushered her in. Thank God I'd been on shift, and I knew what to look out for.

When Jackie called me into her office an hour later, I thought she might praise me for being on time – I'd been leaving home extra early, even though it meant I lost out on sleep.

'So, tell me again where you trained?'

She was leaning back on her office chair as I sat awkwardly on the blue plastic one in front of her desk.

'Well, I had training at my last job, in the health clinic.'

This was not the way I had expected the conversation to start.

'Oh yes, and you did medical treatments there, did you?'

Shit. Had they called Gareth? Did they ask for more details? Did he tell them it wasn't a health clinic?

'We were focused on health and wellbeing, yes, offering a range of treatments—'

'Hattie.' Her voice was sharp.

I stared at her, bolt upright, not saying a word.

'Do you realise how dangerous it is, what you did?'

I started a very wobbly 'wha—' but she carried on talking.

'Sepsis, Hattie? Sepsis? Seen that a lot during your training as a medical professional, have you? Or no – that's right, you are a receptionist. You record.'

I started to relax. Thank the Lord they hadn't talked to Gareth. I could understand why she was angry, but I could explain.

'But she did have sepsis. She had all the signs. I know because my dad had it and so I wanted the triage team to see how urgent it was. I did put a question mark after it.'

'Oh well, that makes it all okay then, does it?' Her eyebrows were raised, and her hands moved out toward me, before sinking down hard on her desk.

I thought she was being a bit over the top. I'd basically just saved a woman's life.

'Well no, but I thought, you know how quickly you can die from sepsis?'

'I understand it's pretty fast. But that's actually by-the-by because she didn't have sepsis at all. She was having a panic attack. No bladder infection either, that was probably the anxiety too. And, as she said to the nurse, she didn't tell you that she had a fever, she didn't have pale skin, and she wasn't in extreme pain. And you know what, Hattie, I have absolutely no reason to disbelieve her, considering how shocked she looked when the nurse started talking to her about "going septic", which, unsurprisingly, did not make the panic attack any better.'

I was stunned. She'd said the same words my dad had said, she had the same look in her eyes as him in the picture, and the bladder infection – it's a classic; they always get dismissed. I looked down at my feet and realised I had blood on the base of my shoe from where I'd stood in the stain by the door of the car. Jackie hadn't finished.

'So, not only did you decide you suddenly had a medical degree and fabricated notes on a patient record, which then went on to cause distress to the patient, but by doing that, it meant that someone with a severely fractured arm had to wait even longer to be seen. The triage system only works when symptoms are reported accurately. Do you understand that?' The eyebrows were up again. Hands now knitted tightly together in front of her, her knuckles white.

I nodded. I could feel my lip going, so I bit into it.

'I don't understand what you were thinking. Dare I mention again that you're still on probation? And I'm hearing this and that about how you're being a bit sensitive to the office banter, you still can't even be bothered to adjust your own chair when you get in, you're still dawdling up the stairs on the way back from your lunch break, and Bhavin said you were slow on the porter shift. I'm getting the feeling you're not particularly into this role. What am I meant to think? What am I meant to do?' She was leaning back now; her hands had moved from the desk to her lap. It was like she had given up trying to meet me halfway, to reach me and understand.

I tried to respond but a hoarse cough spluttered out, my throat groaned and burned like never before.

'Have some water,' she said, in response. Her tone was a bit softer, but still had an edge to it. She handed me a plastic cup from the water cooler behind her.

I took in too much, trying to gulp down the razor blades, started to choke on it, retching a deep cough. Then as I gasped for air, I turned my body away from Jackie, who was telling me to breathe. I tried to get the air in, but I was still choking; my throat was convulsing now. I brought the cup of water up to my lips as I felt a surge from my stomach, but it was too late, and before I knew it, it was coming up and out on to the floor. The sick spread slowly and I couldn't help but spit remnants into the pool as strings of saliva hung from my mouth.

I tried to dry my streaming eyes and nose with my sleeve and tried to speed up time so I wasn't in the office anymore, so it was over, it was done, it was something that happened ages ago, but the smell kept me in that room as Jackie reached for a tissue to cover it, like a white sheet over a body.

'I'm so sorry,' I spluttered out.

'Did you feel okay this morning? Maybe you've got a bug. Bless you, I didn't think—'

'I'm so sorry, I was trying my best. I just—' Tears came as my face crumbled and juddered. I kept trying to wipe them away on the same damp and sticky sleeve I'd wiped the sick from my chin with.

'Look, I think the best thing – I think you should go home. I think you've probably caught something and you didn't quite realise you were so under the weather. Then when you're feeling better, we'll pick this up again and work out the best way forward.'

She handed me another wad of tissues that I planted my face in, trying to catch a proper breath and calm myself down.

'I really need this job,' I whispered.

'I really want to talk about this when you're feeling better.'

I nodded and apologised again, offering to call the cleaners for her.

'You need to go home, Hattie.'

I dragged the tissues harshly over my face as though scouring it would improve the redness and stood up to leave. Anne's shocked face greeted me as I walked past, telling her I was going home now, I wasn't well, and she turned around, as I did, to see Jackie standing outside her office with the door closed, nodding firmly. I apologised again, and the words made everything fall apart.

As I walked down the corridor gripping the tissues, I knew I'd see Aiden, and the minute I did he homed in on me like some sort of benevolent eagle.

'Hattie – mate – are you . . . ?' There wasn't any point him finishing the sentence. It was very clear I was absolutely not okay. He moved quickly toward the staff room door and punched in the code. 'I got this. Don't worry.'

I glanced up at him through the tears and smiled weakly before heading downstairs. He started to follow.

'Mate, what do you need? A chat? A tea? A chat and a tea?'

'I need to go home,' I said, through rasping sobs that I couldn't quite stop.

'Okay, okay, but do you need a lift?'

'No, no, really, I'm fine.'

He stood on the bottom stair and watched as I went over to my locker.

'Can you please text me when you get home?' He put his hand on the banister as he asked, face full of concern.

I nodded, desperate, in a way, to walk up to him and bury my head in his chest, let him hold me, let him tell me it would be all right, but I couldn't. I couldn't let him in. Things were already going so, so wrong. I couldn't risk it. I would hold onto this new life with my teeth if I had to.

'I will, I will,' I said, zipping up my bag and walking past him on the stairs.

When I got into the car, I took two cough sweets to take away the sour taste, and I picked up the scissors and chair leg, cutting into it, hard. I remembered what Aiden had told me about the psychological trick you can use when something bad has happened: pretending you're watching something back, as if on TV. I tried, but it wasn't working: the film in my head wasn't making me feel calm. Rather, I was trapped in the loop, the moment replaying: I was looking up from being sick and catching Jackie's astonished, disgusted eye.

30

#WILD

Ella

Honestly people are so grim

I was nearly sick on about half the clients today

Naturally, I wasn't in the mood to reply.

I got home, ripped off my sick-stained shirt and blood-stained shoes and stood in the shower, crying. The shepherd's hut had no washing machine so I had been very careful with what clothes I'd worn. But now I'd need to make a special trip to the launderette asap as I only had three work shirts and one had already been worn too long. Then I sat on my bed and started to write a message to Aiden. He was the only person in the world that I wanted to talk to.

Aiden

Hey Aiden, soooo I just had the worst day at work I've ever had, as you could probably tell. Long story

short I ended up throwing up all over Jackie's office.
She thought I had a bug but actually –

I deleted it.

Hey it's Hattie. Sorry about before. All a bit dramatic.

The reply was almost instant.

Aiden

Hey, please don't say sorry, are you okay?

Oh P.S. The head injury fainting guy is stable! Made it through so far!! What a legend!

Thanks. I'm not really okay but I will be.

Taking tomorrow and weekend off.

Ah okay. Did you want a quick phone call? Can talk things through or talk shit as a distraction. I hope you're okay! X

My skin fizzed at the kiss. I had spent most of my time in London dating, but there was never anything serious. It was too easy to just keep things casual, stick to one-night stands, flings and easy sex. I learnt early on that my matches plummeted if I put 'disabled' on my dating app profile, so I kept things light and superficial so I didn't have to go there with guys. But here he was, being totally caring and decent and also still very sexy, and I was alone, and The Plan was disintegrating right in front of my eyes. I thought about calling him and I looked up at The Plan, still up on the wall by the kitchen table.

YOU HAVE TO KEEP YOURSELF TO YOURSELF

I picked up the sharpie.

(UNLESS you just, really, really, need him)

He answered on the second ring, and I opened by asking for more news about head injury man.

'I know, amazing, isn't it? Bhavin said he's on the ward and basically thriving,' Aiden said.

'Why on earth are you not with Bhavin now having champagne in celebration, mate? We've basically witnessed a miracle. Potentially the second coming.'

'Ah haha, yeah I should be,' he trailed off quietly and I felt like I'd said the wrong thing. There was a pause before he spoke again. 'I like Bhavin and all – good bloke, I just, I don't go for the drinks and the pubs and all that, so . . .'

'Yeah, about that – did you hear anything about me at the pub? About how I left early?'

He paused. 'Bhavin and Neil told me. To be honest, I'd have done the same as you. Who arm wrestles past seven years old?'

I laughed.

'I'm not a massive pub person anyway . . .' he sighed.

'Where's your haunt then? On a day off?' I asked.

'There's – there's some nice woodland round here . . .' he still sounded quiet, as though he was treading carefully.

'Nice one. There's some nice woods around me, too.'

'Have you been to Pengelli Forest? It's pretty banging. Never seen so much goat willow.'

My go-to was to take the piss out of such a sentence, but from his tone I knew this was the wrong thing to do. I liked the sound of his voice on the end of the phone, and I could see him there, in the forest, his forearms covered in the nature he was breathing in, as though the rain and thunder and flowers weren't inked on at all but grown on him from all his time spent out in the green.

'Tell me about it,' I said, for once without the sarcastic slant that usually goes with the phrase.

'Ah haha.' He laughed nervously. 'In the sigh of wild things, you know? If I must rest, let it be by the Hypericum . . .'

He'd lost me now, and I remained silent. Hypericum? Christ alive.

'Sorry.' Another nervous laugh. 'It's just a poem I like about nature. How going there can really chill you out, basically. But yeah, Pengelli –' he started talking quickly, clearly worried about the fact he'd just quoted a poem at me and it was very much not the eighteenth century. 'It smells absolutely banging, you know, I mean all forests do but that one in particular. There's another not far from there too actually, it's got this badger sett, I've seen their little track marks in the mud.'

'Ah, amazing. Badgers are bloody huge actually, aren't they?'

'Never seen one, but yeah, that's what it says in all the nature books. Bloody huge actually.'

I was pleased he'd taken the piss out of me, giving me permission to gently do the same to him. But as he carried on talking, I didn't feel like I was at some botanical lecture; he talked so much about the smell of things, the smoothness of the bark on wych elm – and I imagined his fingers gliding over it – the spore of adder's-tongue on the back of his hand, and how he'd heard a barn owl, just once, when he'd stayed too late and the dark was creeping in on his skin. It was so clear he lived and breathed this stuff, and it was completely obvious to me that the dark lighting and bitter tastes that come in pubs would simply be so boring to someone who lived so much in his senses.

'We'll have to go sometime,' I said.

'Yeah, yeah of course, but hey – I've just been harping on about the forest, how are you, really? It seemed like a very bad day.'

'Yeah, it was,' I said gently. 'I'm—' My throat burned again. 'Well, I'm . . .'

It was the only way. I couldn't carry on doing this by myself. He felt different. He felt like he could be the one person that could help. He'd only ever been concerned with whether I was all right or not, rather than being obsessed with why I was doing things differently, wanting to know all the details, asking all the questions. The Plan was breaking down badly, and I couldn't even start to work out how to put it back together by myself. I needed someone I could trust, someone on my side. Someone who could wrap their arms around me and hold me steady. It was time.

'. . . I'm disabled but I haven't told anyone. Not in my interview, not when I got the job, not anyone. And I really need to be able to go to work without people knowing. I can't explain it all but I need to have a place where I'm not disabled. And I had planned not to tell anyone, but I'm telling you because I trust you. But you're the only person I can tell, you have to promise not to tell anyone. It affects my muscles and so I'm weaker and I can't run and I get tired and my balance is off and that's why I'm slow on the stairs and when I fell over, well, you know ...'

'Yeah, of course. I get it. I'm glad you felt like you could tell me.' The acceptance of it, rather than silence, felt like sunlight had just burst through a cloud. I rubbed my throat with my hand. 'I'm not going to tell anyone,' he continued. 'It's all okay. But you could just tell Jackie and then – do you think she knows already, actually?'

'I hope not. I don't think so. She mentioned the chair and how I'm late and that stressed me out, but then – basically I thought someone had sepsis but they were just having a panic attack but I wrote sepsis on her notes because my dad had sepsis and—' I coughed again. 'I messed up because I shouldn't have put that and it's a really serious breach of patient safety, you know?'

'Shit, yeah, yeah I get it.' He sounded serious, but still so kind, his voice steadying me as I spoke.

'And she was quizzing me and it all got so much, I threw up in her office.'

'Oh, Christ.'

'But I just can't believe I got the sepsis thing wrong, I'm normally so on it, you know, when I play the game, I get them right so many times! I even correctly guessed someone tripped over a hoover the other day.'

'Wow, that is good. I'm still jealous that you get to know if you're right or not.'

'And so you try and go on a receptionist's computer, yeah?' I teased.

'Well, look, I mean, I wasn't actually – I did not mean to hack your computer, your honour.' I could tell from his voice he was smiling.

'You are forgiven,' I said.

There was a pause. I continued.

'I mean you fixed my chair. Great move. Honestly, though, you're pretty cool, you know that?'

'You're pretty cool, too,' he said.

I was beaming from ear to ear. I didn't want to completely lose my shit and blurt out that I wanted to hold him, sit on him, and then hold him again. I saw us, together, working it all out. We'd sort out the situation with Jackie; I'd get the flat, maybe I'd tell my London friends Oliver and I broke up, and introduce Aiden. Then they would leave, and my new brilliant life would carry on, with brilliant him by my side.

'Do you think we should, you know, go to the woods soon?' I asked.

'Absolutely, I'd love that.'

I was getting all the right vibes, and thought again of his beautiful forearms, with his black, illustrative tattoos, the bolt of lightning, the clouds, rain pouring down his arms . . .

'You know, on a . . . I mean . . . on a date?'

There was silence on the end of the line.

'So – er,' Aiden stuttered.

Shit. What? My heart went cold, and started to beat, fast.

'I mean, I didn't mean to – I just – look, you're pretty sexy, you know?' I tried to sound carefree.

'Yeah, er – shit. I think I've maybe confused – I should have been clearer. I don't see you in a dating sense,' he said.

I tried to sound like it was fine. 'Of course, mates is cool.'

'I just don't think about you like that—'

'No, that's fine.'

'I just don't—'

'Think about me like that. You said.'

'I mean I really like you, but I mean—'

'Yeah. Totally. Step too far. It's okay. I get it.' It was like all the blood had drained from me and yet my heart was still beating, pumping against nothing, squeezing the emptiness through my veins.

Of course he wasn't different. Okay, maybe he got a kick out of helping people. Maybe he figured I was disabled early on, maybe he didn't know for sure and decided it wasn't his place until I told him. But at the end of the day? He couldn't fathom me romantically. Didn't even cross his mind. Inconceivable to him that I would even think I had a chance. A body like mine? Nah. Not with something wrong with it.

31

#SNIP

Ella

[Missed Voice Call from Ella]

[Missed Voice Call from Ella]

Jackie

So sorry but really ill. Sickness and fever.

Okay Hattie take the weekend

Then we'll pick up where we left off

I got the email from the estate agent and filled out the rental form as best I could. I didn't even know if I still had my job, or how I was going to move in this state, but I had to try. I got up and went to the kitchen, put my hand into the bread bag and pulled out a square spotted with green. There were four slices left, each with their own patterns of mould. I sliced off the worst of it and put it in the toaster. I ate it plain and felt it scrape down my throat, making the burning worse.

I knew what I needed. Leaving the door of the hut swinging open, I went out to the car and started to unpack all the plastic boxes I had stuffed into the back all those weeks ago, opening the top and throwing things onto the grass, box by box, unable to concentrate on anything else. The packet was right at the bottom, wedged between a pair of trainers and a stack of photo albums. It took me a few attempts to grab hold of them properly, my fingers slipping with sweat, my cheeks flushed and body aching. When I finally got them, held tightly in my hand, I looked around to see the contents of my car all over the grass, as if I was transported back to the day I was leaving it all behind. I was meant to be starting afresh, and yet here I was, back at the beginning. Same old Hattie, needing her cough sweets just to get through the day. I ripped at the packet with my teeth.

I didn't repack anything. It all got thrown into the car. A box wouldn't fit after I'd emptied its contents in loosely, so I just left it outside. I went to slam the car door but it wouldn't close, so I started chucking stuff further back, folders and pans hitting the window on the other side, until it all started to collapse and spill out again, a blanket hitting the dirt, a photo coming loose from the album and lingering on the threshold. Of course it was That Photo. Of all the ones, it had to be *that* one. The blanket stayed on the grass. The door was shut. I made it back to the hut clutching the cough sweets and the last picture of my dad ever taken, lying in the hospital bed.

*

I don't really remember getting into bed, but I must have. When I woke up again it was dark outside, and I lay in bed for hours, staring at the ceiling. I reached for the scissors and the wood, carved into it and held it tightly until I drifted off to sleep again. The sun had made the hut sleepy and warm. In my dreams I was forever in Jackie's office, throwing up on Aiden, who laid curled up on the floor, and then on long strings of green willow, bark, then the chair leg, the sponge, a cough sweet, Ella. They clung together on the floor, entangled in a watery mess, writhing around as Jackie looked on in horror, and asked me where all of it had come from.

I was losing track of time. I'd kept the blinds closed and switched my phone off. My body tried calling for hunger but when no food came it resorted to short bursts of sleep again. I tried to tide it over with cough sweets, sucking on one whenever I was awake. I was desperate to open the doors and let some fresh air in, but another part of me knew the hotter it became the more drowsy I'd be, and all I wanted to do was sleep. When eventually the headache and nausea were too powerful to shut off with sleep, I got up and sipped at water, took small bites of the stale bread with peanut butter covering the decay. I could smell my own sweat but I didn't shower, didn't change out of my pyjamas or brush my teeth. After my toast and water, I got back into bed and closed my eyes, sometimes soothing myself by running my hand over the dents in the wood from the chair leg, sometimes staring at the photo of my dad until it became blurry.

Some hours later, I had to get outside. I threw on my shoes and headed toward the footpath, still in my pyjamas, covering them with my coat. I felt delirious, even in the fresh air, and headed toward the village. I walked down the country road, trying to avoid the potholes, and nearly fell over as a car went past and beeped at me when I couldn't get on to the grassy bank quickly enough to get off the road. I steadied myself and made sure the car had long gone before I got back on the road, not wanting to catch the driver's eye. As I made it to the post box, red paint peeling, I was feeling lightheaded, and the world was slightly bending at the edges, as if I was in a dream. The corner shop, with its newly painted sign in a bright yellow and neon stars in the window advertising price drops in black sharpie, seemed to glow as I walked toward it.

'Lost your voice?' the cashier was beeping the ten packets of cough sweets through slowly: the only thing I was buying. I'd been in a few times now, and felt it wouldn't be long before the guy, sixty-ish with chapped lips, kind eyes, and a passion for bright green polo shirts, would start talking to me.

I laughed awkwardly and whispered an 'almost'.

'Well, when you're feeling better, what it is, is, me and the Mrs do a quiz night down the Farmer's Arms if you fancied coming, get to know a few people like?'

'Work,' I said with another whisper and a shrug. I held my card out waiting for the pin machine to activate.

'Ah, too bad. Where you working then? You waitressing? We go on late if you wanted to drop in after your shift.'

The pin machine beeped and I reached out for the bag.

'I don't think so,' I said.

The man looked confused and then nodded and gave me a half-hearted wave out of habit. I ate three sweets on the way home, cramming them in my mouth all at once.

THE NIGHT THAT CHANGED EVERYTHING

02:24

'You just need a sleep,' the nurse said, as she opened the door and sent me on my way.

My phone buzzed, and I looked down, expectant.

Battery level critical. Your phone will switch off in 30 . . . 29 . . . 28 . . . 27 . . .

This wasn't the New Year countdown I was expecting.

Ella, please. You have twenty-five seconds now. Just one text. Send me one text and we'll be okay. I won't be cross when I get home. I won't tell you how bad it's all been. I won't post-mortem. I won't go there. Please?

32

#WITCH

I woke up to my own sweat-stained smell that had permeated the entire hut and switched my phone on to try and work out the time. It was 11 p.m. The messages came in like flies to a day-old corpse.

Jackie

Please come straight to my office when you come in

Ella

[Missed Voice Call from Ella]

[Missed Voice Call from Ella]

You haven't said what your new address is –
are you definitely going to be moved in by the
time we come?

Are you sure you're okay?

Call me back x

I'll confirm the address in a few days.

Mum

Hiya love just checking in! Been on so many beach walks, it's bliss. Hope all going okay? Call me when you can xx

Aiden

Can we talk?

Our Son Mr Jonathan

GEORGIA: Hahahahaha

SAM: AHHHHAHAHAHA

PETE: HHHAAAAAA

BEA: HAHAHAHAHAHAHAHAHAHAHA

I could almost hear the hahahahas as I scrolled through the chat, and then swiped it away. I didn't get the joke. I turned to look at the photo of my dad again and could have sworn his left eye moved, like a wink.

I dragged myself into the shower. I could barely look at my body, the body that Aiden rejected. Washing didn't feel like a luxurious act of self-care, a moment of grounding as I took in the smell of the sandalwood-infused soap. It felt like a necessary act to remove the parts of me that were sweat-stained and grimy. That was it. A removal of what could still be removed, fixing what could still be fixed.

I had texted Jackie three words: 'Still not well' and she was yet to reply. Under the stream of water I tried to tell myself that it was going to be okay, but the image of my sick on Jackie's floor kept re-appearing with the same heavy feeling of dread. When I tried to tell myself it was just being ill at work, the knowledge that it wasn't just that, that it was me, being ill all the time, hit me. I told myself I needed to stay away from Aiden – now that he knew, I needed to make sure he never mentioned it, and maybe it was best to give up the job and try to start again but I didn't know where or how or what money I would live on. I turned off the water and tried to take a deep breath but was only met with tightness in my chest. I kept trying to push it away until I started to feel a little dizzy.

As I got out of the shower, I decided I didn't want to go back to bed, not with my dad seeming to move in the photograph and the hahahahahas on the group chat. I would wait until they all went to sleep again.

I opened the doors of the hut. My trainers were difficult to slip on but I managed and walked out into the field. The light from the hut was enough for me to make out some of the woodland in the distance, and the cold air was so inviting. The crescent moon looked magical as its light spilled out onto the few scattered clouds around it; the stars were bright and twinkling against the abyss of the sky. I'd never been able to skinny dip as swimming in the sea at night was always too much of a scary idea – possibly old, subconscious leftovers from an intense lecture series I'd accidentally attended on mermaids – but skinny dipping on land was an option I'd never considered until now.

I was a naked witch in trainers, ruled by the moon, I told myself. The feeling rinsed all the anxiety out of me and I told myself I could do my own spell, right there, in the field, and make it okay, give me strength to see Jackie and stun her with my magnetic energy. She would have no choice but to believe I was transformed and the incident had just been a fever blip.

I raised my arms to the sky and tried to breathe in the moon energy, not being entirely sure what moon energy was. I started to make enthusiastic leaping movements backwards and forwards in the grass, keeping near to the hut so I could still see. I thought about all I wanted to achieve, and about the cosmos, and how I had found it inside me and so I knew I had the power. I started whispering the words, 'I am transformed, I am transformed, by the light of the moon I am transformed.' I started to feel even more dizzy than before but took this as a sign that the magic was working; I was tripping out on moonlight; I was a goddess of the stars. A snapping of twigs rang out loudly and I stopped suddenly, losing my footing. I turned my ankle over, falling onto the cold grass. The thud rattled in my head, and I knew before my vision had stopped spinning that I'd have to crawl my way back to the hut and use the steps to get me on my feet again, if my ankle would tolerate it. I was fairly sure I hadn't broken it, but it stung deeply in a way that told me it'd be swollen by the morning.

As I crawled, naked, toward the light of the hut, a creeping sensation ran over my back; my ears started to pick up noises of footsteps. My heart rang in my ears like an alarm blaring. I moved as quickly as I could toward the steps, and felt, as I reached them, that I would turn round, and see a figure, and scream with no good person around to hear me.

I clambered and turned myself around, sitting down, but the empty field only provided temporary relief. I shrank into the hut, shuffling on my naked, freezing bum, and reached to close the doors. I dragged myself up using the kitchen table and limped about, convinced there was someone hiding inside. Only when I had checked once, twice, and then again, did I pull on a t-shirt and get into bed.

I thought it must have been a bird scratching on the roof, until I realised it was still dark. I woke up as the noise grew louder, and then stopped. When it started again, I sat up in bed and listened, trying to find a rational explanation for the sound. Perhaps it was a fox filing its claws against the walls? Was that a thing? I couldn't really work out where it was coming from and was frightened to move. It stopped again and I stayed completely still, worried that turning on the light might somehow make it worse. I was just about to lie down again, satisfied the noise had stopped, when I heard someone climbing up the wooden steps. I say someone, because it was far too heavy to be a fox. The bang on the door was enough to start my whole body trembling. I was terrified to make a sound in case it was safer to pretend it was just an old hut, terrified to stay quiet in case someone thought it was empty and therefore a place to explore.

The shout made me grab the scissors and hold them in my hand.

A man's voice. 'Wha—?'

Another bang on the door and I turned the light on, still not ready to let them know it was me in the hut, safer to let their imagination run; that perhaps some retired army sergeant lived there.

A call again. 'Wha—?'

I heard him on the steps; it didn't sound like he was going but sitting down.

I became aware of another man's voice, coming closer. I gripped the scissors even tighter.

'Mate, come on, what you doing?'

'Dunno, I thought we could sleep in there?'

'We need to walk home, you twat. Don't go wandering into empty fields. Bloody hell, how am I only half cut and you're a goner, you bellend?'

The noise drifted away and all was silent again. I tried to calm my breathing down but it was only getting more rapid. I was cold and sweaty and I was too scared to turn the light off but worried that keeping it on might make me a beacon for others. I'd never thought that people walking the long way back from the pub might stumble into the field, but now it was all I could think about. I was worried about my car, and images of a man curled up amongst all my things started to make me feel like I was going to pass out, which made me think of my dad again, and the sponge in his stomach again, which made me think of sepsis and the woman and throwing up in front of Jackie. I checked the photo but he was still as ever. Just a blip, I told myself.

My ankle seemed to be swelling by the second. I thought of insects in the grass, things that bite you and can cause infections, and sepsis did the loop again. I felt as though I was going to die or pass out or pass out then die.

I looked through my phone for who I could call but it was

two in the morning and I couldn't explain it all. I tried to grab the wood but it slipped from my hands and clattered onto the floor. There was no great wave of relief or exhaustion that took over, I stayed wired and awake for hours, listening for the smallest sounds, jumping at the noise of moths hitting the window, enraptured by the light.

Eventually, I fell into a hazy sleep as the sun rose, and woke up again at 11 a.m. I'd dreamt I'd been trying to pick up the broken bits of chair from the field outside the hut as a figure in navy blue was running toward me in the distance. As I kept dropping more and more bits of the wood, parts of my body started dropping off as well. Suddenly my hand was amongst the broken chair, then an arm, then a leg. I was lying in it all, my legs next to the chair legs, my arm wrapped around the seat, still trying to pick it up. I switched from being above it all, looking down, to being there, within it, hopelessly failing to put myself back together.

33

#SHIT

Rest-Assured Rentals

Hi Hattie, thanks for sending the form back, but there's quite a lot of missing information, and some spellings I'm not quite sure I recognise. Please can you have another look so we can get you moved in by your deadline?

Ella

[Missed Voice Call from Ella]

[Missed Voice Call from Ella]

[Missed Voice Call from Ella]

Answer Your PHONE

When I got up, I threw another cough sweet in my mouth and limped to the bathroom. I couldn't walk too far on my ankle without the pain getting too much, so I lay back in bed with my leg propped up. I was out of baked beans and bread and only had one potato left. The milk was past its use-by date. I sipped on water. I needed to ice my ankle but with no freezer in the hut I had to make do with soaking a j-cloth in cold water, until it slunk off the minute I moved my leg and started making a wet patch on the mattress.

I scrolled through my phone to see more missed calls from Ella. I looked at the hut, strewn with my clothes, dirty underwear, a crisp packet that had fallen on the floor, surrounded by the tiny papers from the cough sweets like confetti. The bin was full – I needed to take the bag out and put it in the grey dumpster round the back of the hut – but it was overflowing and rubbish was already scattered around the base. Hair tangled itself in the plughole of the shower, and my towel, having only been washed once, lay on the floor, smelling of damp. A fly buzzed in the bathroom and back out to the kitchen, until the noise stopped and I imagined it settling on the rim of my mug, the last cup of tea I'd had before realising the milk was past it. I hadn't washed any dishes, a glob of peanut butter stuck to the plate I'd eaten the mouldy toast from; my glass of water was smeared with my sticky handprints from the sweat of not washing and lying under my duvet for hours, days.

I'd looked up the symptoms of gastroenteritis and texted Jackie again, pretending I had spoken to NHS 111. I told her they'd said symptoms would last about a week, so I probably wouldn't be in work again until the following Monday, but I was working on getting a sick note.

I spent the rest of the day in bed, trying to fill out the form again, living on cough sweets, although the taste was starting to make me nauseous.

Ella

[Missed Voice Call from Ella]

[Missed Voice Call from Ella]

I need to talk to you

I swiped them away.

When my stomach screamed out for food, I hobbled over to cook the potato. The pain in my ankle had lessened enough that I could limp just about all right and I served the potato plain, because I had nothing to go on it. Every forkful turned to mush as I struggled to swallow it down. My stomach had started aching the minute I'd put it in the oven and by now it was hard to ignore, ironically putting me off the very thing it needed. I managed half, and then a wave of drowsiness came over me. I went to lie down for a minute. The next thing I knew it was dark outside, and as I got up again to go to the bathroom, I saw the fly nestling itself into my leftovers.

I looked over at The Plan and wondered how it had all gone so wrong. I'd done everything I could. I thought I had it all worked out – I thought I could work anything out. But now, I was falling, and I didn't know where I would end up, but it didn't feel like freedom.

I went back to bed and fell asleep again, waking up with a migraine. Swirling lights pulsed in front of my eyes, and the sockets themselves seemed to throb in time with the patterns. I reached for my water and drank the last of it, pulling the duvet over my head and hoping I would fall into oblivion again. When sleep didn't come, I crawled out of bed and found a packet of paracetamol in the bathroom, having to squint to see properly and push the tablet out okay. It eased the pain enough for me to drop off again, and I woke up on what I guessed was an afternoon but I had no idea what day. I reached for my phone and found a missed call and text from Jackie saying she needed me to call her about the sick note, a text from Aiden asking me if I was okay, and another few messages from Ella.

Hattie?

You can't keep ignoring me

Then she sent a picture.

And there it was, an image that my heart saw before my brain, and I started to itch, convulsing against my ribcage to try and scratch it away. When my eyes realised what they were looking at, I let out an actual gasp. That blue painted pebble-dash. The stone elephant in the front garden. The hand-painted sign reading 52. The fake address I had given them.

What the fuck, Hattie?

I turned cold and hot at the same time. Everything around me seemed to slow down and yet my insides were on fast forward.

Ella. Okay. I can explain.

Come and explain it to me. Come here.

I can't. I'm ill

The lady says you've been before to pick up post??

Come and meet me or I'm ringing your parents and then I'm reporting you missing.

Don't be stupid I'm not missing

Where are you then?

I looked again at the state of the hut. My head rattled. I couldn't think.

It was no use. I dropped my location and picked up the scissors.

34

#GHOST

God loves a party, so sometimes I imagine the afterlife is re-living every single New Year's Eve you've ever had on a loop. From sunset to sunrise, as a ghost.

I'd travel back in time to 1991, and as a ghost, I'd linger around my cot from around 8 p.m. all the way until the countdown, watching myself as a baby, screaming and crying from the noise of the fireworks. I'd try to pick myself up, soothe myself with a cuddle, but my hands would be useless, of course. I'd watch my mum come in and pick baby-me up and soothe me.

And so it would go on, every New Year I'd be there, ghost-ing about, watching my life unfold all over again. I'd silently sit in the nursing chair through one, two, three years old. Into childhood, teenage years, early twenties.

Until eventually, I'd find myself on the New Year's Eve when I was determined to get off with everyone in the club. I'd watch as Ella and I got ready, as we applied lashes of eyeliner. I'd be in that little club, half pub/half dance floor, and watch as I got off with one, two, three, four people. The drinks would be flowing, the club would be getting crowded, too crowded, and maybe that would be when ghost-me starts to worry.

Because maybe this is the moment in the afterlife where, suddenly, I'm not just a ghost watching anymore, I'm thrown back into my body, and I have to re-live it all.

That's when I'll think 'this isn't just the afterlife, this is hell, and I don't want to have to do this all over again', because the crowd was against me, pushing. I was looking for Ella as that shitty New Year disco ball hung like a piñata above me, and I stumbled as a group of lads came running in. They would have called it a 'brush past' but it knocked me and I regained my balance just in time for a girl to skip past with her arms flailing, and I was shouting, shouting for Ella. But the strobe light started, blinding me, and all I could see were people far stronger than me dancing and pushing and shoving, and I had to go with the crowd and move further away from the door. I was thinking, 'it's okay, any minute now I'll see her hand reaching for me and telling everyone to stop'. The relief when I did find her was like coming up for air. She was dancing and screaming in joy but I was serious and my body was trembling and I shouted in fear: 'It's not safe for me here, it's too crowded. I'm going to fall.'

I went to grab her hand hoping she'd get me out of there, but she didn't seem to see and told me not worry, that it would be all right in a minute. She pushed on dancing with the others, so I was alone and unsteady. I tried to get to the wall so I would have something to lean against, but a girl danced backwards into me and it was too late. I was down, hands out to stop me and people only noticed because I hit into them. I shuffled on my knees on the floor as people knocked into me.

I didn't think I could breathe anymore. I seemed to be only

half a person compared to all the complete people in that room. People seemed to be wondering why I didn't just get up, but no one helped. I crawled over to two people sitting at a table, mascara streaming down my face, and the look of disgust was palpable as I used their table to push against and get up, apologised and went outside. I told the security guard I didn't want to be in this body anymore and WHACK ghost-me was free again, reeling from the scratch of the cold air in my throat.

But I'd still have to watch the next bit. Watch myself crying to the security guard, saying, 'my friend left me'. Watch myself in the freezing cold, outside the club, texting Ella to ask her to come and meet me, but she never replied. Watch myself as I'm looking at my phone and trying to ring her, and there it is, the stumble off the pavement and down onto the ground, hitting the tarmac, the sharp pain in my rib.

I called to the security guard to help me up. 'No, no, you need to lift me, with your hands under my arms,' I shouted to him, my throat burning. He did, but reluctantly.

'You need to go home. You're too drunk.'

'I'm not though – I'm disabled, you don't under— I've – I've really hurt my—' I put my hand to my chest as the pain got sharper.

The security guard called over the taxi and said to take me to the hospital, but I was saying, 'No, no, no, I need Ella.'

'Look, love, you just said you're not pissed, you're hurt, so get yourself seen to.'

He opened the door of the cab and the driver looked at me sternly, telling me to make up my mind.

'Ella,' I call into her answerphone, 'please.'

In A&E, ghost-me has to keep watching. Watch as all I can

say is that something feels broken inside, and I am sat next to a man holding his groin, and the waiting room is heaving and hot. Watch as, when I am finally seen, the pain has subsided. It's a busy night and the nurse is clearly tired, and not particularly interested in trying to comfort me. Watch as her brisk tone just makes everything seem so much worse. Watch as the smell of antiseptic is strong in the air and I say it's making me feel like I can't breathe properly, which comes out all wrong, like I'm making a complaint about the smell of the hospital. It's also not even true, because when I was out in the biting night air, I felt like I couldn't breathe properly either.

Ghost-me has to watch as I lift up my top while the nurse tries to examine me, but I'm making everything difficult again because I'm holding onto my phone like it's a medical device I need to keep me alive – it's getting in the way, and when she says she doesn't think there's anything broken, it's clear that she thinks I'm getting in the way, too.

'Why can't I have an X-ray?' My rib really does hurt, and I fell on it hard. 'And it hurts, inside—'

I'm sobbing again.

The nurse's expression stays the same. 'No X-ray because I've got no reason to think it's broken. Why don't you call someone?'

'I can't get hold of anyone.'

She asks me some more questions, but I keep saying the same thing.

'She won't pick up. I've left her so many texts and messages but she won't pick up.'

We look at the phone as it rings out, the name on the screen – ELLA.

*

That night, ghost-me would thank God I was gone and on to the next New Year before long, that I didn't have to watch what happened the next morning. Didn't have to see myself in my bedroom, cramming cough sweets into my mouth every hour, on the hour.

When I went into Ella's room in the morning, and I tried to explain what had happened, she said she didn't hear me, and assumed I'd gone home with a boy.

'But then I called you – and messaged – over and over,' I said, eyes wide. 'I ended up in A&E.'

'Oh shit – are you okay?' she said, suddenly serious.

'Well, I thought I'd broken a rib, but I didn't.'

Her face lost all concern. 'Oh, okay, so you were fine. Phew!'

'Ella!'

'Hattie – I was drunk, okay, drunk and having a good time, and I just thought you'd got with someone – I couldn't have known.'

'Didn't you check your phone?'

'No! I was dancing. And, really, very, very drunk.' She laughed but I wasn't finding it funny.

'It was so crowded in there, Ella – couldn't you see?'

'You've gone home with boys before. How was I to know?' She ran her fingers through her blonde hair as she asked, her brow furrowed.

My throat felt like it was going to collapse in on itself. 'I was saying we needed to go.'

'Hattie, love, if you really needed me, you should have shouted louder.'

35

#CUT

Ella

Ok. I'm on my way.

Honestly. What.

I sat on the steps with the scissors and wood. It had been just under an hour since we spoke; she would be here soon. My phone sat next to me in its little leather book-like case, with the sound, for the first time in a long time, as loud as it would go. It was a sunny afternoon, and the blue sky above me was cloudless. The landscape probably looked as green as it had ever looked, the hills in the distance so beckoning in terms of space, the woods to the right providing the perfect balance: shade, comfort, a hiding spot. But I couldn't hide now. I had to stay here, on the steps, and wait for Ella. I didn't have the strength to move beyond where I was.

I kept my head down and squeezed the scissors, hard. My hands were slightly shaking from the lack of food; I'd downed another two glasses of water. I could see small scratches on the side of the hut – almost in the shape of a spiral? – where the drunk guy had obviously been trying graffiti with his key.

While waiting for Ella, I was cutting into old dents, the long stick teeming with dark marks. I had been squeezing until my hands ached, and squeezed even harder then, despite how much it hurt. On the steps that late afternoon, the pain set in almost instantly, but I carried on going. When the scissors turned over on themselves and the stick clanked onto the ground, I was close to cutting my hand but managed to move out of the way just in time. Just a scratch; no blood, no matter. I went to pick the stick up, and as I lifted my head up again, the world began to spin. I sat down. Just the lack of food, I thought. I returned to squeezing the scissors, trying to make a dent deeper than ever before.

Her figure in the distance was more unsettling than I'd expected. She would have seen my car, with the box and blanket thrown by the side, and was now looking at me, sitting on the steps. She was walking with purpose. I went back to the wood.

Hearing her voice was disturbing, too. Her 'what the fuck's started from a long way off, and didn't stop until she was just a few feet away, asking if I was going to bother to look at her at all. Lifting my head to her, seeing her long blonde hair, her navy-blue jeans and her striped jumper. Her blue eyes were a mixture of searching and stunned.

'You look like shit,' she said.

'Yeah, I know.'

'I bought you this. Since you're ill.'

She placed the Lucozade down on the steps next to me

with a thud. 'Just have a Lucozade,' I heard, in my mind, all the times I'd said I was tired. And yet this time, I needed the energy, after starving myself for days.

'So what's this about?' she asked.

I put the wood and scissors down on the steps next to me and tried to open the bottle with my hands but struggled. I put it to my teeth, bit down, twisted then wiped the saliva from my chin with my cardigan. I took a big glug of the orangey syrup and kept the bottle in my hand.

'And what's *this* about?' she asked, gesturing wildly at me and the hut.

I took another gulp of the drink, and the liquid ran down my chin. My skin flinched at the cold and I took a deep breath in, letting it out slowly, my eye catching a crow flying off into the distance.

'I just wanted some time away.'

'Most people go on holiday, Hattie. They don't leave their job and their flat and their whole life.'

I stared down into the bottle and watched the collection of bubbles gather around the edge, popping in turn as my hand gently shook. I brought the drink to my lips again but I could feel a tension forming in my throat, and sweat beginning to run down my back, soaking into the band of my knickers, as my jeans, a little big for me, were gaping.

'Yeah, I know.'

Ella was still standing in front of me, the only other human in the wild field, gathering her blonde hair, as though she was brushing it from her face to try and see the situation better, but no matter how hard she tried, it wasn't getting any clearer.

'I knew something was up. So I decided to come up early

and check on you. So I go to that house and that old lady, well she's sure no one called Oliver ever lived there. And then she said a girl had come, in her car, to get some post. And it turns out, you're actually here. So were you seeing Oliver and it didn't work out, or you're still seeing him, or you just made him up entirely?'

I was quiet, head down, looking at the grass, fixating on a small ant scaling a blade.

'Fucking hell. I mean what the fuck?' Her hands were on her hips, her stare arrow-like.

'I just needed a break.'

'And when were you planning on coming back? Honestly, Hattie, after everything I've ever done for you.'

The ant had disappeared while I blinked. I tried looking for it, searching for a flicker in the undergrowth, wondering how far something so small could travel in such a short amount of time. I could feel Ella's eyes on me and tensed up in anticipation of her coming nearer. I didn't know what I thought she was going to do, but she was already far, far closer than I wanted her to be. I brought the bottle back up to my lips and took small sips, and the fizz tapped out on my tongue.

'If you just wanted to move out, live somewhere different, make some new friends, you could do that in London, but it— I mean, I don't get it – we were a team! I helped you out so many times.'

I swallowed as the stinging in my throat danced on.

'I needed to be away from London.'

'Forever?'

'Yeah.'

'Why?'

Ella sat down on the grass cross-legged, her hands neatly in her lap as though instructed by a school photographer. She stared at me, waiting for something to click. I felt the answer bubbling in my throat; I felt the burning grow and grow until it was ablaze. I couldn't look her in the eye.

'I think we need—' Her tone was softer now, more hesitant. 'I think I should take you to a doctor. I think maybe you're a bit unwell? Is that what it is? Because they can do all sorts now, meds and stuff, and you'll be okay in a little while and you can come back to London.'

'I couldn't get in here –' I pointed back at the door, 'because the owners never thought, never even considered a disabled person might be a guest one day, might struggle with the door, which they knew was a bit stiff.'

'Okay. Yes. Let's. Let's see a doctor about this . . . little blip and then you'll be okay.'

'I don't need— I needed to get away from everyone because it was— I couldn't keep explaining . . .'

'Explaining what?'

My voice was still croaky, and my throat painful, but I tried. 'This is why you shouldn't be here.'

'Please tell me what's going on.'

'I needed to go – go away from my disabled life and start again and go away from you because you're not— it's not your fault but you do things that make me feel so shit.'

The words came out like a water breaking: the relief followed by the pain, the feeling that an important part was done but there was still so much more to do. Agony waited behind each breath.

'What?' She looked genuinely confused.

'So, one of the things – one of the things was – well, I was already planning on leaving, and I'd come up with my pla— I already wanted to leave, and I was going to make up Oliver and everything, but then I had moments where I thought I'd miss you too much and wondered if I'd actually go through with it. But it was confirmed when I saw you put all the photos of me, of my legs, in the "no" pile when you were making that pinboard.'

She scoffed. 'What?'

'It's a lot to explain. But I saw you and I knew I couldn't take it anymore.'

'Honestly, what are you talking about?'

Her defensiveness lit a fire in me.

'You see? This is the problem. You were on the floor with your big corkboard getting ready for your party. You were arranging all the photos, going through them all, you remember, piles and piles of photos. We were laughing because you'd spent about four hours printing them off in Boots and then you weren't even going to use them all. So there you were, going through the piles, and there was the "yes" pile – the ones that were going on the board – the "maybe" pile and then the "no" pile. I saw you. I saw you do it, time and time again, every single picture where my legs were showing, you put the picture in the "no" pile. And I felt so sad about that, but I knew you weren't even thinking – you did it automatically.'

She stared at me with her mouth slightly ajar.

'And then I said, "hey – you can include photos of my legs you know", and you just ignored me.'

'I don't think I ignored you.'

'Well, did you answer?'

'I didn't really think it needed an answer. To be honest, I'm not even sure you said anything.'

'I did say. I know I said because I find it so hard to say, it physically hurts.'

She was staring at me, silently.

'But why would you think I'm doing this to hurt you? I'm not malicious, Hattie. Why would you think that? After all our years of friendship?'

I felt the guilt squirm in my stomach. 'I don't think you're doing it on purpose but it's not only about the photos; that was just one example. There's been loads of bad tiny things and then very bad big things, big things that made me feel like I needed to get out, get away from you and start again. It was too painful.'

'What kind of big things?'

'A big thing like New Year. A big thing that made me think, this is never going to get better,' I said.

She sat there, staring.

'The New Year you said you didn't hear me, but I told you, I told you why. And you didn't come with me. And then I was in A&E,' I said.

'Oh Hattie, not this, not the one where you freaked out and thought you'd broken a rib but you didn't?'

I downed the rest of the Lucozade in one violent motion, forcing it down my aching throat and into my stomach. Then I threw the bottle in the vague direction of Ella and it landed, pathetically, a few inches from my feet. Fucking sports. Fucking arms. Fucking Ella. This isn't what I wanted to happen, she should have just left me, but she had to come and find me, didn't she? I picked up the scissors and the stick.

Ella started talking again. 'Or do you mean a different one? A different one where I apparently messed up and wasn't allowed to have a good time by dancing? You know, you really need to talk out loud more, less of all this going on in your head.'

'But I am exhausted at having to explain all the time,' I started waving the stick at her as though she was that pink piñata from years ago, 'and what I'm trying to say is: what if I couldn't talk, what then? Would you finally start looking, and thinking, and not assuming?' I could feel a strange, dancey, angry energy, and I stood up as though I was going somewhere. Christ knows where I thought I was going.

'But that's— what the hell are they?' She was pointing at the stick and scissors.

'I'm using it to make my hands stronger, see the dents?' I was smiling now. 'Instead of having to ask people to do my office chair at work.'

'What, at the hospital? Of all the people that would be understanding of your needs . . . just tell them.'

'You are always waiting for me to speak. It is always me that has to raise my voice. You never think about it otherwise. And you don't get how hard it is to try to explain, and be met with awkwardness, or pity, or not be listened to. And,' my voice went louder, 'when you do ask me, you expect me say it's all okay, because if it's not, you act like it's a problem, or that I'm making something out of nothing, like our stupid fucking flat on the stupid fucking second floor.'

'No, you're right, I don't get it. And I thought you loved our flat.'

'Exactly, Ella. Exactly. Look. What if I couldn't speak?'

'But you can.'

I dropped the stick and kept the scissors, leaping to the side, like I was getting onto a stage, the anger, or energy, or excitement – I wasn't sure anymore – rising in me, ignoring the shooting pain in my ankle.

'So let's say I'm dead and I can't speak, so the pathologist has to find out what's wrong with me. They have to look, don't they? They can't rely on me to speak.'

'But you're not dead, Hattie.' She almost rolled her eyes.

I'd stuck my tongue out to mimic being dead and said, 'Yesh I am.'

'You're being a child. You're not dead and you can speak.'

'What if –' my tongue was still out, 'I –' I raised the scissors up to mime the action, 'cut it –' the scissors were jokingly open around my tongue '– off.'

I'll never forget the way the colour drained from her face. The razor sharp, blinding pain lasted only a few seconds before the shock took over. I could feel something hot rush out of my mouth, down my chin. I had been surprised at the intense feeling of spongy resistance, sure I was in fact only gently pressing, pretending.

I dropped the scissors on the ground and remember being confused that the blades were scarlet. I was shocked at how quickly my mouth seemed to be filling with blood, running out, down my top, my shoes, the grass. I put my hand up to try and catch it, and my fingers were red in seconds. I remember Ella grabbing my phone and putting it in her bag, and then pulling my arm, and running, trying to drag me along as I limped. I remember her asking me where we were, what was the address, exactly, could I write it down, we needed an ambulance. I remember shaking my head, us getting in the car, her trying to find the location drop thing I'd sent on her phone, but giving up because all she was doing was pressing all the wrong buttons in her panic, opening her calculator, her photos. I remember her driving, me reaching and pressing the wad of tissues from the glove box into my mouth. I remember her saying over and over, 'What have you done, Hattie, what have you done?'

36

#SHOCK

I don't understand why, if the human body has the ability to block out pain when in shock, it can't carry on doing so when it's starting to come round to the idea it's got a serious injury. Lose the sweating, the nausea, the fainting – keep the absence of pain.

Ella didn't make it to the hospital; in fact, she wasn't ever planning on driving all the way there. She'd decided we needed to get somewhere with other people, a little-less-middle-of-nowhere before she made the call. I'd managed to remain conscious until she got to the village. I remember the green blob of a polo shirt on the man, running out of the corner shop, before running in again to call an ambulance. Ella was apparently standing over my collapsed body in the car, holding onto the tissues, keeping my tongue out of my mouth and pressing hard. The paramedic on the phone had warned of the risk of me choking on my own blood. The shopkeeper had helped Ella get me out of the car and put me in the recovery position while still managing to keep the tissues pressed on the wound. I didn't come round until I was in the ambulance.

Science will say it was the injections of whatever adrenaline the paramedics gave me and the oxygen tube around my nose that revived me back to consciousness, but I am telling you now, it was the pain. It was like a swarm of bees had stung my mouth and were trying to get nectar out of the swellings. I screamed out, I remember that, because the movement made it all the worse. I became aware that my tongue was still pulled out of my mouth, and a blue-gloved paramedic was holding onto my jaw.

'Hey, hey, easy. Try not to move your mouth.'

I promptly ignored him and tried to scream again, but he kept his hands fixed around my face.

'Hattie, we want to give you some pain relief but Ella here says she thinks you're allergic to some things, she says because of your muscles? Can you give me a thumbs up if you have allergies?'

I tried to feel for my phone in my back pocket but was again reprimanded for too much movement.

'Really need you to keep still, Hattie – just a thumbs up with your hand.'

Ignoring them, desperate to relieve the agony, I tried again to speak, saying 'phone' and trying to mime a call, which immediately filled the ambulance with more requests to keep still, although it eventually clicked and Ella looked in her bag for it.

They opened the cover to show me the screen, pressing the button to turn it on, but that was enough – I pointed at the side with slots for cards and they found the white piece of paper with my medical details on.

> WARNING: May be allergic to some medications. Please check the following list before administering.

It felt as though it took them an hour to read through the A4 paper that I had folded up tightly so it could fit in my phone case. I was sure I was going to pass out again, and in many ways welcomed it, but somehow my body was keen to remain conscious, leaving me to experience the full horror of excruciating pain and the knowledge of how much worse being sick was going to make things, which of course made the nausea all the more intense. The idea of stomach acid pooling in the cut was enough to make my whole intestinal tract try to crawl out of my mouth.

When the pain relief finally hit, my body let go and I was in a conscious but out-of-it state for the rest of the journey. I vaguely remember Ella on the phone to my parents – I assumed – and envisioned my mum and dad and Martin arriving on the ward on the back of a giraffe. I sort of remember realising we were headed to my A&E: the largest, closest one to where we were, as due to the nature of the emergency, minor injuries wasn't going to cut it. For a short while the two paramedics kept their bodies but their heads were replaced by pink balloons bobbing around. I remember thinking: 'that makes me the only one with a mouth.' I wondered how badly I'd managed to injure myself, if anyone would believe it had been an accident; but, if the laceration was severe, it would at least mean all that time spent cutting into wood had been worth it, and I was getting stronger.

37

#BOARD

Lying in bed, surrounded by a blue curtain, I had come a long way from being four years old, wanting the guy in the bed next to me to stop moaning in pain, and for my mum to be with me. Rather than wanting the patients around me to be quiet, I was trying to guess what was wrong with everyone by sound alone, which was, in many ways, a levelling up of The Game. Or that's what I was thinking, until I remembered mistaking a panic attack for sepsis and started to feel sick all over again. The light above me was bright in that artificial way that made me want to curl up under the thin bedsheets forever; the room was filled with the sound of beeps and curtains opening and closing. I could never fully relax as I kept thinking footsteps were coming toward my curtain, about to swish it open and subject me to more pain, or questions, or both. I thought about the photo of Dad that lay in the bedsheets in the hut, that photo of a dying man in a hospital bed now tucked into the empty bed of his daughter as she wound up in hospital. I wondered if he had found the lights too bright as well, if the noise of the hospital made him agitated, begging for some peace and quiet. I supposed he got it in the end, and found myself pulling the bedsheets further up and over my head, shutting my eyes even tighter.

Mum and Martin were on their way, but it was the last thing I needed. I'd tried to text them to stop them coming, telling them I couldn't talk anyway, I'd be out in a few days, but apparently the hotel was already booked and they were heading up in the car. The nurses had given me a whiteboard with a pen to write with, and I enjoyed the low level of expectation people had of me because of it. I had an IV drip for fluids – an initial blood test had shown everything to be pretty out of whack after spending about four days surviving on cough sweets, and my ankle had been officially diagnosed as a sprain. It was elevated with ice, my lower legs wrapped in compression stockings that I deemed to be unnecessary. I was also being forced to take small sips of a weird pink-liquid-food-milkshake with a straw, trying to keep it on the safe side of my mouth only.

On the whiteboard, I drew a large tongue and tried to work out how long the cut was. They'd sealed it together with dissolvable stitches and put a large amount of cotton padding in my mouth.

Since I arrived at the hospital by ambulance, I had avoided the horror of seeing my colleagues on the desk, but my name would have popped up to anyone working out back, checking admissions. I was still on a lot of painkillers when they brought me in; the memory of it was broken and hazy. I checked my phone case to see if they'd replaced the list of medications that are dangerous for me, but they hadn't. I wondered where it was.

I seemed to be in a gown, but I didn't remember taking off my clothes. I tried to look around the floor by my bed to see if there was any sign of them in a bag, but there was nothing. I thought about the scene outside the hut – the blood on the grass, the pavement where the shopkeeper and Ella had put me in the recovery position, and wondered if I'd left a mark of blood there too. I wondered if the shopkeeper was thinking of me, if I would end up in next week's pub quiz. *Whose blood marks the pavement outside my shop, and for a bonus point, how did it get there?*

Trickiest one of the lot, I reckon; no one would know my name. I sketched out the line I thought I had cut in my tongue with hatching marks, rubbing away the corners. Perhaps three inches? Perhaps a lot less than that. It was difficult to tell; the amount of cotton padding in my mouth felt like I must have ripped the thing in half. I vaguely remembered them saying they didn't think I'd need surgery, but someone from the team would come and check. My sense of time was off; I couldn't remember if they had already checked the evening I was admitted or if I was to expect them today.

There had been a lot of people around the bed, different people from different departments, and questions about my disability. It was a lot of talking, a lot of questions and a lot of asking me to stick my tongue out. It was still too painful to move properly, and they seemed a little bit concerned I might have caused some permanent damage. My head was still scrambled and in shock from the fact I'd misjudged things so badly.

As I tried to go over the events again, it dawned on me that I had no recollection of how I got from the A&E ward to here, and I realised with horror it could have been Aiden who had wheeled me in. I picked up my phone and double checked his missed calls to make sure there wasn't one from last night, or a text. Thankfully his last call was before it happened. I was sort of sure if he'd wheeled me through, or heard I'd been wheeled through, he would have sent me a text. I hoped so, anyway.

By the next morning I was more coherent, having had the drip in me all night, and they had reduced my pain medication enough that I wasn't so drowsy. It was the afternoon and Ella, Mum and Martin had been with me most of the day.

When Mum and Martin arrived, Mum immediately came over and gave me a hug, her short, pixie cut hair brushing against my cheek, her fleece reassuringly worn, faded, and smelling of the same laundry powder she'd used since I was small. Martin stayed back a little, his long grey hair tied back behind him, his waterproof trousers muddy like he'd been in the garden and rushed to the car without a second thought. Looking concerned but unsure of what to do, I gave him a small wave and he relaxed, smiling warmly at me, but giving me time with Mum. The concern on Mum's face was difficult to see, and I knew that she was seeing shadows of my dad lying in a hospital bed as she looked at me. She told me I looked 'so small and sad'. She stroked my hair, and I couldn't think of how to explain what had happened. I couldn't think of a way to tell her that, actually, the main reason I was so sad was that they were here, and my new life had crumbled, propelling me back to where I was when I was four. Small and sad. A New Life this wasn't, but I wasn't ready to completely let go of it all and surrender.

Once of the first questions my parents asked me was where Oliver was. I wrote: *We broke up.*

Ella had left us to it for a bit. Mum had sorted her a room in the same hotel as them and I wasn't ready to admit everything to them. I was too exhausted to go through it all.

'And is that why you did this to yourself, love?' asked Mum.

No it was a joke that went wrong

They looked at each other and Mum put her hand on my hand.

'Funny sort of joke, sweetheart.'

Not my best

And I know you always say

We don't do anger here

'When you were younger, love.' Mum laughed, but her eyes were searching.

But I'm angry I've ended up in here

Just for a bad joke

When I'm fine

Mum held the energy drink for me to sip. She said she was glad I was okay, but they wanted to know everything that led up to the tongue, and they asked me so many questions my hand started to get tired from all the writing. I managed to tell them a version of the truth, that Oliver and I had broken up, that I was living in an Airbnb for a bit but I'd got a new job, not the dog walking one, the new job was on reception here, but I'd been off sick with a stomach bug.

'Do they know you're in here?'

I shook my head and put the board down, hoping they'd stop asking me questions. They told me not to worry about things, that I should tell work where I was, that I should tell Oliver too, that if I wanted to stay here in Wales that would be okay, if I liked the job and could keep it, but they were sure Ella would have me back in London and that it might be good to have people around me. I nodded to all their words and closed my eyes while Mum stroked my hand.

'That's it, you just rest for a bit now.'

When I opened my eyes again, they had gone, and my phone was flashing with a message from Ella.

Ella

Spoke to your mum and Martin. I went along with the Oliver break up thing, but you need to tell the mental health lady you made him up okay? She'll understand.

Oh btw, I think Martin went to talk to your boss on reception.

Oh, fantastic news.

What?

Don't worry, I think they need to know you're in here, but it doesn't matter anyway because you'll be back in London soon, eh xx

I put my phone down and pulled the thin bedcover up to my face. IV in my hand and stitches in my mouth, I whispered, 'Sorry body. I didn't mean to hurt you,' before a nurse came in with more pain meds, and sent me off into a deep, dreamless sleep.

38

#AVA

'Now before you freak out when you look at your phone, I've told the guys on the penguin group that you're a bit poorly, and I'm with you, and they obviously need to cancel their visit. I'm happy to pretend Oliver broke up with you if that's the line you want to take with them.' Ella was looking very pleased with herself.

I looked at my phone. She had kept the details brief, saying I was in hospital after 'a bit of a crisis', she was with me, and I needed a bit of time to recover.

SAM: OMG

PETE: Hattie?

GEORGIA: What's happened?

Need the deets

I'm okay but will explain later

I wrote on the whiteboard: *I wish you hadn't done that*

'Oh, so you were planning on them still coming? Did you want me to pretend I'm Oliver?' she asked. She had a point, but I was, obviously, in a mood.

I don't even like that group chat

She simply raised her eyebrows at me. I hovered my pen over the board and wrote again.

Does Georgia like where she works?

Ella looked confused, but before she had time to answer, I rubbed it out and wrote another question.

How Pearl's Lena getting on at school?

'I dunno, great probably.' Ella wasn't particularly interested in this line of questioning.

Where exactly is Pete living?

'Bloody hell, Hattie, I don't know.'

Exactly. And neither do I

Pearl had been right; we could all act like a pack of wolves sometimes, desperate for details. But we never actually *talked* on that chat. It had been such a long time since we'd had a proper conversation. When I said I was tired, they just brushed past it. We could all have been in our own personal versions of hell and writing 'hahahhaaa' every three days, sending the occasional GIF, and no one would be any the wiser.

'Well, Georgia's just messaged me privately asking what's happened? Do you want me to ignore her?'

I looked down at my phone to see she'd messaged me too. I gave Ella a shrug and messaged Georgia, again, that I'd explain later.

'Look, she's trying to call me now,' said Ella, as though it was my fault. Ella was smart enough not to answer, but clearly wanted to. As silence hung between us, I let out a deep breath.

She stayed sitting there, not looking at me, scrolling through her phone. Mum and Martin popped by soon after and stuck around for a few hours before heading off for lunch. I was pleased when they all left me; it had turned into Ella and my parents reminiscing about the good old days, while I sat there trying to think of any sentence that would get me out of the looming visit from the psychiatrist. I could have done without them going over old holidays and catching up on how Ella was getting on in the salon while I tried to plot my escape route.

When the nurse came in, I still hadn't thought of anything, but, in desperation, I decided to play it breezy.

Hey! You know what, cancel the psychiatric assessment? Changed my mind, I wrote on the whiteboard.

I gave a strong thumbs up and tried to smile as blood dribbled down my chin.

'We can't not have you seen. You've got the best coming, you know? Nice one, I promise. It won't be long to wait now.'

I tapped the word 'cancel' with my pen and she simply ducked out again and drew back the curtain. I reached for a tissue to rub away the writing, a white flag of defeat. I would just have to sit there and say nothing.

Minutes later, the curtain drew back again, and a woman in a navy suit and lanyard was standing in front me and introducing herself as a member of the psychiatric assessment team. Ava was the best dressed therapist I had ever seen. NHS pay is hardly rolling in it, but money can't buy you style. Her navy suit was perfectly tailored to her body; she wasn't tall but seemed to have the calm confidence of the tallest person in the room, like she was able to see the lay of the land in an instant. She had a small gold nose piercing and wore a bright white shirt. Her bright white trainers were slim enough to look smart but, being trainers, cool enough to look easy going. Adjusting her glasses, which were framed only on the top of the lens, with little gold motifs in the corner, she looked down at my notes and said she understood I'd be using the board for most of the session, and to take my time.

'We have as long as you need,' she said, smiling, apparently finished with my notes already as she put them on the bedside table.

I knew that we almost certainly didn't have as much time as I needed, that there was probably a very short window she had before she made her assessment.

'What would you like to talk about?' she asked.

I was slightly taken aback that she didn't start with a question about why I thought it was a good idea to have scissors in my mouth, but I knew it wouldn't be long before we got there. I shrugged.

'Perhaps you don't want to talk about anything?'

I drew a big tick on the board and showed it to her. Therapists had never done me any good. She nodded and reclined in her chair.

We sat in silence for the next few minutes, and then Ava shut her eyes. I assumed she would open them again soon, but she didn't. Had she died? Did I just kill her? I tapped my pen on the whiteboard and she, to my relief, opened her eyes again.

Are you okay?? I wrote on the board.

'Oh yes, quite fine. Just having a little rest.'

She shut her eyes again and laid back in the chair. I waited.

Convinced she would open them again soon, I sat staring at her. But as the minutes ticked past, she genuinely seemed to be having a rest. I was aware that this could mean she wasn't that bothered about me, and I was just another piece of paper she had to sign off on, but I was still suspicious. I shut my eyes too. And then quickly opened them again. She still appeared to be asleep. I shut them for a little longer, and then BAM, I opened them and tried to catch her out. I shut them again and then opened them very, very slightly, but, alas, her eyes were still shut and her legs were still out in front of her as she leant back in the uncomfortable hospital chair. Fine. If this was a game, then I was going to win. I closed my eyes and told myself I wouldn't open them again until she spoke. I tried to zone into the busy ward and find a rhythm, a rise, hum and fall that I could concentrate on, but the noise was too jagged, like a radio losing signal. It must have been ten minutes before I heard the sound of the curtain being pulled back. Mum and Martin were standing, unsure, on the edge. Looking over, I expected to see Ava reclined as before, but to my surprise she was sitting up, alert.

'Sorry, love, we're going to pop back to the hotel for a bit, okay?' said Mum. 'Leave you to it.'

As Martin pulled the curtain back, I started to write on my board.

Have we finished? I was keen to get this shit wrapped up.

'Do you want us to be finished?' replied Ava.

I nodded.

'Is that because you don't like me? I can find someone else? Although, it might take a while to be seen.'

I found myself shaking my head. This time, I didn't want to start all over again.

'Well, just say if you change your mind. Makes no difference to me.'

She settled in her chair again and closed her eyes. What the hell was she playing at?

A loud groan came from a bed somewhere on the ward. I tapped on my board to 'wake' Ava up.

I guess he is recovering from appendicitis. You?

I thought I might as well use her medical knowledge, even if she did specialise in mental health, to my advantage.

'Could be. But he'd be post-surgery by now. Shouldn't be in that much pain.'

Punctured lung then???

'That's more like it. Ever had one?'

I shook my head.

'Me neither. Sounds bad though, doesn't it? Like a football inside you, deflating.'

We were quiet again.

'Any other theories going?' she asked.

I paused for a while.

I think Martin – my mum's partner – threatened to sue my boss – I work on A&E reception downstairs

I had been working on the theory since Ella told me Martin had gone to speak to them. His love for his career in employment law – even after he stopped practising – was well known by Ella, having to suffer through many a monologue from him as we were growing up.

'Hmm, okay. We can get to that. Just so I don't get it wrong – it's "Mum" and it's "Martin", yeah?'

Dad died when I was three. They left a surgical sponge in him. Got sepsis.

'Nasty business,' Ava nodded solemnly.

I think about it a lot

'You do?'

Yes.

'Have you talked to anyone else about it?'

Therapists. But they don't seem interested in the sponge.

She looked confused.

'Really? Poor show on their part. I'm interested. Big time.'

She was the first therapist who had ever said that. With the whiteboard pen gripped tightly to my hand, I started to write down the story.

39

#CARD

I tried to squeeze the writing as small as possible to get the whole story in and had to rub out parts to make more room. Once I had finished, and Ava had read it, I rubbed it all out and simply wrote: *So yeah. I still think about it. A lot.*

'Let's try to think about why you think about it so much. Close your eyes if you like. Take your time.'

I tried. I really did. I imagined Dad collapsing in the supermarket. Him lying in the hospital bed. The photograph. His eyes. The stolen surgical sponge sitting in the shepherd's hut. I felt as though I could only see the periphery of it all; the centre was blurred.

I can't.

Ava told me it was okay, that this was probably going to take time, maybe a few sessions. I thought she was just going to sit with me for twenty minutes and write up a report, but apparently that wasn't what she had in mind at all, and this threw me to the point that I wasn't entirely sure what to do next. I had been planning to get rid of her quickly.

The curtain suddenly shifted back to reveal Ella, who looked shocked to see somebody else in the chair.

'Oh! Shit!' she said, realising that this was probably the 'mental health lady'. She disappeared before Ava or I could say anything.

'And that was . . . ?' asked Ava.

Ella. She is the one I was with when it happened.

I pointed to my mouth, because apparently, I thought it needed explaining.

'In your notes it says you say it was a joke gone wrong?'

I nodded. *I was only meant to be pretending to cut my tongue off. But I accidentally snipped it a bit.*

Ava smiled again.

'Yeah, just a bit, eh?'

Have I gone mad?

'Well that depends how good a joke it was. If that was the punchline, what was the set-up?'

I paused again, wondering how to explain it. We were silent for a long time as I stared at the whiteboard.

I was saying, imagine I don't have a tongue

Because I'm tired of explaining everything to everyone

And I get so frustrated

But I didn't mean to cut it

'It must be very tiring having to constantly justify yourself. I can understand that.'

Ava leant forward and was gently serious, completely focused on me. There was a pause.

'You're tired of it, aren't you? Tired of it all.'

I nodded.

'And you're angry too, aren't you? Have you ever done

anything like this – not this – I know, this was a joke – but any . . . outbursts? Big moments of angry energy?'

Broke a canvas at school

My phone at uni

Recently smashed up a chair

Smashed up my phone at work too

And I scream in my car

'So it builds up and bursts out, but what about letting it out in small bits, at the time? Not smashing things up, but being pissed off, complaining to a mate?' She was leaning forward as she spoke, her fingers mimicking an explosion when she said the word 'bursts'.

I wanted to write 'we don't do anger here' on the board, but I knew it would take a lot of explaining, and I was feeling exhausted. As my pen hovered over the whiteboard, Ava held out her hand.

'It's okay. Rest for now. I'll be back to see you tomorrow, okay?' She squeezed my hand and then she was gone, her navy-blue suit disappearing behind the curtain. I closed my eyes; they were suddenly heavy as though she had hypnotised me. Or maybe, she'd just seen what was already there.

I wasn't really sure why the nurses had decided I needed the curtain around me at all times; I hadn't seen the rest of the ward as they'd given me strict instructions to rest, wary that my ankle could easily get worse if I started moving about too soon. It seemed pretty extreme that they'd given me a catheter, and the way the nurses checked it made me convinced it was more to see how hydrated I was rather than anything else. The IV drip in my hand was becoming itchy under the tape. I had successfully managed to keep myself constipated to avoid using the bedpan they'd offered me, not least because I was barely managing to drink the liquid food supplements they'd given me. My tongue was inspected a few times a day, and I was kept on a low dose of pain relief.

When I didn't have to move my tongue, it wasn't painful, just an ongoing discomfort. But when I tried to drink, the sharpness would return, and it was made worse by the antiseptic mouthwash I was forced to swill afterwards. When they made me stick my tongue out for inspection, it was almost unbearable. I was told that the tongue can heal itself incredibly quickly due to the large amount of blood supply it gets, but I had to give my body everything it needed to heal. The main bulk of cotton wool had been removed from my mouth now, and the stitches were holding; I'd been warned if I didn't start drinking the food supplements they'd have to consider putting a feeding tube in me. I doubled down and tried to pretend it was a drinking game, taking large gulps with my eyes squeezed shut. In some ways I wished my tongue could be dry enough to scab over, so I could see for myself that it was getting better.

After texting Mum and Martin to say the psychiatrist had gone, I flicked through the messages on the group chat, feeling more annoyed than ever at Ella and relieved when I got to the bottom of the thread to see they had moved on to another topic of conversation. Scrolling through my phone, I found myself looking at an old missed call from Aiden and wondered if I should message him. The memory of our last phone call still made my stomach squirm, but I found myself longing for his voice. I was so embarrassed about getting the wrong idea, and at the same time, wishing I could just carry on the belief that maybe he liked me for just a little longer. The mix of pain, anger and yearning for him was making me fidgety, and I clicked on and off his name on WhatsApp as I tried to work out what I should do.

Before I could decide, Mum and Martin came back with Ella. They bumbled in with two balloons, flowers and cards. I drew a smiley face on the board because I knew I wasn't doing a very good job of pretending to be pleased. The balloons were placed behind the bedside table, getting caught on one of the wires for the call bell, but Mum managed to sort it. I was pleased that neither of them were pink. The flowers were large, too large, and I obviously didn't have a vase, so they rested them on the bedside table, meaning there was no room for anything else.

'Open your cards! And then let us know how it went with the mental health lady,' said Ella.

Mum and Martin's card said 'GET WELL SOON' on the front with a message inside saying they would be here for me whatever I needed. I smiled and rested it awkwardly on my lap as there was nowhere to put it. Ella's card said 'WITH SYMPATHY' and on the inside she'd written 'just like the first card I ever got you!!!' I smiled again and placed it down, writing 'thank you' on the board.

'Do you remember that?' Ella asked Mum.

'What's that, love?'

'The first card I ever got Hattie was a "With Sympathy" card, because my mum said she couldn't run as fast as everyone else.'

The soft laughter from Mum was cut short as I knocked the cards off the bed, reaching for the board.

That's not what you told me, I wrote.

Martin tried to step in, saying it was a long time ago now, and that it was a sweet thought of Ella, at only eight or nine.

'Wasn't it?' she said.

You said it was a card because I got detention

'Ah yeah, that'll be it then, like Martin says, long time ago now.'

Did you buy it because I was disabled?

She laughed. 'Oh bloody hell, wish I hadn't brought it up. How did this meeting go about your mental health?'

I found myself reaching for my throat and swallowing as my heart started to race.

She's coming back tomorrow

'Was she helpful?' Her face was fixed with a smile.

Do you feel sorry for me?

Mum tried to jump in this time.

'We all feel very sorry that you're in hospital, in pain.'

Ella, can you go now?

Mum jumped in again, telling me they could all go if I needed to rest. Ella carried on sitting in the chair, looking at them, not me.

No, can you two stay? I want to talk to you about something.

40

#ADMIT

Oliver never existed.

The good thing about a sentence like that – when you're in hospital for suspectedly cutting into your own tongue as an act of self-harm, undergoing a mental health assessment, with a sprained ankle from falling over after going outside naked and pretending to be a witch (not that I confessed to that part) and being pumped with various nutrients because you've been doing such a bad job of looking after yourself – is that the assumption is that you hallucinated Oliver.

I made him up on purpose.

Relief is definitely too strong a word for their reaction, but they were certainly breathing a lot less sharply than before. Not that they didn't have questions, though. They had so, so, so many questions. We sat, they asked, I wrote my answers: short, little sentences that only gave them more questions to ask, but sometimes I couldn't give them what they wanted.

'But I don't understand. You and Ella had a falling out? What did she do?'

It's hard to explain.

They left it there, going on to the practicalities of where the hut was, how long I'd been living there, did they need to tell anyone it was empty? I still had three weeks left until my stay was over, so it wasn't worrying me. I could pick up my things when I got discharged. They asked where I wanted to go after this, with them or back to London. I said I didn't know. The truth was, I wanted to stay in Wales. I didn't want to give it all up but the likelihood was that I had lost my job and I had to start coming to terms with the idea that The Plan was over.

Did you speak to my boss?

They looked at each other, and Martin spoke first.

'I might have had a word.'

They didn't know about my disability

'Yeah, Jackie – is it Jackie? – did seem a bit surprised at that, but it gave me even more reason to threaten them. Failure to perform proper health and safety checks, failure to understand their staff and failure to provide a workplace environment that doesn't lead to self-harm. There's a case there, I'm sure of it.'

It wasn't self-harm

'Well, you might want to think about that actually. Because if the psychiatric report said it was, then that'd really be a case.'

Mum jumped in. 'But we weren't actually serious. We just thought it might be worth making them think about what they've done to you, give you a bit more time off. And then if you leave, it's on your own terms, right? We aren't actually going to sue them.'

Martin slumped in his chair. 'No, no, of course not.'

So what did she say?

'She said she'd have to look into it, and she was meant to be getting a card up to you at some point. She had no idea you were in here. It's best they know.'

Do you think I'll be able to keep the job?

Mum was gathering her things. 'Up to you, love. Do you want it?'

When they had said their goodbyes, told me they loved me and would see me tomorrow, I drew another smiley face and wrote that I loved them too. When I was alone, I hugged that whiteboard.

Despite having a lacerated tongue, I was relieved of the pain in my throat the minute they handed it to me. I thought of being back at work, with all that talking, all the notes, how fast paced it was. I compared it to lying on the sofa back in Devon, using the whiteboard for longer than I had to 'just to be on the safe side'. I gave into the idea, desperate for rest.

I picked up my phone again and flirted with the idea of responding to a few of the messages on the group chat, but it wasn't time for that yet. I'd do it, I knew I'd do it, but just not yet. I clicked on Aiden's name again, and then clicked off it, and back on, in the weird little way I had been doing. Aiden had always had his 'last online' and 'message read' feature turned off, which I found particularly annoying when I was desperate for any kind of interaction, something that made him feel less far away. As I reflected on this, I realised I missed him too much, and that it was going to take some time to get over him. But I would allow myself the chance at one more meeting, even if it was just to end things on a more positive note and give me some closure on the whole thing.

Hi Aiden, it's Hattie. I'm sorry I haven't been in touch. Obviously I haven't been in work, but it's not been because of the stomach bug or my meeting with Jackie or anything. I don't know if you heard from the girls on the desk or anything but I'm actually on the ward as a patient. It's nothing serious, I'll be okay. I've sustained an oral injury –

Who on Earth did I think I was? Sustained an oral injury? *An Oral Injury.* I needed to check my pain meds.

I've accidentally fucked my mouth up so I can't talk, but if you've got time when you're on shift or whatever would be good to see you – I'll be going back to live with my Mum for a bit and pretty sure I won't be coming back, so, yeah. Don't want to leave things on a bad note, be good to say a proper goodbye!

The explanation mark was the best I could come up with, knowing I couldn't put a kiss, but a smiley face looked sarcastic after talking about saying goodbye. I just wanted to clear the air, and leave on okay terms, after hanging up on him and then ignoring him. That wasn't fair of me; I'd overreacted. My heart jumped as another message came in, but it was from Ella.

Is everything okay? Did you have a good chat? Martin offered to pay for me to stay longer in the hotel, work says they'll give me a few extra days as compassionate leave xx

Hey, yeah was good to chat to them. Ahh that's good – but up to you – if you need to get back I understand! X

No I'll stay a bit longer xx

I feel a small jolt of disappointment at the news.

When Ella and I were living together in London, I had met up with Pearl from Eco Society. Pearl had told me that she felt like we never really talk on the group chat, and sometimes felt uncomfortable. She was still part of the group, of course, but she was a mum trying to balance single parenthood and nursing. She lived on the other side of London and never made it when we all went out as a group. I was pleased that we'd manage to find a time to catch up for a child-free coffee.

I had tried to turn the conversation more toward Pearl after that, asking how she was doing and how the nursing was going, but she only gave short answers. Her eyes looked tired.

'Have you ever had anyone come in with a surgical sponge stuck in them?'

She laughed. 'Like your dad, you mean?'

I nodded, eager to hear any details.

'Not as far as I'm aware. You mention that a fair bit, you know?'

'I think about it a lot.'

'You should talk to your mum about it.'

'She doesn't open up like that. Not easily.'

'Do you?' she'd replied, in an instant. I laughed it off, but my heart sank when she finished up and said she better be heading off. I'd rung her a few times after that, but she didn't pick up, and I felt a bit like I might be bothering her.

But being in that hospital, and seeing all the nurses dart around, I imagined Pearl getting home after a shift and picking up Lena from her mum's, and I wished I'd kept calling. I wished we'd carried on that conversation, but for now, all I could do was go over the same words she'd said – 'Do you open up? Do you open up? Do you open up?' – until eventually I opened my mouth wide, stuck my tongue far, far out of my mouth, so the bloody stitched flesh of it was completely on show, and took a picture with my phone. That was it, for the moment. I just took a picture and put my phone on the bedside table.

I looked over the bed to see Ella's 'WITH SYMPATHY' card on the floor, and tried to work out how I should feel, wishing that Aiden would reply. I felt like maybe he'd listen, or at the very least, tell me about the flowers deep in a forest, far away from the hospital.

41

#AIDEN

I dreamt of that forest. The one with the goat willow that Aiden had told me about. Although I didn't know what goat willow was, so I basically dreamt of lots of goats grazing under a thicket of trees. Either way, by morning, I was desperate to hear from him and was gutted I didn't have any messages on my phone.

When the nurse came in the next day to check my blood pressure, she told me I should be able to start speaking again soon. I gave her a thumbs up and held onto my board a little more tightly. When she went to check my ankle, and asked me to move it in circles, there was another groan from a bed next door.

Is it a punctured lung?

She gave me a well-practised, non-committal 'maybe' and went about draining my catheter.

'We'll get this taken out later too, okay. Get you up on your feet again.'

I struggled with her jolly tone. I had been sedated when they put it in and found it difficult to imagine the mechanics of the thing. How far did it go up? Would I have to birth it? Or were they just going to pull it out, like yanking a sock from a dog's mouth? Would the event be ticketed or was it a free for all? I felt like I should have a say in the matter. The urine vampire, seemingly delighted with her loot, left with the promise of seeing me later.

At which point Ella bustled in. I went to write on the board, and hesitated. I thought about speaking, moving my tongue gently in my mouth, and decided to stick to writing.

Was the card because you felt sorry for me?

'I'm not apologising for feeling sorry that you're in hospital.'

The 1st card . . . Year 5

She sighed.

'It was so long ago, Hattie. We were nine.'

I stared at the board for a long time, trying to work out how to say it.

There's a part of you

I started. But paused again. I wanted to tell her that it felt like there was a part of her that pitied me, but when I actually needed help, she wasn't there. I began to write the rest of the sentence, but then I heard the sound of a bed being wheeled into the ward.

'Here you go then, back safe and sound.' The porter was manoeuvring the bed into position. I couldn't be sure, but I didn't want to miss my chance.

Thinking I recognised the voice, I quickly scribbled: *Can you open the curtain?*

'Why? Do you need—'

As I waved my arms about, Ella got up from her seat and pulled the curtain back. For the first time, I saw the other beds, the other patients, but not who I was looking for.

My heart jumped at the flash of orange. It wasn't Aiden; it was Bhavin. I started to write on my board to ask Ella to get him for me because I thought he would know if Aiden was on shift, but he was walking out of the ward too fast.

'Bhavin!'

The word croaked out in a half-shout and my tongue flinched. I tried again.

'Bhavin, come!' As he looked round, I knew I needed to start explaining, and fast, because I currently seemed to be treating him like a dog.

'Hattie – you spoke!' Ella was delighted, but I didn't look at her.

'Where ish Aiden?'

Again, my voice wasn't strong, and my tongue wasn't quite healed, but it was working.

'Hattie, my God, I – er – sorry, what?' he asked, tentatively walking toward the bed, flitting his eyes between me and Ella, who looked bewildered.

'Aiden. Ish he working today?'

'She's not too well . . .' Ella tried to soften his confused expression, but Bhavin stayed focused on me.

'Aiden's on the ward.'

'Can you ashk him to vishit me? Shay it'sh Hattie. Tried to text but no re-sh-pon-sh.'

He walked even closer, next to the bed this time.

'No, no – you don't understand – he's a patient, on the ward – upstairs. Got sepsis.'

I had never said the words 'wheel me to him' before, and I definitely didn't expect to say it over and over again, getting louder and louder before I saw a wheelchair arrive. I'd tried to simply jump up and run to him but nearly fell over with dizziness. Ella was full of questions as I got in the chair, but I ignored her.

'LET'SH GO!' I shouted, triumphantly pointing forward, forgetting that I was holding onto my catheter, and quickly withdrew it from the air as the liquid sloshed in front of me.

'SHTAY-THERE!' I shouted to Ella, and before I knew it, I was being wheeled down the corridor, heading towards him, completely forgetting about the whiteboard and my pen.

42

#GIRAFFE

As Bhavin wheeled me into the ward, I saw that Aiden was sleeping, and a guy about the same age as him – who I quickly discovered to be Wally from security – was sitting by his bed.

Apparently, Aiden had been admitted before me, the day after we spoke on the phone. It turned out his new tattoo had been troubling him for a while but he thought it was just taking some time to heal. In fact, it was infected, and after spending the entire day at work, he went home to his studio flat, dived into bed, and woke up at 2 a.m. with just enough strength to open his front door and call an ambulance. He was collapsed on the floor when they found him, having not made it back into bed after releasing the lock. He'd been wheeled in and luckily, due to a quick diagnosis of sepsis, managed to avoid ICU – just – and the antibiotics were working. He was sleeping a lot, exhausted, but his fever had come down.

He was curled on his side with his hands up to his mouth, the IV antibiotics visible in his hand. I traced the mark my drip had made, and asked Bhavin and Wally if we should come back later, but Wally said he thought he'd like to hear our voices, if only in a dream. When I asked if his family had been called, Wally shook his head, explaining that he was an only child and his father left when he was young.

'His mum . . . his mum isn't too well either,' Wally said tentatively. 'She keeps things. Too many things. Aiden grew up living with old newspapers, hairbrushes, eggboxes, tiny silica gel packets, broken appliances.' I could tell from the way he spoke that Wally must've seen it once, when they were back in college. 'Obviously, he never had anyone round really, but . . .' He paused, 'Trust me, you wouldn't want to live there.'

Wally went on to explain that according to some hearsay, the hoarding had only got worse, starting to spill out into the garden.

'He was so happy to have the space of his own – his new flat – but bloody hell, scary to think what would have happened if he hadn't managed to call an ambulance.'

'Yesh. You're a good mate, to be with him, like thish,' I replied.

Bhavin shifted uneasily and Wally looked at him in the eye, before turning back to me.

'I do what I can.' He shrugged.

There was a heavy silence before Bhavin spoke.

'Yeah, dunno, think we're quite different. Wanna make sure he's okay though. Some of the other porters don't really – yeah – well, just wanted to make sure.'

Bhavin's beeper went for a second time and he said he couldn't ignore it any longer. 'I'll have to take you back,' he said, starting to wheel me away.

'No, no, I'll sh-tay a bit longer, reckon I can wheel myshelf back.'

With little time to argue, he left, and I watched the gentle breaths of Aiden as he stayed sound asleep.

'What wa-sh that about – with Bhavin – about being different and the other porter-sh?' I asked.

Wally sighed. 'Early days on the job, some real twats worked here. Used to confront Aiden in the corridor, threaten him and that. Like playground bullying, but at work. Aiden kind of shrank into himself after. Not that he's ever been the loudest. But yeah.'

My eyes widened and I looked over at Aiden, aware I was on the point of tears.

'I—'

My phone went, with messages from Ella.

The nurse just came to drain your catheter

She not happy

Where are you?

On my way – two seconds

'Aiden, you've got sh-epsh-is and you're fa-sht a-shleep but if you can hear thish then it'sh Hattie and I'll be back to she you later, don't worry if you sh-tart sheeing giraffesh okay I think it'sh normal.'

My voice wobbled on the last sentence. Dad saw giraffes before he died. Trying to 'lick his life away'. I didn't want Aiden to start seeing giraffes. I didn't want the last— my eyes filled with tears and I shook my head as if to get rid of the thought.

'He's gonna be okay, Hattie,' Wally said, gently.

'I know, I know,' I said, unconvincingly.

'Get him something, like a card or chocolates or whatever, for when he wakes up?'

I looked at Wally, feeling a bit confused at this sudden request to buy Aiden a present.

'It's a way of telling the universe, "I believe he's gonna be okay, and you better make sure he is, because I've bought this to give him".' Wally spoke with complete sincerity, and ended with a very self-assured, 'Trust me,' that made me believe that it would work.

'Yeah, okay. Okay I will. To make sh-ure he get-sh better,' I said.

Wally nodded, content, and I wondered for a second if he was, in fact, some sort of shaman. Before I could really consider this, though, Ella was messaging again, insisting that I return.

Just went to look in corridor

Are you coming?

Yes any minute now

?? I can't see you

The words 'hey what else is new?' floated into my head, and with them came a flood of light from a forgotten place, some overgrown corner of myself that seemed out of bounds.

I wasn't in the corridor at all, of course, having stopped at one of those slightly strange hospital card and gift shops. In the store, I spotted a keyring – in the shape of a clunky, badly painted car. It was probably one of the tackiest things I'd ever seen – and would break within minutes of use – but there I was at the till, holding it in my steady, outstretched hand.

43

#TUG

It's not ideal having your catheter removed by a nurse who's annoyed with you. The best scenario would be to have it removed by someone who idolised you and treated your urethra like a passageway to God himself. Instead, the nurse disconnected the tube, 'released the pressure' that was apparently being held by some sort of tiny balloon in my bladder, and then promised me it wasn't going to hurt before yanking it out and, when I winced, admitting that she'd lied.

'Sometimes it's worse when you expect pain.' She shrugged, as she snapped off her plastic gloves. 'Delighted to see you're talking again – I think it's one more session with psych and then we'll do another round of bloods and you should be good to go, since you've decided you can get out of bed now.'

'I needed to help a friend with shepshis,' I said. 'I have a lot of experience with shepshis. It's very sherious.'

'You're not wrong. That's why that tongue needs another check before you go,' she said.

I had put the keyring I bought for Aiden on the bedside table and was going through periods of staring intently at it while silently asking the universe to make sure he was all right.

'He can't die, okay? He needs to get better so I can give him this, okay?'

The idea of getting news that Aiden had suddenly taken a turn for the worse was making me feel sick, and I scrolled through my phone to try and distract myself. As an Instagram reel of a whippet in a yellow raincoat played, I got a message from Mum.

> In the hotel with Ella. She says you're talking now? Need to think about where you want to go when discharged?

I couldn't even fathom it.

When Ava arrived a few minutes later, she found me with the 'WITH SYMPATHY' card sitting exposed on my lap.

'It'sh from Ella,' I said.

Ava looked at the card, the message inside, and the little bit at the end about coming back to London soon.

'But you don't want to go back, do you?' Her eyes were kind, a slight smile on her face.

'No. I had to get away,' I said quietly.

'And why was that?'

Seeing I was finding it hard to speak, she handed me my board.

I wanted to be non-disabled
Because I felt like it was causing all these problems
And whether it was Ella not getting it
Or a stranger adding a stereotype

People weren't seeing the real me

I thought back to all the tiny things Ella had done and how she didn't seem to hear when I tried to talk to her and didn't notice when my voice got croakier and croakier, coming out in a cough, because I was so tired of trying to explain, trying to get her to understand.

'It jusht got too much,' I said.

Ava paused and looked at me again, a gentle, kind expression on her face, but with a focus and depth of thought behind her eyes that held my attention.

'You know why you keep thinking about that sponge, don't you?'

When she saw my eyes fill with tears, she motioned to the board again.

It couldn't speak.

She nodded. I rubbed out the words and carried on.

So no one said, 'You should have told us you were in there'

She wasn't nodding anymore, but staring at me.

I'm tired of telling people that I'm in here.

'Where, Hattie?'

I put the pen down and pressed my hand to my chest.

'Here.'

The word was a small, quiet cry. The cry became a sob that I couldn't stop. She took the board from me and passed me a tissue from the side. Moving her chair closer to me, she said nothing. A trusted witness who saw the wound for what it was, and knew it needed air.

44

#TRY

I had quite a few more sessions with Ava in the hospital. She let me go over everything, right from the beginning. Luckily my voice had quickly returned to something I recognised as my own.

'It's not like I was running away from the past or anything,' I'd said. 'I was running away from the now. The everydayness of it. And then when she chose the party over me that New Year, when I was really, really afraid, I just couldn't do it anymore. But I slept on it. Tried again. And then the next morning, she wouldn't hear it. Didn't want to talk about it. And it just kept going, because even when I was considering ditching The Plan altogether, there was the thing with the pictures.'

'Her reluctance to engage. It's a problem, Hattie.' I nearly started crying again. The acknowledgement of it. After all this time. Ava went on. 'I don't think she's doing all these things to hurt you. I don't think she's a bad person.'

I nodded. 'I know.'

Ava looked at me sternly. 'She doesn't mean to hurt you, but she still is.'

'The trouble is, though, that goes for a lot of other people too. Everyone does stuff like she does, all the strangers on the tube everyday rushing past me, not thinking "there might be someone on this tube with a disability", other friends who don't know how to talk about it. She's my best friend and she knows me the best. She doesn't mean it, but I can't deal with it. So I had to start again and be not disabled so it didn't happen again.'

Ava paused for a minute. 'There's a lot there to talk about. But let's stick with her lack of apology for hurting you. Her lack of wanting to talk about it. If you accidentally step on someone's foot, you might not have meant to, but you hurt them. You should say sorry and try not to do it again.'

I gave a shrug and breathed a loud sigh. 'I don't know what to do.'

'Let's think about that birthday party with the piñata. She helped you then, but she doesn't seem to help you now.'

'No, not so much.' I shrugged.

'Let's pretend every single birthday party she has a piñata. And every single time, you fall.' Ava was thinking it through. 'And then we get to adulthood and she still insists on having the damn thing, even though every time you fall over and get hurt. So every year you have to raise your voice and say, don't spin me round, don't crowd around me please, actually I'm going to sit out this time because . . .' She paused again. 'And at some point, you think, Ella, you know what, maybe you could just not have the piñata. Maybe I don't have to be the one making adaptions and speaking up all the time. Maybe you could think, "actually this piñata isn't that good".' She dismissed it with her hand, as though it was in front of her and she was whacking it away.

'Hmm. Yeah,' I said, despite a part of me wanting to say that on her birthday, you could argue she could do whatever she wants. But I held back and followed along. 'That's a good way of putting it. I don't think she really ever considers my disability. Not properly.'

'But have you actually, fully, clearly sat her down and said that?'

'I try – that's what I mean, I try to say but then . . .' I sighed. 'It gets too painful. She doesn't listen. So I don't.'

'Yeah. I know. I know. But what you need to do, is really clearly say it, and let her think about it. And have the conversation. And if, once you've done that, she still chooses that stupid party game over you – she still doesn't change her ways – then you've got a point here. I think the friendship is going to be tricky to save. But you need to give it that chance.'

45

#BEADS

Another day in the hospital, another session with Ava. She came in as I was fiddling with the keyring for Aiden, doing my little prayer that he was okay. Wally had popped in earlier to tell me he was still improving, and I gave him my number so he could update me if anything went wrong.

'I bought him a gift,' I said proudly, holding up the tacky keyring with pride.

'That's the way,' he'd said, in the same sincere tone that made me sure he was connected to some sort of other world, but asking out loud would have, of course, made me seem deluded.

'What's with the keyring?' Ava asked, as I pressed it into my palm.

'Just a gift thing,' I vaguely answered, putting it down.

Somehow, Ava instinctively knew when to push, and when to let me have my secrets. She changed the subject, announcing we were going somewhere different for this session.

'This could well be our last little meet up,' she said, as we walked down the corridor. 'You're doing pretty well physically, huh? They're keen to get you discharged. But I need to write my report.'

'Will the report say that I am, undoubtably, The Best?' I asked.

'Potentially. Can't say for sure though.' She smiled, and we turned the corner towards the children's hospital playroom.

'Ava, honestly. I'm nearly thirty.'

'Now is not the time to worry about looking cool,' she said, gesturing at the hospital gown and my unwashed hair.

It was a fairly basic room, with small tables dotted around, some books, a few toy blocks and bean bags in the middle. The walls were filled with drawings, a big tissue paper forest on one with colourings of all the different animals that might be living there. In the corner, there were some kids playing with puzzles, by which I mean throwing the pieces as far as they could across the room. In the opposite corner, Ava waited by a tiny table with a box of beads in the middle. She helped me down onto my seat.

The minute I looked in the box, I found I was crying again. I seemed to be doing a lot of crying since I put scissors in my mouth. Who would have thought?

I'd told her the thing about imagining tiny embryo-me, in the womb, stringing my chromosomes together like beads.

'One part of one of my chromosomes ... I can't remember which now, is duplicated,' I said. I took one of the red strings out of the tangle in the box and started threading beads on, all different colours, and then put two yellows on, breaking the pattern. 'So it's like this. But I didn't realise I'd made the mistake.'

Ava laughed kindly and tied the string into a sort of necklace for me.

'I like it,' she said. 'Only, *you* didn't actually make the mistake, did you?'

'Well no, I . . .' I looked at her, more tears forming in my eyes. 'I guess I didn't.'

Ava took a new string and started twisting it so a knot formed in the centre. 'So this idea you had, to start somewhere new?'

'I was going to be able-bodied. But then I couldn't hide, and people started thinking I was lazy, or bad at my job, but I couldn't risk them finding out the truth and going through everything I'd gone through in London again, and then, it was starting to get obvious, so I had to back away, but it was too late and I made too many mistakes.'

'You blame yourself a fair bit,' she said. 'When you get discharged I want you to find a therapist and work with them. Because there are definitely some things you need to look at. Like wanting to live as an able-bodied person? I do get it. You did it because of how people were treating you. But there are some real problems with that kind of thinking. It's not intrinsically better to be able-bodied, you know?'

I knew she had a point, and I felt the strangling sensation of guilt around my stomach. 'I just . . . didn't know what else to do.'

How had I got it all so wrong?

'Like I say. Another therapist. Long term work. Not just about all this, either. I have a sneaking suspicion you need someone to help you think about your dad, too.'

I found myself unable to keep looking at her at this point and focused on a piece of fluff on the carpet. She let me off the hook.

'But not now, and not with me. A different time. What I do want to say to you, though, is the world has done you a disservice, and made you feel less than. Made you think things about yourself that aren't true. Like how you're the problem that needs changing. It's bullshit, Hattie.' She reached her hand out toward mine, and I looked up at her.

She paused and looked around the room. 'Did you ever come to playrooms like this, when you were a kid?'

'Maybe sometimes. It's not what I remember though. I remember waiting rooms, and things I thought were games, but were actually just ways to monitor me.' I thought about the time they painted my feet and asked me to walk along a long sheet of paper.

'Sneaky bastards,' she said, digging in the box for more beads. 'So what do you think they're doing?' she said, gesturing over to the kids.

'Playing?' I said blankly. A little girl made a swooshing noise as she chucked another puzzle piece.

'Sure. I think they're also kind of pissed, probably, because they are in hospital, and that's boring and shit.'

I gave her the same blank look.

'You could do with a bit more of that, couldn't you? Being comfortable with feeling angry, letting it out in little bits, rather than keeping it inside until it all comes out?'

'As a kid I wasn't really allowed to be angry. Mum would say, "we don't do anger here". So I don't really know what to do with it. Because my mum didn't know what to do with it.'

'It's an important emotion. Gotta feel it. Own it.'

I took one of the beads out of the box and threw it on the

floor. The kids looked up at me for a second and then went back to their own game. Ava laughed gently.

'It's going to take a bit more than that. But do tell your therapist about all the breakages, you know? How it gets so intense you just let it out in a scream or smash something up. It's important.'

'It's embarrassing.'

'That's the point.'

I threw another bead on the floor but she didn't laugh this time.

'Okay. I promise. I'll tell my new therapist.'

'Good. Right, so, let's just think about everything that's gone on. It's like this.' She put beads on the string up to the halfway knot. 'This is everything that happened until you enacted The Plan. Your chromosomes, you being born, your dad, your mum, you breaking your leg, going to school, past therapists, that night in the club . . . Everything. And you can't change it because look, the knot has been tied on that string. The beginning has already been.'

The kids in the corner continued to throw bits of puzzle out into the room, but I could hardly hear them. I was so focused on Ava and her calm voice.

'So we say, okay, it's happened.'

I nodded.

She rooted around in the box and gave a satisfied smile when she found a broken bead.

'But what you did with The Plan . . . you decided to edit out a part of yourself, like breaking a bead and only using a part of it. No matter how hard you try, it's going to fall off the string. So it's going to be hard to really, truly, fully live your life.'

She held up the string, beads on one end, nothing on the other.

'But being whole … being the whole of me … it wasn't working.'

'I know that's how it felt. You tried to adapt. You were told you were the problem, that you were too slow, not strong enough, so you chipped away at yourself, contorted yourself into a whole new shape. There was never anything wrong with you, but being told you were broken? That's what made you break.'

I was crying again.

'And why shouldn't other people change their ideas, be more inclusive, instead of you adapting your entire life?'

I had given up trying to wipe my face; the tears weren't stopping.

'So instead, you can say: from now on, it's all of me.' She put more beads on in a different order. 'And that does mean a lot of work from you, because you need to keep talking, and not just shut down, but it also means realising when you deserve better, and knowing you are right to ask for some very basic needs to be met, like feeling safe. Feeling listened to. Feeling seen.'

She stopped threading the beads and asked me if I understood what she was saying.

'Well, bit patronising isn't it, explaining it with beads.' I could only hold my mock-serious face for so long before laughing, and Ava laughed too.

'I don't know whether to stay in Wales or just pack up and go live with my parents for a bit.'

'Well, you still need to recover. But after that, your life, your beads.'

'I wish you could be my therapist forever,' I said.

'Nah you don't. That'd mean you'd be here forever. And that's not what you're going to do, is it? Because,' she said, pointing again at the string, 'you've got more things to do. And it's all out there, Hattie.' She smiled. 'Now, like you said, you're nearly thirty, what are we doing in the children's playroom?'

She helped me up from my seat. As we started to leave, one of the kids, a little girl with her arm in plaster and a lilac dress on, shyly came over to the table, and picked up the necklace I'd made at the beginning of the session.

'All yours,' I said, as she looked a little worried she might be doing the wrong thing.

'I love it!' she replied. With those two yellow beads sitting next to each other and disrupting the pattern, she gleefully put it around her neck, and went back to throwing pieces of a puzzle.

46

#FREE

The rain set in heavily overnight, pattering loudly on the single-glazed window of the ward. There wasn't the usual sound of snoring coming from the bed across from me, so I assumed they must be awake too, staring at the ceiling of their little blue curtained chamber, wondering how much longer it would be before the dawn.

By the time I got debriefed by the discharge nurse, I had been awake for hours. Ava had referred me to a psychologist and advised regular sessions going forward. I was also to have a conversation with my GP about medication.

'Is it on my notes as self-harm?'

'Er – according to the report – an accident.' I smiled. 'Oh, for your discharge – I have to put where you're going to?'

I thought of being curled up in the spare room in Devon, with my hands all cosy, blanket up to my face.

'The same as my parents. But keep my GP as here, for now.'

While I waited for all the admin to be completed, Ava came to visit me one last time.

'No session today, don't worry,' she reassured me. 'I just wanted to give you this.'

She handed me a white card and, before I could open it, put her hand on mine.

'You've got a lot of work to do, you know?' Her tone was serious. 'You can't just shut down and not talk to people. We aren't mind readers, you know?' She was almost telling me off. 'If someone asks you how you're feeling, or what's happening, you have to tell them. Especially if you're feeling angry, you have to try and explain why, and back yourself that you have a right to express it.'

I nodded. She was right, of course. I wasn't sure how I was going to do it, but she was right. I stared at her and nearly started crying again.

'You can do it, Hattie,' she said, as though she *had* just read my mind.

And then she was gone, drawing back the curtain as a feeble 'thank you' shook itself into the air.

I looked at the card, another 'WITH SYMPATHY', but Ava had added an '^OUT' in black biro between the words. As the nurse came in with my completed paperwork, I opened the card.

. . . Just respect.

X

47

#TONGUE

Martin

Paperwork done, I'm free to go

Just having lunch, then we'll be with you

Brill

BTW I never got a card from Jackie

What exactly did you say to her

I know you were just trying to help

But have you made things worse

Did you want to get your job back then?

I want to know if it's an option

Leave it with me

No – don't do anything else!

I can talk to her

Mum

Can you tell Martin to leave things with Jackie?

Mum??

Our Son Mr Jonathan

PETE: GUYS

Mum

[Missed Voice Call from Hattie]

Mum please

Our Son Mr Jonathan

PETE: Mr Jonathan is dead

BEA: WHAT

GEORGIA: NO

Mum

Sorry love he's on the phone at the mo

Martin

You better not be calling Jackie

Our Son Mr Jonathan

PETE: He drowned, apparently

BEA: How can a penguin drown?

GEORGIA: Did the zoo call you?

Martin

All sorted

!! What does that mean?

Mum

He says it's all sorted x

What??

He says he'll explain when he sees you in a minute! Xx

Martin

Trust me

Jackie

Hi Hattie. I'm so sorry to hear you've been unwell. Was going to come and see you but didn't want you to feel pressured. Can we have a chat when you're feeling better? Would like to talk about your return to work.

Our Son Mr Jonathan

PETE: Yeah just now

SAM: Hahahaaa I can't believe you fell for that

PETE: What?

SAM: Was winding you up

PETE: SAM

OH MY GOD

Why would you LIE LIKE THAT

GEORGIA: OMG I was genuinely sad for the penguin

I clicked off the chat and looked at the picture I had taken of my tongue. It made me feel a little sick, and for a moment, I clicked back off it again and found myself clicking on Aiden's WhatsApp picture. There he was, smiling away in a forest. I hadn't heard from Wally, which meant all was still okay, and I was still doing my daily wishes to the universe. I knew that what Aiden needed more than anything was rest, but a part of me wished he would message me, just so I could hear from him, and feel a little more certain he was all right.

I wanted to hear from him so much more than I wanted to hear from Our Son Mr Jonathan. The penguin joke was kind of the epitome of it all – nothing was real on there. Lately, I'd been contributing to that, big time. I didn't want to carry on like that, and if they didn't want to hear about what was really going on, well, what was the point? I clicked back on the image of my tongue, and with a surge of adrenaline, hit share.

Our Son Mr Jonathan

I didn't just 'hurt' my tongue

I cut it

with scissors

and it looked

like this

The picture was worse than I remembered. All that sore flesh and blood. I had never posted something so raw, so clearly not a joke, on Our Son Mr Jonathan and, despite the pulpy horror of the image, it felt so, so good. It felt like, for once, I wasn't editing anything out.

48

#AWAKE

Wally

> Aiden much better. Still sleeping a lot, but reckon he'd definitely be with it enough to get your gift, if you came up to see him? Am off home now.

Mum had bought me some clothes, something that I could wear out of the hospital and back to the hut, where I could pack up. Ella came with them when I got discharged.

'Um. That picture you sent. What was that?' She was speaking gently, clearly horrified at what I'd done.

'I took it a while ago. It's healed now,' I said, obviously dodging the question. I knew she was desperate to ask where I would be living after spending some time with Mum and Martin, but I fielded all questions with a simple 'one step at a time, eh?'

Progress was going to be slow. I had more of an idea of what to say to Ella, and a way of moving forward, but I hadn't quite worked it all out in my head yet. She left for her train back to

London with a big hug, and I thanked her again for getting me to the hospital, for staying, for everything she'd done.

'You'll be better in no time,' she said, looking at me with her head at a slight tilt.

'Well, like I said – it's small steps.' I could feel my body tensing as I spoke, but I managed to get the words out, to reiterate that this wasn't going to happen quickly.

She smiled, but it looked forced, as though she wanted to say something else, but had decided not to. 'Text me soon, okay?'

I nodded and she turned, leaving the hospital ward with the door swinging behind her.

'You good to get in the car then?' Mum asked.

I paused, thinking about the text from Wally.

'Are you two okay to get a coffee?'

'Always. But I thought you were ready?'

I walked slowly along the corridor on the way to Aiden's ward. I'd been given a stick after a few practice walks up and down the corridor had been slow as I still felt a bit dizzy. Mum was keen to go with me to the ward but I said I'd be okay, promising to call her if I needed anything. My tongue was almost back to normal, but I would still be on soft foods for a little while and my ankle only twinged slightly if I put too much weight on it.

The strip lighting blinked as I stood outside the lift, and after making it to the upper floor, I passed some more terrible poetry, and then a hospital map just before Aiden's ward. Suddenly, the thought that he might be awake made me incredibly interested in the location of every fire exit in the building. When I went through the doors and saw him at once, sitting up in bed, I thought about turning around. I could just text, go and live in Devon for a bit, see how it goes. I could thank Jackie for the offer to chat but turn it down. But then, of course, he saw me and gave a little wave, and there I was walking over to him. He was skinnier than before, having lost a fair bit of weight, but his smile was just the same, and I was relieved to see life in those verdant green eyes of his, even if they looked more tired than usual.

I opened with a long monologue of questions, asking if he had this symptom or that symptom and did he think he was going to die at the time and were the paramedics nice to him and did they give him drugs that made everybody have a balloon for a head and what about the giraffes did he see the giraffes? And had the infection cleared and was he eating and did they take regular bloods or did he think they were fobbing him off a bit because they do need to take regular bloods with something as serious as—

He joined in on the last one: '. . . sepsis. I know, I know.'

I sat down on the chair by the bed and handed him the keyring, suddenly wanting to play it cool but feeling embarrassed about getting it because I thought Wally was connected to a magical realm and I wanted Aiden to live so much I thought I'd do whatever I could to make sure that happened.

'This is from the hospital gift shop. It's gross I know, but it's a car, like when we moved the man's car.'

There was a pause.

He nodded a calm 'appreciate it' and we did an awkward fist bump.

He hadn't got my text; it turned out his phone was still in his flat and Wally had sorted out everything with work while he was admitted.

'Told me you were in here and all – hurt your tongue or something?'

'Yeah, I actually – do you know what? It's a long story. But I'm slowly on the mend.'

I explained I was actually just leaving, and we chatted small nothings about the hospital food, sick leave, the weather in Devon. The sunlight came in through the windows and Aiden talked about how much he was missing being outside, even just for a little bit each day, because he likes to feel the weather on his skin and look at the sky, see the birds. It was a quiet conversation; he didn't have the same energy as before or the same stories brimming in his chest. The phone rang out at the nurses' station and was answered quickly. We listened to the conversation as though we were waiting for her to finish, when in truth we could have talked at any moment. When it did end, the agony of the silence between us was enough to make me habitually check my phone, even though I had been avoiding it since my message on the group chat. The messages had flooded in, but I'd swiped them away.

'I need to be going soon. I just wanted to see you, you know?' I said.

'Yeah, good . . . are we good . . . about . . .' He looked so tired.

I stood up to leave, knowing that all he really wanted was for me to nod, say, 'yeah, yeah all good,' and go. But a sadness trembled through me and I didn't want to hide it from him anymore.

'. . . you could have given me a chance, is all.' I took a deep breath in but it fractured and a tear ran and hesitated on the brink of my chin. I should have just left it. I didn't mean to come here and talk about that. I felt like I shouldn't have come to see him at all.

He went to move towards me but his antibiotic line snagged on the bed and he juddered back.

I reached over to the keyring. 'Sorry. That was— you probably don't want this either, actually.' I picked it up and wiped my face.

'Yeah, I don't like it, to be fair,' he said with a smile, but I didn't feel like laughing.

'Cool. Well then.'

'I don't—' he started.

'No, no, it's okay. I know.' I could just start again in Devon.

'Because I don't fancy—'

This was getting agonising. Why was he still talking?

'There's really no need to ram it home, mate.' I gave a nod and a small wave to try and leave on a neutral note.

'Fancy anybody. Ever. It's not . . . I'm not . . .'

His cool exterior had vanished. Sweat was starting to glisten on his temple. I took a step toward the chair and tried to soften my expression.

'. . . designed . . . like, some people just don't ever want to have anything like that with anyone, and I'm one of those type of people. I think. I mean, I know. But I . . .'

'It's okay. Go on,' I said.

'It's just hard to know how people are going to react. I don't think many of the guys I work with, well, it's all quite, who pulled who, you know? And they don't really like that I don't join in, but I'm just not interested in it. At all. In sex or romance or any of it and I try to just not talk about it or I just change the subject. Because I know I'm just going to get, you know, shock or misunderstanding, calling me Virgin Boy, and I can't be dealing with that. I've been there before and I'm not going there with lads I don't even like that much anyway. And like, Bhavin's fine but he's not like *you*, not like you're a mate, like a proper one, that I care about loads. And I hope we're okay, Hattie, because I really do like you and it's going to suck if just because I don't feel one subset of feelings we can't see each other at all, because it is love that I feel for you, like proper friendship love which is a real thing, properly.'

And I could see it, then, in his eyes, the gravity of what he was saying, the amount he meant that he did, truly, love me.

The Game was well and truly over. Call myself a good guesser? Didn't see that coming at all. And why not? Why could I see a bald lady in a wheelchair and decide she's having chemo for arthritis rather than cancer, correctly guess a broken arm from tripping over a hoover, but I couldn't see Aiden's lack of romantic interest in me as anything but a personal, specific, disability-related rejection. Why did I not even consider that he could be asexual?

'Man,' I said. 'So, what you're saying is – you just, really, really don't like the keyring?'

His laugh was like a window opening, a fresh breeze coming in from outside, allowing me to breathe.

49

#BACK

As Mum and Martin pulled up next to my car, which was parked a short walk away from the hut, I felt a little bit like I was a murderer taking the police to where I'd hidden the body. I was hoping they would leave me to it, let me go to the hut by myself, but I still had my walking stick and was noticeably unsteady on the ground. There was little conversation on the walk there, apart from when I pointed it out as we rounded the bend, and Mum gave a very weak 'lovely'.

I managed to convince them to stay in the field while I sorted the worst of it out. Thank God it wasn't raining; it was another bright day and birdsong filled the air. I pointed weakly to the woods – I wanted to tell them how calm it had once felt under the canopy of the trees, how I knew it didn't look like it now, but for a while the plan really was working, and I was doing pretty well in my little incubator by the hills. But it was too difficult to try and convey, so I just said how nice it was in the trees and that they could take a walk if they wanted. They both said they'd stay in the field, clearly reluctant to leave me.

I slowly made my way up the steps, stick in hand, and

unlocked the door, holding the key turner tightly. The smell of mould coming from the unwashed dishes, the bag of rubbish I never took out and a damp towel on the bathroom floor was overwhelming. It looked smaller than I remembered, too. I started by gathering up the clothes that flooded the floor and heaving them into the suitcase, not bothering to check what was dirty or clean because everything that had been sitting in there needed to be washed, twice.

I turned the tap to its fullest to try and speed the washing-up along, but all I managed to do was soak my t-shirt when I whacked a spoon under the faucet in the hope of power-washing it free of baked beans. The gentle knock that came twenty minutes later was inevitable.

As she came inside, Mum didn't make any comment. She just got on with the job in hand. Even when she stripped the bed to find the photo of Dad, she paused for a minute, and then just quietly put it on the table.

'Don't forget this, eh?' she said gently.

'I never could, Mum,' I replied, in what had meant to come out as a sweet sentiment but instead sounded irritated. I didn't mean it to. 'I meant that, like—' I tried to explain as I tucked it in the front pocket of my suitcase.

'Let's just finish up and get out of here,' she interrupted, with the same gentleness as before.

I sprayed the bathroom with the cleaner under the sink, leaving water marks with every hurried swipe of the cloth. I came out and shut the door behind me, announcing it was done.

By the time Mum dragged the suitcase outside the door and took it down the steps, waiting at the bottom with her hand outstretched, I could feel my body aching for sleep. I almost didn't notice what Martin was playing an imaginary game of rounders with, assuming he'd picked up a fallen tree branch from the bottom of the field.

'Strange-looking thing, isn't it?' he mused, as he turned it over in his hands.

I stared at the chair leg for a second. I didn't tell them what it was and I imagined that the scissors had been dragged away by some fox, thirsty from the smell of blood. I feigned curiosity and asked to see it. I ran my fingers over the marks as traces of dirt rubbed onto my fingers.

'Take it with us?' he asked, walking forward in the direction of the car.

Ideally, I would have dropped it on the ground and announced I was glad to be leaving. Ideally. I spent most of the journey running my hand over the dents in the wood.

Back home, the messages on the group chat were filling up – I hadn't looked at it since I sent the picture. Ella had tried to ring twice and had texted asking if I was going to respond to them. I hadn't even replied to Jackie yet. I just wanted to do two things: sleep and lie awake with my eyes closed. Mum tried to convince me to spend the day sitting in the lounge, even just watching the telly, just so I could get out of bed. When an old episode of *24 Hours in A&E* came on, I turned it off and put the blanket all the way over my head.

Mum and Martin had bought the house in Devon when I went to uni – a new start by the coast, they'd said – and coming back I felt like I was back to being a student, returning home completely exhausted with a load of work to do. Back then, life was just getting started; there was so much still to see and so many people to meet. But underneath all that promise was a gnawing sense of doubt. 'Where will I be, and what will I do?' I used to think, especially as I headed toward my final year. That was nearly ten years ago and I was still asking myself the same questions. How had I done it all so wrong?

I kept looking at my phone, but there was nothing I wanted to reply to. I wished I'd gone and got Aiden's phone for him – or asked Wally to get it. I thought about calling the hospital to check if he was okay. I pressed the number into my phone a few times, but never dialled.

Ella ended up calling Mum in the end to check I was okay. She told her I was asleep, even though I was wide awake, lying in my room with the door open.

'Thought you might need a bit more space, eh love?' she said after hanging up the call. 'And that looks nice, there.'

It was sweet of her to say it, even though she didn't like that picture of Dad in the hospital bed, and probably didn't particularly understand why I'd put it in a frame on my bedside cabinet. A part of me didn't really understand why I'd done it either, and I thought back to Ava telling me I probably needed to talk to my new therapist about it. She was almost certainly right, yet again. But that wasn't a task for today, or any time soon.

That day, it was enough that I managed to say, 'Thanks, Mum,' without any weird annoyance coming into my voice, and give her a hug.

It was late when Martin went up in the loft; I didn't recognise the sound at first. I slowly opened my bedroom door to see the ladder on the landing, the creaking floorboards getting louder.

I'd been sitting for hours staring out of the window, watching the day go dark. There was a small patch of grass outside their house, but it was coarse, not the same type of green as in Wales. It was like the salt in the air had grazed each strand. Although being so close to the beach, the view was actually a little closed in; the quiet road and the bungalow next door, white pebble-dash with the roof stained with seagull droppings.

I left my door ajar and watched Martin come down from the loft a few minutes later, carrying two big plastic bags, and then go back up again to bring down a box. He saw me watching just as he put the ladder back. The lamplight from my bedroom creeped toward him, meeting the edges of the light from the hall, a soft dark shadow between them.

'Did I wake you?' he said, worried. I shook my head as he picked up the bags.

'It's all your old schoolwork, thought you might like to look?'

Mum came out onto the landing as he spoke, and I sat with them in my room as we went through the box: English exercise books full of hilariously bad stories, unfinished maths homework and (in my opinion) harsh school report cards, particularly for geography. When all our cups of tea had been drunk and most of the box had been emptied, I looked for the bags. Martin had left them on the landing and seemed reluctant when I asked for them.

'I don't know if it'll . . . it might be a bit late,' he said.

I ignored him, not quite understanding the warning. As soon as I approached the bags, I realised what they were, and stopped.

'Did you keep it?' I said, standing still.

'Yes, love,' Mum replied softly.

I hadn't looked at those canvases since the day of the art exam. I carried the bags back to my room. Mum and Martin followed, and as I sat on my bed, they perched on the window-sill to the right of me, watching tentatively.

'I thought they'd gone in the bin.'

'That's where you wanted them, but you know, it was your final exam, you'd worked so hard, I couldn't just leave them at school to be thrown away. I think your teacher was quite pleased I'd gone to pick them up,' said Mum.

One by one, I pulled each canvas out of the bag and laid it on the cream carpet of my room. Then, when usually we would all have been asleep, we sat together to see that body recreated, complete with the middle canvas, stained, smudged and broken. We had never sat staring at anger for such a long time. It wasn't what we did in our house.

'I can't believe you kept it,' I said. 'I mean, I put my foot through it.'

'I know,' said Mum. 'But your foot is a nice foot.' She had meant it as a sort of joke, but as I looked at the way it had broken through that fabric, in a way you could never recreate, I felt like she was right.

'Do you remember, at the hospital, they made you walk in paint once? To see the arches on your feet?' Mum said.

It came back to me – the chill of the green paint between my toes, the way it had been sold to me as a game, but then the doctors started to furrow their brows and measure the splodges. It didn't feel like a game then, and I'd wanted them to stop. I'd sat there silently as Mum used wet paper towels to clean me up and put my socks back on.

'I'd wanted to take that home at the time. But the doctors

wouldn't let me, said it was for them. But this? This is much better. It's the action of it, not the mark left behind. Yeah, my girl's got a kick to her.' She smiled and did a little wink.

'I wish you'd told me that at the time,' I said, sadly. 'I felt so guilty. Every time I was angry, it was, "we don't do anger here" and I—'

'It's because your dad said, towards the end, "don't be angry at what's happened".' Her fingers were knitted together tightly in her lap, her eyes dewy.

I looked at her, astonished.

'I never told you that though, did I? I sort of— I accidentally changed it into something else – I realise that now. At the time I felt like I was keeping the promise to your dad, but that's not even what your dad meant, he meant that we shouldn't be bitter at the bad luck of losing him. I was just trying to think of him, too, as a parent, but instead I just told you, accidentally, to keep your feelings inside. I hope this isn't why— I've been so worried – racking my brains since you mentioned it in the hospital – is this why you did what you did? Is it my fault, love?'

'No, no, Mum,' I said, with a tear falling down my cheek. 'It's not . . .' I took a deep breath. '. . . the point is, from now – maybe we can all express ourselves a bit more?'

Martin put his arm round Mum and she wiped the tears from her eyes. I looked at the canvas on the floor again, still amazed at their reaction, and stepped over the squares to join them.

50

#BEACH

It was a whole week before I set foot outside the house and made it on to the beach.

'Hey body, we're gonna try a walk, okay?'

It was a bleak day for August, spitting rain that flicked onto the waves. I'd managed to buy some chips from the shop on the high street but they were unappealingly lukewarm. My hair kept getting in my mouth and caught a glob of ketchup as I was trying to eat, which then stuck to my cheek. It was early, and due to the weather, there was hardly anyone else about, just a dog walker in the far distance, hood up to avoid the rain. The sea was the same grey as the sky; the curve of waves mirrored the clouds.

I knew I needed to look at my phone and work out what I was going to do. Replying to people had started to seem like a possibility, so I found a little place to sit: a hollowed-out part of the cliff with a ledge that saved me from having to stand. I took my phone from my pocket, only to see that it was ringing, on silent. Aiden. My heart quickened.

'Hello you,' I answered.

'Hey mate!'

He had more energy in his voice, and he said he was pleased to be out of hospital and back in his flat. The rumbling noise of his tumble dryer in the background was loud enough to distract me from our chat. He told me how much he loved taking hot sheets out of the dryer and pulling them up over his head, then pointed out I was hardly speaking from a 'specialist sound recording studio' myself.

'It's the seagulls.'

'Noisy sods, aren't they. Like geese. Did I tell you about the geese? That's my tattoo – geese flying.'

I nodded and said 'hmm' every now and again, secretly thinking that sounded like a bit of a shit tattoo. Definitely not worth the trouble.

He started telling me about the events leading up to his admission to hospital, and I felt nervous at hearing how close he'd come to not making it to medical help in time.

'I just thought, you know, there's doctors here, if I look that ill, they'd tell me.'

'What?' Seagulls squawked in the sky above, but as the noise faded, I tried to grapple with what he'd just said.

'I said, I felt rough, but you know, I work at a hospital, a doctor would tell me if I looked too serious.'

I flew into my response. 'You went into work, while feeling awful, and just assumed they'd notice you were secretly battling a raging infection, rather than just telling them you felt like shit?'

'No, well I did go and see my GP a few days before but they reckoned it was okay, so I left it, although it did kill.'

'So at work, you didn't think of asking one of them for a second opinion? You just thought they'd be able to guess? Why didn't you just say it out loud?'

When I heard myself say it, the realisation came in a small but audible laugh.

'I mean, fuck it,' I said, throwing the chips onto the sand and letting the seagulls have them.

'Wait, why you are laughing?'

I caught my breath enough to speak.

'I cut my tongue,' I said. 'I cut my tongue with a pair of scissors. Can you believe that?'

There was a pause on the end of the line.

'Jesus.'

'And even Ava,' I was shaking my head in disbelief, 'she said it, you know, that I do still have to speak. To tell people things. People can't read minds. And I thought, well yeah, but how? Like I got it intellectually but I didn't *get it* get it – and then I literally just said it to you.'

I emerged from the shallow cave and started heading towards the promenade, scattered with uncharacteristically empty benches for the season, a couple of food stalls open, but quiet, hopeful with chalked offers written on their board. I did a slight skip as I walked.

'God, hypocrite! Ava was bang on,' I said. 'You can't just give up on communicating and hope everyone will see. It's true that you should have told them again and again *and* it's true that they should have taken you seriously in the first place. That GP did let you down, that's shit. God. Mate. Isn't it all so hard?'

A pause from Aiden. 'Right, yeah. Sorry. Who's Ava? Can you explain?'

And with the slightest resistance in my throat, sitting on the promenade looking out at that August beach as seagulls dove down into the sand, I did just that.

51

#CUPBOARD

I spent a month in Devon in the end: the period of time agreed by my GP and me for my extended sick leave. After that, I'd talk to Jackie about a phased return to work and hopefully start my therapy. In terms of my recovery's trajectory, it was hard to convince Mum and Martin that I was feeling a lot better while spending a lot of time sending messages and making phone calls in the cupboard under the sink. I'd crawled in there the day after I spoke to Aiden, instinctively yearning to find somewhere similar to the hollowed-out part of the cliff, but not having the energy to make it out to the beach every day. I told myself I would send a message to the group chat while in the cupboard, and as I crawled in, and found it to be small and contained, it seemed doable. Then I would leave my phone in there and check it again at the end of the day. It was my communication cupboard; it had walls and limitations. Structure. I could shut the door on it.

'I knew a lady who came into A&E wearing a flipper,' I said, when Martin tried to get his head round it. 'It's just a thing I have to do so I can do the thing I have to do.'

He smiled politely.

I opened the group chat and scrolled up to see the messages that came after the photo of my tongue. Everybody was obviously confused. Confused and alarmed. There were a lot of questions. But after that, there had been nothing. A silence yawned open as they waited for me to explain. In that cupboard, on that day, I felt like I could.

Our Son Mr Jonathan

That was the truth of the situation

The very gross truth

I've been lying a lot

But that was the truth

SAM: Hey it's okay as long as you are okay?

GEORGIA: It was very very gross

BEA: Still don't really understand but yeah hope you're okay

And then, a private message from Pearl.

Hey girl.

Saw your message on the group chat. Almost felt inspired to send a picture of Lena's bloody knee from where she fell over (again) today!

Secondly: That's quite the wound. Did you want to chat?

Hahahaa!

I'd love to chat, but not yet.

Of course, whenever.

If I don't pick up I'll try and ring back

We'll find a time xx

And I really, really meant it. Because I hadn't been a good friend to her, assuming when she didn't pick up that she was too busy. But just because she's busy shouldn't mean I should give up on the friendship. I was going to do better there. Much better.

Then it was silent. The phone stayed in the cupboard all day, and when I went back to check on it in the evening, there were no new messages. But the next morning, someone had sent a meme and said it reminded them of Friday night, and I didn't get the context. They'd moved on. It was time to message Ella.

It wasn't one big conversation. I didn't roll out of the cupboard in tears after a great long chat about everything. Some days when I spoke to her, I tucked myself into a ball, other days I sat with one leg hanging out onto the kitchen floor. Mum and Martin moved the kettle into their bedroom. For the first few conversations, she wanted me to explain why I wasn't coming back to London. I told her that I was excited for the new start, and Aiden had been a good friend.

'There's lots of things we get about each other,' I remember saying, which made her go quiet. 'And that sort of leads me on to why I left.'

She started by saying that we'd already been through it, and she didn't want to go over old ground. I said there was actually a lot of new ground to cover, but we could save it for another time? She agreed and seemed surprised that I decided 'another time' meant the next time I called her, a day later.

I started by tackling New Year.

'You knew all those people were going to be pushing me. And I told you it wasn't safe. I was terrified. And you say you didn't hear me, but the next day, I mean, you didn't even apologise.'

'I just . . .' She paused. 'Like I know it was crowded in there but I didn't think it was that bad, and maybe you were just feeling worried. But I didn't hear you say that we absolutely had to leave, or that you were terrified. And I wanted to enjoy New Year.'

'But do you see the problem now?' My hand found its way up to my throat again.

'I do. I just think it's tough, like – you say you want to go, but maybe I don't want to and I don't know why I have to do what you say every time, if I'm honest. But I think you'll agree that . . . that I do help you out a lot. Probably more than most people would. Like I said to you before, I was there for you every morning we went to work together, even though we always missed the tube because you're slower on the stairs and it made us late, so then we started leaving earlier, and like, I could have just had a lie-in, you know, but I didn't, I was there with you and I'm not sure you even realise all the things I did to help?'

My throat burned and my eyes welled up with tears. I said I needed to go. But the next day, I tried again. I tried telling her it feels, sometimes, like she thinks she's an angel for being friends with a disabled person. That it feels like she doesn't want to talk or be challenged on anything. She didn't want to understand me better as we grew up. She feels sorry for me in an abstract, patronising way, rather than really seeing the things I find difficult, having empathy and helping find solutions. I told her that trying to talk to someone who doesn't want to hear it is exhausting.

She said I'd got it wrong. Said she thought I was amazing, so inspiring, and I said it made me feel uncomfortable to hear that word, because I was just living my life, she shouldn't feel inspired by that. I suggested she read a bit more about the problem of the word. She said that surely I knew she meant it in a nice way, I said that I did, and that was the end of that particular call.

Another time she said she knew it was suspicious, the whole Oliver thing, and I asked her if that was because there's a part of her that doesn't believe a boy would want to be with me. She sighed at that, said of course not, and asked me when I was starting therapy. She said she knows I'm going through a hard time. I said it's okay if she doesn't want to be friends any more, after what I did, she said she still wants to be friends. I didn't know how I felt about that, but I just told her she could change her mind whenever.

'We aren't tied to each other, you know?' I'd said.

Another time, I asked her to google some stereotypes around disability and she scoffed at the suggestion.

'I know you, Hattie. I know you better than you probably know yourself.'

'Ella.' I hesitated. 'I don't think you do.'

After a long silence, she sighed and said she'd do a google if I really thought it would help. I thanked her and said I knew it was hard to have so many conversations around the same subject.

When she called again the next day, I thought perhaps she'd done the googling, but instead she just wanted to gossip about Gareth. We talked about the salon for the rest of that call. On another call, she said she found it hard to trust me now, after all the lies. I said I understood that, and apologised for the way I went about things. I thanked her again for getting me to the hospital.

On the last call from under the sink, she asked when we could just go back to talking like normal again.

'If I'm honest, Hattie, before all this we never talked about your disability. You just got on with it. Like a brave and stoic soldier. I really admire that about you. It was . . . you know, a good thing.'

My tongue squirmed in my mouth and I swallowed. 'Yes, but it was my plan in Wales to not tell anyone I was disabled, and it didn't work, did it?'

'Well, I mean – they probably do need to know, like you need to tell people – but if you don't want to talk about it then yeah, I get it, that's great. We can pretend you're not disabled in London if you like? That's what I meant really. Stoic. Just getting on with it.'

I squirmed. I thought of Ava and the beads.

'No, no, that's not what I want. Anyway, you'll still know, and you'll still have opinions about what "being disabled" means, opinions that maybe you need to look at.'

My eyes were squeezed shut as I knelt my head on the inside of the cupboard, curled up in a ball.

'Look, all I know is it was really good before and then you moved away and it got bad and it should go back to how it was.'

'No, it didn't work before. You didn't listen or consider me properly.'

'Consider you properly? Hattie. I've known you all this time. I know you. Who you really, truly are.' She was annoyed, and clearly tired of the conversation.

I couldn't help but feel she wanted to be the best friend, the best knower of me, without any real effort. I had given her lots of chances, and she still wasn't listening.

She had started talking about the first day we met, looking at that snail shell.

'We were friends straight away.'

'I know,' I said. 'We were nine.'

I thought for a long time about where I wanted to live next. I could move back to London, not with Ella, but back into the city. I'd be able to see a bit more of Pearl, maybe, but I knew I'd miss Aiden.

I spent a long time staring at the dark stick with all the cut marks I'd made in it, and that made me feel like I didn't want to go back to Wales at all. Aiden could be a pen pal, perhaps. I wasn't sure about going back to my old job either; a big part of me just wanted to leave it all behind.

Then I thought about picking somewhere new altogether, Scotland maybe, until the thought of having to start again, meet new people and find another job, became overwhelming. And then I got a missed call from Jackie. I called her back.

'Hattie,' she began, in the gentlest voice I'd ever heard, 'there's a lot I want to say, but I first need to let you know that you are on speakerphone and Linda from HR is with me in the room.'

'Hi, Hattie,' Linda said.

'Hello, Linda.' I assumed Linda was there to oversee my termination, like the Grim Reaper's supervisor.

'I would like to begin by formally apologising for the way we as an organisation may have made you feel during your employment with us and would like to reiterate that no employee should come to work while they are feeling unwell, and that the sickness procedures as outlined in your contract should be followed. I'd also like to state that our hospital is an equality opportunities—'

'*Equal* opportunities,' Linda interrupted.

'Yes, sorry, equal opportunities employer and we would never terminate a contract solely due to the disclosure of a disability as this would be in breach of the . . .'

I was scrolling through Instagram at this point. I wasn't getting fired, and I had the job if I wanted it, but these words meant nothing in terms of how it would be working on the desk, the whispers, the gossip, the complaints of being late or slow. I still had to decide if that's where I wanted to be, so I ended the call saying that.

And then, two things happened.

Firstly, Jackie sent me a text from her private number:

Hi Hattie. I just wanted to add we had a lady come in to thank you and another staff member for your care, after she presented with some mental health concerns. Said Hattie on reception made her feel just as valid as everyone else for being there, and was glad people like you worked in the NHS. She said you and the other staff member 'helped her find her other flipper.' (?) She seemed to think you'd understand that. Anyway, we do need people who 'get it', you know?

And then, Aiden sent me a picture of the most beautiful spot in a forest, with this huge old oak that looked like it was out of a children's picture book and massive moss-covered stones that you could sit on and take in the way the light fell through the branches. He said he'd love to show me it for real, if I was thinking about coming back properly.

I was still taking things in stages, but my gut told me where I wanted to be.

52

#STICKS

The first time we went to the woodland was for a burial. The green of it all was particularly vivid, with sunlight beaming through the leaves, drying the trees after a fresh, brief downpour. The air smelt earthy, but the ground wasn't boggy or difficult to walk through. It felt smooth underfoot, with subtle, light casts of our wellies left in every footprint.

I told Aiden about what I wanted to do, and how I'd discussed it in therapy and it seemed like it might help. He offered to make a cross. There was a slight chill in the air, but the spot we chose was open to the sunlight and bathed us in a soft warmth as we looked at the ground. Aiden had wrapped himself in a large, soft, green scarf that echoed the green of his eyes. He nuzzled his nose into the fabric as I pointed to where I wanted it to lie. Aiden took out the little trowel from his pocket and started to dig.

I held that wooden stick in my hands for the last time. All those marks I'd made, it looked nothing like a chair leg anymore.

'Here lies a deformed, beautiful thing,' I said, after placing it in the ground.

'It can rest now, eh?' Aiden said gently.

'Yeah,' I said. 'It's not all on me. I don't have to change or get any stronger.'

He put his arm around me and the softness of his scarf brushed against my cheek. We walked away from the spot, deeper into the tall trees, over curved roots that ducked and dived into the soil.

I have a new therapist, Emily, that I see every week. It was hard seeing someone new because I had to start all over again. After I talked about my childhood, she said, 'Well, Hattie, we certainly do anger here.' She asked me to write a list of everything that makes me angry, and I had to read it to her, over and over again, and get used to feeling that way. Like Ava said, it's a process. And as Ava also said, there's a whole load of stuff about my dad I need to work on with Emily too.

'You seem to see him as intrinsically connected with death,' Emily once posed, stopping me mid-sentence. 'I just wonder, do you ever allow yourself to really connect with the fact that he lived?'

Well. That had me sobbing, didn't it? A whole load to unpack there. But I'll get there, with time.

I've been feeling pretty guilty about wanting to be able-bodied, but Emily says I shouldn't feel guilty, I should just try to understand why I did what I did, and why it didn't work. I think I'll be seeing her for a while yet.

I feel like I have a better understanding about what happened with Ella now. I didn't want to hurt her, because I thought, in truth, it was all my fault. But I got it all wrong. I was so tired then; I didn't know what else to do. But I know now that I can't give up on my voice. I'm going to need to work on that, but in time, I'll raise it higher than ever before.

I still feel the need for cough sweets at work – now that everyone knows I'm disabled – but I'm trying to taper off. Anne still rolls her eyes when I'm occasionally late. I've already had another chat with Jackie about what she feels is 'a reasonable adjustment' and what isn't. Sometimes I feel compelled to ask Martin to call her again, not that it would do anything. The matter of my sickness is a 'closed episode' – they made me sign a thing and all – and had me sitting in that same training room for a 'refresh' when another batch of new admin staff came in.

Some people find it no trouble at all to adjust my office chair, others passive aggressively tell me how to do it every time they help. When a male employee came over from another hospital to do some training, he definitely thought I was hitting on him. I fell over again the other day, because my shoe had come untied and I don't have the balance to stop and do it without a chair, as I was trying not to be late. I had to crawl toward the desk to get up again, and Daphne asked if I was all right about a thousand times for the rest of the day, even though I'd said I was fine. The next day Anne made a comment about making sure my laces were done up before I went off to lunch and I asked why she'd said that. That's quite a good tactic I've learned – 'oh, why do you say that?' It makes them have to spell out the reason behind the comment, and then I can tackle it. That time Anne said, 'because you went flying the other day!' and I said, 'thanks, but I don't need reminding.'

In better news, Melissa has invited me on a dog walk with her whippet and I think I might go along with her to a pottery class one day. I love helping the patients, and someone came in the other day just to say thanks, because I sat with her for ten minutes instead of taking my break. I didn't mind; she just needed to know she wasn't alone. I go to the cinema a lot on my days off and flirt with one of the guys that works there. He gave me extra popcorn last week, which was a real win.

My flat is small but perfect for me. It is on the ground floor with a shower and very nice wooden floorboards. In the mornings I put the kettle on and look out of the window at the flowers that are planted on a little patch of land by the flats. They are wildflowers that blow gently in the wind. I don't have to take big breaths in to calm myself down before work, I'm just happy to drink my tea and head out the door. The downside of the flat is I can hear the upstairs neighbours banging a lot, but I just turn my music up. Sometimes I think I should get a mega speaker and shout out encouraging words like the person who sits at the back in boat races. 'KEEP IT GOING NOW, COME ON!'

I brought back some of my old school stuff from the loft to show Aiden. He was particularly keen on the comic of *The Fourth Little Pig* (working title).

'We could make this into a film,' he'd marvelled. 'Like a cool indie one.' It was nice to see him so excited by it.

I don't think about Ella too much anymore. I feel a bit bad saying that, but it's the truth. We spoke on the phone when I got back to Wales, I sent her some pictures of the flat. She wanted to just move on from it all and would tell me about a guy she was seeing, or what Gareth had done at work. I'd tell her about A&E, about some show I was watching on telly. Where there was once so much to say – some of it excited and babbling, some of it hidden and repressed – but always so much, so much that I wanted to get out when I heard her voice, now there was just an empty space, like a clearing. I think she feels the same way about me; she said there wasn't 'much to report' when I asked her how she was. Sometimes I send her articles that I think are interesting, sometimes they're about disability rights, sometimes they're about ageing children's TV presenters. She replies with a thumbs up or a laughing face, but I'm not sure she reads them. That's okay, she doesn't have to.

The den is in woodland a few miles from the hospital. Aiden and I built it with branches that had fallen from various winter storms. They were still lying there in late spring when we started building. Aiden had managed to get hold of some blue rope that we used to tie the branches together and strengthen the support.

The other day, by the den, Aiden started quoting the poem again. It's about nature and birds flying; that's why he got that tattoo. Turns out it was him who chose that poem to go in the A&E waiting room – they had a staff vote thing a few years ago.

He quotes it all the time. The guy really loves a poem, but I still think they're mostly shit. Not that one though, I quite like that one. I listen while he recites his favourites. Wanky, isn't it?

We finished it that day – the den. It's pretty simple, don't get me wrong. It's the shape of a teepee, but a wonky one. It's small, too, we can only just about fit in, and the little wooden stools Aiden picked up in Homebase don't exactly go with the rest of the design. Not that I'm complaining – I didn't even have to ask for a chair to sit on, he just bought them for the both of us. I'm quite pleased with the way we've covered it with moss and smaller branches so it blends in.

When we put on the finishing touches, he told me to go and stand in it.

'Nice, nice,' he said, nodding calmly with mock professionalism. 'This is a sound structure, Hattie, no mistake.'

'Bloody love it, mate,' I said, tilting my head up to look into the apex.

We heard voices coming from elsewhere in the woodland, getting closer. Aiden ran in to the den, putting his arm round me in a huddle.

'Intruders,' I joked. 'Keep cover.'

The voices came closer as the couple walked along the path, breaking sticks underfoot. Aiden peered out at them from the gaps in the branches, and whispered, 'What do you reckon, mate, can they see us?'

53

#IN

We were dressed in pink, skipping through a catalogue of verdant green. The forest floor was scattered with rich bark from fallen twigs that had come down in the previous night's storm, the air was fresh and earthy.

Pearl was filming and her daughter, Lena, was giggling at the top of her lungs. Every time she did this, we had to stop and start again, but we didn't mind. Aiden kept saying he'll probably cover 'this bit with music anyway', but would like the 'forest sounds just in case'.

'See?' Pearl said to her daughter, gently, 'we want to hear the forest for the film.'

'But it's so funny to see them dressed as pigs!' was her sweet eight-year-old response.

Pearl had been staying with me for a few days and genuinely didn't seem to mind that part of her stay was taken up with Aiden's grand plans for *The Fourth Little Pig* indie film. She had to go back to London soon because Lena was going through a lot of hospital appointments because the doctors have noticed she's quite clumsy with her hands and falls over quite a lot.

'Imagine if she does have the same as you,' Pearl mused, as we watched Lena up in front, skipping along with Aiden.

'It would be so strange,' I said. 'Only because of how rare it is. But it could be.'

'Ah, there are still so many unknowns.' Pearl sighed.

'You must be pretty tired of it all,' I said to her, my hand on her shoulder.

'It has been a lot – but we'll be okay.' She smiled, a genuine smile. 'Have you heard from Ella?'

'Ah – no, like I said, we don't speak so much now.' I kept my eyes on Aiden and Lena as I spoke, feeling a little uncomfortable thinking about Ella.

'She found out about Lena's hospital appointments and messaged me, you know?'

'Oh, that's kind of her,' I said, with little emotion.

'I suppose,' said Pearl, clearly wanting to say more. 'She said, "fingers crossed it's not a disability".'

I felt my body tense again in a way it hadn't for a long time. I took a deep breath, trying to work out what to say, but Pearl carried on talking.

'And I know she meant, "fingers crossed Lena's okay", but that's not what she said, is it? So I – I had a bit of a go at her.'

'Oh God, did you?' I looked straight at Pearl, my eyes wide, my heart lifting.

'I just said she needs to have a real think about the way she says things, and even if Lena is disabled, she'll be okay, because it's nothing bad, there's still such a life—' Pearl paused. 'Sorry. Obviously, you are more than aware.' She laughed.

I couldn't help but smile as Pearl carried on.

'And I told her, I told her, Hattie did the right thing, you know, to take a step back.'

'Woah – what did she say?' The heaviness in my body had gone, and an energetic bliss was descending on me.

'She said, "Hattie's not well", and I said, "Oh, she really is".'

'Mate! Yes!' I exclaimed and reached out my arms to hug her. She held me tightly for a few moments and said she wasn't sure whether to tell me. 'Oh, I'm thrilled you did.' I laughed. 'Fucking thrilled.'

With twigs breaking under foot, we caught up with Aiden and Lena, who had found a slug in the grass.

'And you see, we might have missed that, but you spotted it,' Aiden said to Lena.

I looked from the grey little thing making its way along the woodland floor all the way up through the grass and the moss and the leaves to a space in the canopy of trees, where I caught a flash of a bird gliding through the sky. And I thought of all the things I couldn't even see but were here with us in the forest – the ants on the bark, the crows nesting between branches, the foxes hidden, fast asleep.

It was a familiar sound that broke me out of my little day-dream, the skidding on the dirt, the thud, the wellington boots clunking into each other.

'Oh sweetheart, hey, hey,' called Pearl, running over to where Lena had wobbled over and fallen, just a few steps away from Aiden and the slug.

I walked over and Pearl knelt down and offered her hand to get her up, but Lena stayed down, covering her face with her arm, letting out a small, frustrated cry of 'argh', muffled by her sleeve.

'Are you hurt?' asked Pearl, her hand on the back of Lena's head, face full of concern. 'Sweetheart, can you get up?'

Lena reluctantly moved from the ground, her face red and a tear on her cheek, as her mum helped her up.

'See, it's all okay, no need to cry,' Pearl soothed.

I was cautious, not wanting to intervene between mother and daughter. Not wanting to make Lena feel more on show when she didn't want to be. But the tears welling in my own eyes willed me to go on.

'Sometimes, there is a need to cry, though,' I said.

Pearl looked up, a bit puzzled at my glassy eyes and wavering voice.

'And sometimes, Lena, there's a need to stamp your feet like this,' I stamped my feet into the dirt, 'and say, "arrgggghhhhhh, this body is a bit wobbly".'

After a beat, Pearl was on board.

'Oh, silly Mummy, she's right. Do you want to try? Look, I'll do it too,'

Aiden joined us. So there we stood, all of us, stamping our feet into the ground, saying, 'argggghhhhh this body is a bit wobbly'.

'And then we say, "but I'll hold on to it!"' I said, wrapping my arms around myself, tears still threatening to fall.

'Yeah, I'll hold on to it,' said Aiden, doing the same with his arms. Then Pearl followed too.

And Lena didn't say the words, because it can't happen all at once, but she did put her arms tightly around herself and look up at me, smiling.

Acknowledgements

Straight off the bat, thank you to YOU for reading this book. I am so grateful to YOU, and I mean that Big Time Tombola. (Big Time Tombola is the same as Big Time, I've just added my own spin on it, as a Brand New Phrase. It means I get to use the word Tombola a lot more than I would be able to otherwise. What a word, what a way to pick a winner.)

I wrote this book because, as a disabled woman, I didn't feel represented in a lot of literature. I really hope this changes and there will be a lot more books with non-stereotypical disabled characters in future, and more disabled authors are supported to write about whatever they want to write about.

On that note, a real shout out is also needed to everyone who has experienced ableism, in one or all of its many forms. I know how difficult it is, I know how tiring it can be, I know how hard it is when so many people don't even recognise it exists in the first place.

Thank you to my agent Hayley Steed who 'got it' from the very beginning and helped to make it what you have in your hands today. You really changed things for me in a brilliant, beautiful way. I can't believe I get to have you as my agent,

Hayley! You are phenomenal. Here's to more books (are you ready, darling?).

Thank you to Christina Demosthenous and all the team at Renegade. Your faith in this book has changed my life, which sounds very dramatic but it has, Big Time Tombola. You have helped make this a better book, and I'm so grateful. Thank you for all your support, insight and encouragement.

Thank you to all my friends. Listing my friends' names makes me very anxious in case I forget someone so I'll just say that friendship love is real love – we don't talk about it enough but it's beautiful. I'd be lost without you all.

Thank you to my family, especially my mum for all your support and love, and for giving me a roof over my head during the pandemic when I had to shield. That's when I started writing this book.

And finally, thank you to my bed. I love my bed so much. It is always happy to have me, and since that is the end of these acknowledgements, I will be having a nice long nap in it very soon.